Y0-DOM-183

Everybody Dies

Gail Graves

PublishAmerica
Baltimore

© 2010 by Gail Graves.
All rights reserved. No part of this book may be reproduced, stored in a retrieval system or transmitted in any form or by any means without the prior written permission of the publishers, except by a reviewer who may quote brief passages in a review to be printed in a newspaper, magazine or journal.

First printing

This is a work of fiction. Names, characters, places, and incidents either are the product of the author's imagination or are used fictitiously. Any resemblance to actual persons, living or dead, events, or locales is entirely coincidental.

PublishAmerica has allowed this work to remain exactly as the author intended, verbatim, without editorial input.

Hardcover 978-1-4489-3586-4
Softcover 978-1-4489-5970-9
PUBLISHED BY PUBLISHAMERICA, LLLP
www.publishamerica.com
Baltimore

Printed in the United States of America

For my family. You are, after all, what life, love and sacrifice are all about. Thank you.

Prologue

Charles Theodore Henri Antoine Meinrad, Count of Flanders and Prince of Belgium, was born October 10, 1903 to Albert I, King of the Belgians and Duchess Elisabeth of Bavaria. He had one older brother, Leopold III, heir to the Belgian throne, and one younger sister, Marie Jose, who eventually became Queen of Italy.

Charles, of noble birth and majestic lineage was dedicated to the good of his people. Though he was not crown prince of Belgium, Charles reigned in his brother's stead when Leopold was rejected by the people. Charles nurtured his wounded country after World War II, cultivating programs that would help restore prosperity.

Charles was not afforded the luxury of a love match, as was his brother Leopold. No official marriage is recorded for Prince Charles, however there are rumors concerning the choice of his heart.

Everybody Dies

Survival is the most basic instinct born to mankind. To love and be loved is the driving force to that end, and the only emotion capable of motivating a willing relinquishment of that right. Freedom is but a fleeting phantom, desirable but mostly unattainable. In the pursuit of freedom lies the adventure.

Chapter 1

Like a great pre-historic python, the locomotive snaked its way through the quiescent Appalachian peaks and valleys. One glowing eye, throwing light from its massive head, searched the tracks as it chugged endlessly on. Gobbling the light as it forged ahead, it left a trail of darkness and belched out puffs of steam that dissipated into the countryside behind.

Anna had wanted to see New York City, with all its bustle and excitement, for as long as she could remember. Times Square, the Statue of Liberty, Central Park. Everything. Someday she would live there and see it all. She had been in New York less than half a day and couldn't get away fast enough. Now it slipped into the distance and the nightmare she was living slithered into the recesses of her mind.

The night train from New York City to Chicago stopped in Buffalo at the new Central Station, then Boston, New Haven and Niagara Falls along the way. Anna's sleep was light and troubled; she woke and looked out the window at each stop. Each time she looked out, the sky was lighter.

During these difficult times of the great depression Anna should have been excited by the opportunity to travel and live with wealth and prominence, but under the implausible condition in which it was offered, she was determined to return home. It wasn't that she had much of a home to return to, but she had no intention of being forced.

Anna finally gave up on sleeping and went in search of a restroom with a mirror. She closed the door and held onto the knob while she gripped the window sill on the opposite side to steady herself against the chugging and lurching of the train. She braced her foot against the toilet while she rubbed her teeth with her finger and rinsed her mouth with the metallic water from the miniature sink. She doused water on her face and scrutinized herself in the small oval mirror. Maybe she should start carrying an overnight case with her everywhere she went. You never know when you'll get thrown in someone's backseat and hauled off somewhere without your toothbrush. She straightened her hair and lightly bit her lips, wishing for fresh lip color.

She found a seat by a window and sat watching for the next stop; in Cleveland she would have to change trains. The Terminal Tower loomed in the distance. She clutched at her stomach to stifle a loud rumble and hoped there would be someplace close by to get something to eat before she had to board the next train.

Clouds of steam hissed and the whistle sounded as the train slowly pulled into the station. Two men were on the platform talking to an official and pointing to her train. A tall blonde and shorter dark haired man…yes it was them, Diederik and Maurits! How did they find her and how did they get here first? They did have an airplane and getting a train schedule to Chicago, with all the stops along the way, wouldn't be difficult, but how did they know she was on this train? These men were good…and very determined! Brakes whined and people began gathering their belongings.

Maurits looked right at her as she passed! He grabbed Diederik by the arm, dragging him and pointing at her. She jumped away from the window and started for an exit. At least she didn't have to worry about luggage.

She pushed the door open and stepped out to the front deck, grasping the railing as they passed the sign for the train she was supposed to connect with. Diederik and Maurits were gaining on her as the train dragged up to its port. The brakes squealed and billows of steam hissed. The train finally lurched to a stop and she stumbled down the stairs on the far side of the train, opposite the platform. She slipped and skidded on the spotless, glossy tile, darting around and between the bustle of early morning travelers as she started back to find the other train. She quickly boarded and found an aisle seat, away from the window.

Anna was still dabbing moisture from her face with her bare hand when the train pulled away. It wasn't supposed to leave for another 30 minutes. She fingered the dip in the center of her collar bone and pressed on her heaving lungs, the drumming within slowly returning to its normal cadence. No sign of Diederik and Maurits. She sighed a deep breathe of relief that caught in her throat when she realized they would probably be waiting for her in Chicago!

As sincere and legitimate as her two abductors seemed, she still had a hard time swallowing their story. And the people they hired to capture her were certainly less than respectable. Josephine had often accused her of being too gullible, but Anna had no intention of getting involved in this state of affairs.

About 40 minutes into the trip the conductor came by collecting tickets. He shook her gently and she woke with a start, dropping her crumpled ticket to the floor.

"You're on the wrong train Ma'am," he said, straightening out the wrinkles and reading the destination. "This one is headed back to New York by way of Pittsburgh."

"What? No! What have I done?" She jumped to her feet. "Can you stop and let me off?" She clutched at his arm. Fields of alfalfa and Holsteins whipped by the windows on both sides, in a blur of black, white and green.

"You're gonna have to wait till we get to Pittsburgh now and catch another train back to Cleveland. They'll probably charge you for another ticket. Sorry Ma'am...You might want to go to the telegraph office and send a wire to your people, let them know you're gonna be late."

She dropped into her seat breathing the lemon verbena hand soap on her palms as she massaged her brows. "What do I do now? Let my people know?" She muttered in disgust. "I don't have any people." Josephine would never miss her and since her Mother died she hadn't been allowed much social opportunity to make friends.

She squeezed her eyes shut tight, trying to focus on her options. Even if she were able to slip past them at the station in Chicago; if she ever went back to her apartment Diederik and Maurits would just find her again.

Jazz music played softly over the system. The smooth muted trumpet echoed sympathetically in the empty loneliness of her heart, while Louis Armstrong's deep, raspy "Enzo" voice comforted her. Enzo was the only family she had now. Even Enzo probably would think she changed her mind and decided to go to Europe…or that she ended up "sleeping with the fish."

It had been nearly three months since she had packed her few possessions and announced to Josephine that she was moving out. There were no tears, no asking her to stay. She had merely nodded and replied, "It is time. I wish you the best."

She wiped her eyes and smiled when she thought about that first day she walked into Enzo's place looking for work.

Chapter 2

Chicago, Illinois
May 1930

Dust clung thickly to his plumy feather duster as Enzo stretched to reach the cheap vineyard prints hanging on the walls of his little dive on the south side of Chicago. He had immigrated to America in the early 1920's with his mother and younger brother and had earned their way from New York to Chicago by 1926.

He worked hard at anything anyone would pay him to do. In just four years he had earned enough to own his little pizzeria outright. He made the best pizza outside of Italy and his place quickly became popular among the seedy tenants of the area. He saved money by doing most of the work himself. Someday he would have enough money saved to have a nice place on Michigan Avenue.

He was suspicious when a skinny young girl walked into his place asking for a job. From her deep auburn hair neatly twisted and pinned in back and her Coco Chanel leather handbag to her conservative black pumps, he could tell she had class. She was not a street girl.

"What're you doing in this part of town?" He eyed her suspiciously.

"I live here." She righted a sugar jar that tipped when she knocked into the table behind her. "I have a place, an apartment," She pointed with one hand as she brushed spilled sugar into a mound with the other. "Right over…" Confused and flustered, she didn't know which way she lived.

"Close by." She swept the sugar off the edge of the table and into her hand, scanning the room for a garbage bin.

"You live here? Where?" He peered over his glasses as they slid to the end of his nose.

"I…I don't remember." She quickly emptied her hand into the pot of a wilting fig tree when he turned away. "I just moved in." She fumbled through her purse trying to find the card with her new address.

"Who sent you here to spy on me?" He demanded.

"Spy?!" She dropped her purse spilling lipstick, a powder compact, keys and comb with a clatter. "No. I'm on my own. No one sent me. I need work." She lunged for her lipstick as it rolled under a chair. "Spy? Why would…" She blew a fuzz puff from her compact and stuffed it into her purse. He definitely needed help.

She was too young, too innocent, too bumbling. She was no spy. He should just tell the spoiled rich girl to run on home to mommy and daddy and patch things up, she didn't belong here. This was no place for a naive young lady to be "on her own."

"I don't need anyone; I wait on my own tables and sweep my own floors." He turned away shaking his head.

"Please, you won't be sorry. I can make your life easier. I am a very hard worker." She followed, stuffing the rest of her things back in her purse.

"What experience do you have?" He impatiently turned back to her.

"Experience?" She shrank, loosing what little was left of her confidence. She was 18 now, with no professional skills. Her mother and Aunt Josephine had taught her grooming, music, etiquette, and social skills, but had not taught her anything marketable. Being a waitress was not her mother's vision for her. But dying when her daughter was only 15 was not part of that vision either.

Enzo turned away again waving her off, "A hard worker at what, painting your fingernails?" She dropped into the nearest chair, tears welling up in her eyes. She winced as she slipped her right foot partially out of its shoe, easing the pressure on a newly forming blister.

"How am I supposed to gain experience if no one will hire me? I'm smart, I could learn." She mumbled to herself as she dug deeper into her purse, looking for her handkerchief. Enzo grabbed a bowl and slopped some spaghetti into it. He had a heart as big as his belly. He held out his handkerchief to her as he set the bowl on the table next to her.

"You look hungry, eat." He ordered.

"I don't take charity." She pushed it away.

"My employees eat my spaghetti!" He bellowed. She looked at him with confusion. He smiled as he pushed the bowl back to her. "The broom is in the back room."

"You are hiring me?"

He held out his handkerchief again. "Don't start crying again. I can't pay much. But if you work hard and be pleasant, you will get tips." He fell back as she threw her arms around his jolly girth. She dropped back quickly, blushing and nervously collecting her things. She snapped her purse shut and forced a smile, embarrassed by her own impulsive behavior.

"You won't be sorry." She wiped her cheek and hurried off toward the back in search of the broom.

"Eat first," he bellowed again, "The meatballs, they are getting cold."

"Put it back in the pot. I will earn it first, then I will eat."

"Tomorrow, if you come back, lose the heels." He smiled sympathetically.

* * *

Anna stood on a stool with a carafe of water, resurrecting the limp ferns hanging in the corners when the bell on the door jingled, signaling the beginnings of the rush dinner hours. The air filled quickly with the buzz of happy chatter as the tables filled with hungry patrons, most of them regulars. She moved promptly from table to table, taking orders and filling water glasses. Fredrico and Lucius usually sat in the center of the room where they had the most contact with Anna. Dear old Mr. Alantro shuffled in and sat patiently waiting at his usual "table for one" in the corner.

"And how are we today Mr. Alantro?" She smiled brightly. "You're looking very robust this evening."

"I am quite well, thank you my dear." He shakily lifted his hand and she took it with a squeeze. "I have received a post from my son in Texas just this morning. He is bringing the family for a visit!" He excitedly pulled an old worn photo from his breast pocket.

"Could we get some water over here?" Fredrico called out. She held up her first finger to them without looking away from the old family photo.

"They're lovely. I'm very happy for you." She smiled, the look of longing on his face swelling a lump in her throat. She turned to the center where the two customers she dreaded the most were seated.

"I'll take your order if you fold your arms...no touching!" She warned, stopping just more than an arms length away.

"We'll have a large sausage pizza and a little attention." Lucius winked.

"The pizza, I can help you with." She smiled. "I'm sure you find yourselves more entertaining than I could ever be." She winked back, turned and started for the kitchen with the orders when she caught a slap from behind. She whirled around but before she could so much as make a threat, Enzo was there dragging them both out the door by their collars. Enzo was quite protective of his delicate new employee, like the mug his mother had carried from the old country that he kept in the cabinet, rather than on the shelf with the everyday mugs. He had a 'no touching' rule for her as well.

When the last order was finally filled, she sat only for a moment to slip off her shoes and wiggle her toes before grabbing a cloth and chair to clean the windows. By the time the last customer went out the door, she had finished sweeping the floor and began to polish it to a radiant gleam.

If her work ethic wasn't enough to keep her around, her jubilant harmonization with Enzo's robust rendition of Denza's "Funiculi, Funicula" definitely secured her position in his restaurant, as well as his heart.

He was not only impressed with her, but surprised; he didn't think she would last a full day! She didn't exactly fit the image you would expect to see at Enzo's place. She was like a Mona Lisa on velvet.

* * *

As the weeks past, they got to know each other better. He learned that she had no parents to run home to. She never knew her father; he died before she was born. She and her mother had been living with her Aunt Josephine for as long as she could remember.

Josephine wasn't actually her aunt, but a dear friend of her mother. When her mother died, Josephine lost interest in Anna other than to keep up her music lessons and put a roof over her head. Josephine's home wasn't as large as some on her street, but it was elegantly furnished and full of rules.

Anna was never close with Josephine and was made to feel like she was a burden—allowed to stay on only because of a promise made to her dying mother. So she decided it was time to fend for herself. Anna's apartment was dark and cramped, but it was all she could afford. It had been two months now since she had gotten her own place and her job at Enzo's and hadn't been in contact with Josephine since.

Anna straightened the doily under the radio, clicked it on and slowly adjusted the tuner to WGN just in time for the morning newscast. The doily her mother had crocheted, as her only link to her family, was her most treasured possession. The radio was second. Sheltered as she was, she kept up on important events such as the crash of the stock market and the arrest of Al Capone just over a year ago for a range of gang related crimes. She preferred learning the facts without the gruesome pictures that were continually plastered all over the papers. She knew all about Johnny Torrio, Al Capone, Bugs Moran, Frankie Yale and many others but wouldn't know one from the other if she met them face to face.

She sat on her only chair, a simple pine with no sculpture or padding, at a small table with peeling red paint chips. She gazed out the small window, her window, as she finished her simple breakfast of hot cereal and juice.

The table, chair, a small faded rag rug and a small dresser with no handles and one broken drawer were left there by the previous tenant. It was no Buckingham Palace, but it was her own place, no one watched over her shoulder. She could jump on the bed, stay up all night or eat with her fingers if she wished. She didn't wish to, but knowing that she could, made it home to her.

She gathered her dishes, swaying side to side to the music as she washed, dried and put them away in the small cupboard. She took her purse, made one last twirl and turned off the radio. She smiled as she locked the door to her meager castle, there wasn't really anything inside worth stealing, and hurried off to work.

* * *

Anna waited impatiently for the last customer to leave. She hoped hey couldn't see through her façade of gratitude for their patronage as she smiled and thanked them for coming in this evening. She had already swept and cleaned all the other tables and was anxious for them to vacate the last occupied space so she could finish up and be on her way.

Anna liked to go to the Vendome Theatre on the weekends to hear Louis Armstrong and his jazz musicians. She missed being able to play Josephine's Steinway, but with the lack of access to classical music, jazz was growing on her and she found herself going to the Vendome more frequently as time passed. Once she had enough experience as a waitress, she planned to make application to work at the Vendome. The pay and the atmosphere were better there. But for now she was happy to have any job and a place of her own.

"Why are you in such a hurry to leave? You must have big plans tonight!"

She liked Enzo, he was good to her. She suspected that he had ties to the mafia, which made her a bit uncomfortable, but she didn't feel threatened by him. She was hesitant to tell him where she was going. She didn't want to offend him by frequenting the competition, more out of concern for his feelings than fear of him.

"Well...it is Saturday night." She shrugged.

"Run along then." He smiled. "I can finish up here myself." Martyrdom thickly infused with the twinkle in his eyes.

"Thanks, I owe you one." She kissed his cheek, grabbed her purse from under the counter and dashed into the dark street to hail a taxi.

As she reached for the back door of the cab, a gentleman lunged from behind her and grabbed the handle first. "Excuse me!" She raised an eyebrow with one hand on her hip.

Holding the door open he smiled and gestured for her to get in, "We can share it."

"What makes you think I want to share it? How do you know we're going the same direction? You don't even know where I'm going." Anna protested as he gently pushed her in and she slid across to the other side. He dropped in, pulling the door shut behind him. "2128 South Wabash." He announced to the driver. He looked to be in his early 30's and well dressed—expensive but not trendy. He was confident, but not showy, not particularly attractive, but he had a winning smile.

"Where are you going?"

"To the Vendome." She leaned up to make sure the driver heard. Her destination should take precedence.

"Dale Winter is performing at Colosimo's tonight. She hasn't been back here since her husband got...well you know...ten years ago." He reached up to the driver, handing him a folded bill. "I'm in a bit of a hurry. Can you get me there fast?"

"Wasn't Giacomo Colosimo, Dale Winter's husband? The one who got...you know?" she asked shifting her brows knowingly.

"Yeah, Big Jim."

"Diamond Jim." Anna countered. She was only eight years old at the time, but the distress it had caused her mother and "Aunt" Josephine made an impression. He was not a good man, he promoted gambling and prostitution, but being gunned down in public was quite disconcerting. Rumor had it that his partner and nephew, Johnny Torrio, had ordered the execution. Their way of doing business had become common in Chicago, but was still disturbing. "Aren't you afraid to go there?"

The man's intense black eyes interrogated her with a long look as if analyzing and memorizing every feature of a possible enemy. "Why should I be afraid to go there?"

"Colosimo was a criminal and his restaurant has been owned and run by those associated with crime families ever since. Don't you listen to the news?" He looked at her with furrowed brows and a crooked smile, was it confusion or amusement. "Surely you are aware that he was killed right there in his own restaurant...probably by his own associates!"

"Word has it that Frankie Yale wanted to expand his New York territory into Chicago and whacked Big Jim, but Torrio was stronger than

Yale expected. He didn't let Yale muscle in on his territory." He replied, still eyeing her cautiously.

"Torrio and Yale were old friends. Besides, if you ask me, Mr. Capone did the 'whacking' himself." She rolled her eyes at the obnoxious term for taking a life.

Her companion, now thoroughly amused, sat back, smiling at her. "Alright, I'm asking you. What's your theory? Why do you think," he gestured with his hands, palms up, in disbelief, "Mr. Capone was the perpetrator, evading justice and all suspicion…except for you…all these years?" He turned to look out the back window, exposing a scar on the far side of his face. He touched it in response to her horrified look. "A war wound, in France." Her eyes softened with admiration.

"He ended up with everything, the restaurant, the territory, everything. Oh, Mr. Capone is clever; he is very good at evading justice." She gave him a knowing look. "I'm surprised you don't keep up on these things more." A crowd gathered outside Colosimo's just ahead. "I suppose a war hero, like yourself, goes wherever he wants, even in Chicago." She added smiling.

He wasn't nervous to be here and the large crowd pressing to get in gave evidence that a good many people this evening were not afraid to be here. It was very tempting for her to experience this new venue.

"If you aren't Mr. Capone's enemy, you don't need to be afraid of him." He reassured her as their car pulled up in front of Colosimo's Restaurant; the gentleman opened the door and stepped out.

Never having had any contact with the man, he shouldn't have any complaint with me, she thought. I would love to hear the famous Dale Winter. She slid across the seat toward the door and stopped. Do I dare? Why not? Is it safe? What about the Vendome? At her hesitation the gentleman moved to close the door. I may never have this chance again, Dale Winter! I can go to the Vendome any time. She quickly stepped out onto the crowded sidewalk. He shut the door and disappeared inside. She inched her way toward the large round entrance. Once inside, she edged toward a darkened corner to quietly listen to the music. She couldn't afford dinner there and the tables were mostly full, anyway.

So this is the famous Colosimo's. It wasn't terribly wide but it was very deep, with an ornate stage at the back end. A wide sweeping staircase rose to each side of the stage with red velvet curtains and gold accents. Gold and crystal chandeliers hung from great gold trim circles on the ceiling. Throngs of people crowded in, filling the room with smoke and stench. A couple at a table to the right sat arguing, she stood leaning over angrily in his face. He slapped her. She whirled and left. Anna cowered further into the corner, clutching her purse more tightly.

Three men sat at the table to the left smoking cigars and passing a bottle around, filling their goblets. A fourth man joined them, a hideous man, with a wide upturned nose and chubby cheeks. He put a plump, hairy hand on one of the seated men's shoulder as he pointed to a side door. They all got up and followed the pig faced man to the door. He opened it, briefly revealing a large elegant office with a massive oak desk and what appeared to be an immense gun cabinet, before they disappeared inside. Maybe coming here wasn't the best idea.

Lights dimmed as curtains drew back. Fats Waller and his Rhythm were opening the show this evening. Anna edged up through the crowd, closer to the front. Fats' big round eyes rolled and bushy brows rose and fell humorously as he sang "Ain't misbehavin' savin' all my love for you, for you, for you, for you…" His fingers hopped and skipped, playfully chasing up and down the piano keys. He had a nice style, lighthearted, fun. His hands were nearly a blur as they raced and circled, picking out an amazing ragtime.

The gentleman next to her slopped his drink on her as the pig faced man pushed past, out the side door and into the alley, his gun in the back of a rowdy. She felt in her purse for her handkerchief to wipe off her arm and sleeve. Perhaps the man had spent a little too much time, and money, down in the speakeasy and was being "bounced" before he could draw attention to his illegal condition. Or worse, maybe he owed Capone money he couldn't pay or had done something to make Capone angry. She wanted to run but the crowd pressed tighter.

If she could just edge her way back toward the front door. There was a muffled banging sound from the alley. Had they knocked over garbage cans or were those gunshots? She wouldn't have noticed the noise in the alley, with all the music and voices inside, had she not seen the gun. Over active imagination or not, this wasn't the place for a young lady, alone. She pushed through the crowd, her heart beating out a ragtime of its own. The smoke and heat became suffocating. She burst out onto the sidewalk and gulped the fresh air.

A gentle summer breeze tossed a leaflet at her feet. 'Dale Winter at Colosimo's' read the headline and underneath was a picture of the gentleman she had shared the taxi with earlier, his arm around the famed singer. She snatched up the paper and jumped into the nearest taxi. Her heart thudded within her tightening chest. She had explained her theory that Al Capone had killed 'Diamond Jim' Colosimo, to Mr. Capone himself!

Chapter 3

The train lurched and Anna nearly jumped to her feet. She rubbed the sleep from her eyes. Those around her slumbered on, or continued reading, except to glance at her curiously. The man in the taxi with the scar across his face glared at her from her dream.

The woman next to her offered her a little pink fan with cherry blossoms. Anna worked it vigorously as large beads of perspiration formed on her brow.

Chicago could be a harsh place. Gangsters open fire on each other; people come up missing all the time. Why was she so anxious to go back there? Maybe she should just move on, start over where no one could find her.

She settled back into her seat and closed her eyes as her heart slowly returned to a normal pace. They wouldn't look for her in Pittsburg. Maybe this mistake was actually a blessing. She could relax some what, at least until she got to Pittsburg and had to start an entirely new life!

How could an average girl from a sedate ordinary existence, end up on a train with nearly $500 in her garter, running from two men from Belgium who claimed she was some distant relative to royalty in the Netherlands? Until last Tuesday the most urgent worry on her mind was how to scrape together enough money to pay her rent. She had never thought much about wealth or political importance and now she was desperately running away as both were being thrust upon her against her will. She carefully analyzed the events of the last four days, trying to figure out any alternative explanation to the unbelievable one that was given her.

* * *

Business was slow that uneventful Tuesday night and that meant Anna wouldn't be receiving the tip that would pay her rent. Anna's back was to the door as she tried to clean up a spilled drink without cutting herself on the glass. She didn't even notice the two men come in and seat themselves, nor could she hear what they were whispering about.

They were anxious to find the girl they had been searching for. The girl they knew so well, not her face or personality, but her name, lineage, and things she didn't even know about herself. Could this be her...cleaning the floor? They smiled and looked back at each other, raising an eyebrow in approval. "His Highness shouldn't find this such a difficult task!"

"And if this is what her life consists of, we shouldn't have much difficulty ourselves." They laughed quietly.

As she picked up the last piece of glass she felt a jolt of pain from the jagged edge tearing the skin of her finger. She turned to the garbage to throw away the broken glass and noticed for the first time the two men in suits in the corner. She dropped her note pad into the pocket of her apron and grabbed a cloth.

These men weren't the typical men that ate at Enzo's, usually the only men that came in wearing expensive suits went straight to the back, to see Enzo. They were never there for the pizza. These men weren't Italian and they weren't wearing the pinstriped pinch back suits and spats that were popular in Chicago. They had an air of wealth, position, superiority, what was it? She couldn't put her finger on it, but they were different. What ever it was, she hoped it meant there would be a big tip.

She wrapped the cloth around her finger and squeezed to try to stop the tender wound from bleeding. As she walked to where they were sitting she bit down and squeezed harder to make the pain stop. She arched her back and forced a smile, "May I help you this evening?"

The men stood and smiled. "We certainly hope so. Are you Anna Elisabeth Frederik?"

She lost the smile and her eyes tightened. "Yes," she answered cautiously. She forgot about her throbbing finger. She had only lived here a short time and knew very few people. She had never seen these two before.

"Please, sit down. We have a matter of great importance to discuss with you."

"I'm sorry, but I'm on duty until eight."

They weren't smiling anymore which was unsettling, but they weren't threatening either, which was somewhat intriguing. Her mind was spinning. What could this be about?

"Can I get you something to drink?"

"Thank you, no. We will be back at eight o'clock."

They bowed slightly and headed for the door. Anna pretended to go back to work, but watched them from the corner of her eye until they were out of the restaurant and out of sight.

She wished she hadn't told them when she would finish working. She had no idea what they wanted and wasn't sure she wanted to know. She hoped they would be late so she could slip out before they came back.

They returned at 7:45.

She finished up, untied her apron and hung it on the hook behind the door to the kitchen. As she approached their table, they stood and removed their hats. The three of them sat around the small table.

"Good evening, I am Maurits and this is Diederik." He hesitated, not sure exactly how to approach their offer. These things were usually arranged through the parents. When Josephine was contacted she abruptly ended their conversation informing them that she no longer was responsible for the child. He decided to openly set forth their proposal. How could she oppose such an offer when this kind of life was her alternative?

"We have been commissioned by Albert, King of the Belgians, to arrange a marriage between you and his second son, Charles."

Well, that was the last thing she expected to hear. She had imagined a number of scenarios in the last couple of hours since they had first appeared. She hoped they had come to offer her a position at the Vendome. She liked to sing and play the piano, but how could anyone know that. Furthermore, she was schooled in classical, not jazz. She knew she was only dreaming to hope they would ask her to perform there, but she never even dreamed of this offer! How could they expect her to believe such a story? And why?

They told her of the wealth and privileges that would be hers. She listened politely, trying to decide if this was a prank. Her mind raced to think of who might have put them up to this; she knew it couldn't be real. Things like this just don't happen in real life! Whoever it was, she wasn't falling for it. She stood, shaking her head. "I'm sorry…"

Maurits stood up quickly, the back of his knees shoving against his chair. The sound of the wooden legs of the chair scraping loudly across the oak floor drew the attention of the few other guests in the room.

"Please accept this gift from His Royal Highness." He quickly offered as he pulled a small box from his pocket, oblivious to the interest he created around them.

Anna flushed red and dropped back into her seat. She waited until all the eyes in the room were bored with what was happening and leaned forward to whisper. Before she could say anything, Maurits opened the box and lifted out a gold necklace with a large teardrop emerald and handed it to her. It was beautiful. Pale green sparkles flitted about like fireflies as it caught the light from the sconce on the wall. Its brilliance made it look like a real gem, but its size gave it away. This little joke had gone too far.

She stood and dropped the offering on the table, still unable to believe what she was hearing. "If you will excuse me please?" She turned to leave. Maurits snatched the necklace and caught her arm.

"Take it and think about it." He insisted. "We will return tomorrow for your answer. Please," he said pressing the necklace into her hand, "At lease consider it. This is very important." His eyes gripped hers in a humorless snare. He was serious, very serious.

They left. The two dark images stopped at the curb under the street light. What were they saying to each other? Why were they doing this? They crossed the street and faded into the night, the bauble in her hand confirming that she had not imagined this strange encounter. She jumped at Enzo's deep, scratchy voice next to her.

"What did those men want with you?" he asked.

She told him everything and asked him what he thought of it. He didn't know what to make of it, but promised to ask around. He said the necklace looked very valuable and offered to keep it in his safe in the back room until they returned tomorrow.

On the long walk home Anna replayed the eventful day in her mind. The men had an unusual accent. They pronounced their words with such precision, no slurring of words and no slang. She couldn't remember where they said they were from and she didn't recognize the accent, but it definitely wasn't British. They were probably from somewhere in Europe though.

When she was a little girl her mother told her stories about England. Her parents had come to America from England just before she was born. She loved hearing stories about kings and queens, royal balls and parties. As she got older she had assumed they were just fairytales to get her to sleep at night.

It would be exciting to go to Europe. She twirled and swayed as she imagined herself at a royal ball, living in a spacious palace. She could almost hear the music and see the splendor. Then she imagined herself with King Henry VIII, and shuddered; wives loosing their heads for displeasing their husbands or for taking a stand on politics or religion. She was actually quite happy in her tiny apartment!

The next day was rather busy and Anna had almost forgotten the incident from the night before. Business began to slow before the dinner crowd, so she picked up the broom and had just started to sweep, when the two men walked in. She put the broom against the counter and went into the back room to get the necklace. They were still standing near the door when she returned. She tried to return the necklace, but they insisted that she keep it.

"You don't understand. I am refusing your offer."

"You do not understand. Refusal is not an option." The shorter one hissed.

"Anna, are you alright? Enzo called from behind the counter. "Are those men bothering you? You want I should throw them out?"

"Thank you Enzo, no. They're leaving now." She called back without taking her eyes off them. They were starting to scare her now. She tried to hand the necklace back again but neither would take it.

"How do you know my name? Who put you up to this?"

"As we explained to you before, our king has…"

"I know what you told me and I don't believe it. Enzo has connections and he will protect me. I suggest you leave now…and don't bother me any more."

She stared up at the shorter one, trying to look threatening. His jaw was set and he was determined not to back down; so she shrugged, put the necklace in her pocket and went back to her sweeping.

The taller one nudged his companion and motioned with his head to leave. "Do not make a scene."

* * *

The dinner crowd was even larger than Anna had expected. By the time everyone left and she finished cleaning and helping Enzo close up, she was exhausted. She couldn't wait to get home.

She usually ate a bowl of pasta during her break, but they were so busy she hadn't taken a break. She was too tired now to stick around and eat. Her stomach was rumbling, so she grabbed a slice of pizza to eat on the way home.

She was so absorbed in savoring every spicy bite of her pizza that she didn't notice the black Ford Model A Town Sedan following her. She could smell basil and garlic on her fingers as she licked the sauce from them. Working for Enzo certainly had its perks.

She turned down the deserted alley that she usually took as a short cut home, and her shadow leapt out in front of her as headlights veered down the alley right behind her. She pressed against the brick wall to let it pass, but it stopped next to her and both back doors flew open. Two men jumped out and caught her as she tried to run. Her scream was muffled as one grabbed her face and upper body. The other scooped up her legs and dragged her into the back seat where they sat, one on each side.

"We got her Tony, let's go!" One yelled as they slammed their doors shut.

"Why are you doing this?" She tried to wrench her arms free.

"It's our job, lady." said the man driving.

"Your job? Someone hired you to get me? You must have the wrong person; I haven't done anything. I don't know anyone, and I'm not involved in anything!" Her voice rose with each statement.

"You're the right person, now shut up." said the burly guy on her left. He kept rocking forward and looking out the window, picking at a worn spot on his knee and buttoning and unbuttoning his vest.

Why was this happening? What did they want? It had to be connected with her foreign visitors, but how? Had Enzo told his relatives about the necklace? The necklace, it was in her pocket! She never put it back in the safe. She couldn't let them know she had it with her, unless maybe she could bargain with it.

"Are you going to hurt me?"

"Not if you cooperate." He pulled a watch from his vest pocket and replaced it twice.

"Who hired you? What do they want me for? Please tell me what is going on."

"Look lady, cooperatin' includes shuttin' up. So shut up!" He leaned back and tried to light a smoke but the match kept going out.

She turned to the man on her right. "What ever they are paying you, I'll pay you more. I have something very valuable, and I will get it to you if you let me go." She hissed desperately.

"Huh uh, cause ya see, we don't double cross nobody. Now you can shut up like he says or I can shut you up. Ya got me?"

Just stay calm. Take a deep breath and stay calm, think. She drummed on her knee. If she let panic take over she couldn't think. She stared out the front window. Make a plan, do something before they get away from the busy public, down by the river or out some lonely road. Panic was winning. A police car pulled up beside them. Do something, anything, draw some attention! She lunged forward and grabbed the wheel plunging their car toward the police car. It took off a mirror and some paint before the driver gained control. The men beside her grabbed her and pulled her back, but that was all it took. The flashing lights came on and they had to pull over. When the officer came to the window, he ordered all of them to get out of the car.

"Please, help me. I don't know these men. They are taking me against my will." She begged as she stumbled out of the car.

"Alright, stand over there." He drawled and calmly pointed to the sidewalk. "Let me talk to these boys." He was so calm. Why wasn't he shocked that they had done this! He cuffed the nervous guy on the back of his head.

"Tony's gonna pay for my car. Look at it! Look what you lunk heads did to it." He buffed the scrape with his sleeve.

They all knew each other. This officer wasn't going to help her. The driver opened the door to join the others. It was the pig man from Colosimo's! Were these Capone's men? Was this policeman on Capone's payroll as well? Surely Capone didn't consider her and her theories about him a threat.

She folded her arms in a feeble attempt to stop biting her thumbnail. She needed to get out of here fast. She edged to the back of the sidewalk when a group of people walked by and blended in with them, walking on the far side of the group until she was out of sight. She ducked into a hotel lobby, went quickly out the other side and caught a taxi home.

The first thing next morning, she went to a jeweler to have the necklace appraised. She needed to know what she was mixed up in. He said it was worth $500.00! She sold it on the spot. Now she could pay her rent—for the rest of her life! She went into the restroom and put the money in her garter. She was afraid to carry such a large amount of money in her purse.

When she got to work, Enzo didn't act strange or surprised that she was there. Maybe he didn't have anything to do with the incident last night. He had been good to her, so she didn't think he would turn on her. But she had only known him for a short time, how much loyalty and trust can you build in a couple of months? Maybe she should tell him what had happened. Since he obviously wasn't the cause of her abduction, he would surely offer her protection. Of course, she would have to wait until she could talk to him alone.

It was a very busy day and she was exhausted by closing time. Enzo was in a hurry to leave; he had an important meeting. She would have to talk to him tomorrow.

For safety reasons, as well as being too tired to walk, she took a taxi home. She tipped her purse and shook it until a pile of coins gathered in the bottom corner. She counted out the required amount and then dumped the few remaining coins in the driver's hand as a tip. The taxi pulled away and she was just turning the key in her lock when two men came around the corners on each side of her. Not again! Her heart leaped into her throat. Was every thug in town after her? Get the key out of the lock and get inside! Her shaking hands nearly dropped the key. You can't lock them out if they have the key, she cursed herself. She frantically pushed inside and tried to shut the door, but they were right behind her. One of them got his foot inside. She stomped on it and threw her shoulder into to the door, but she might as well have been trying to cage an angry bull. They slammed their way in, knocking her against the wall behind the door. She swung her purse at them, hitting one of them in the arm as he blocked his face. He grabbed it and tossed it aside; the other ducked his shoulder into her stomach and threw her up over the top as he stood up. The more she kicked and tried to rise up, the further he pushed her over his back, as he charged out the door. Flailing wasn't working. She hooked her elbow around his throat and thrust herself upright. He dropped her to her feet and before she could catch her balance they had her in the back of the car that had just pulled up.

These were the same three men that had captured her last night. She had found a way out before, but she would have to come up with something else tonight. This time they were wise to her tricks; the two men beside her kept a tight hold on her arms. Perhaps if she could lighten the mood, they would relax a little.

"We've got to stop meeting like this boys. People will talk."

"Just shut up. And no funny business." Growled "Mr. Nerves" as he rocked back and forth, looking out every window, tightening his grip on her arm.

"So," she grasped for conversation, "are you boys from around here?" She smiled.

She got only silent glares in return. They drove in silence to the airport; no opportunities presented themselves for escape. They pulled up near a Travel Air Mystery Ship model 6000 mono-wing. She gaped out the window. She had never seen one of these, let alone this close up! She momentarily forgot about her present situation.

Tony, the driver, got out and left. When he came back he was with one of the two men that had come to the pizzeria. The two men with her in the car got out, the quiet one held the door for her. It was starting to make sense. Those men had hired these thugs to get her and bring her to them. Fear left her completely as anger boiled to the surface.

She folded her arms and refused to get out of the car. There was no way she was going with them to become one of many wives to some fat old prince of wherever in Europe they were going. Tony reached in, grabbed her arm and dragged her out. The other two took hold, one on each side they hauled her to the airplane. The stairs were too narrow for three side by side. As they dropped to single file she grabbed the railing and held tight. The nervous guy pulled a pair of handcuffs from his pocket and clipped one ring to her right wrist and held the other ring in his left fist. He plunged up into the plane dragging her behind with the metal cutting into her flesh. They buckled her in and handcuffed her to the seat.

When they finished paying off the men they had hired to bring her to them, the European men came aboard. They introduced themselves again. The tall blonde was Diederik and the slightly shorter, dark haired man was Maurits. They both appeared to be in their mid to late twenties.

Diederik sat next to her while Maurits sat across from him. There were three seats side by side on each side of the fuselage, facing in to the narrow isle going down the center.

The engines roared louder as they began to taxi to the runway. Anna gripped her seat and squeezed her eyes shut tight as they accelerated for take-off.

Diederik touched her arm, "Have you flown before?"

Anna shook her head without opening her eyes.

"We have a very qualified pilot and our aircraft is in excellent condition." He reassured her. "You are perfectly safe. You needn't be frightened."

The rattling rumble stopped as the wheels left the ground. They leaned to the back of the aircraft as they soared upward. Once they leveled off, Maurits knelt on one knee in front of Anna and unlocked the cuff from her wrist.

"Would you like to play a game of cards with Dirk and me to pass the time?"

She shook her head and looked away. How could he act like they were friends? These men had hired mafia thugs to abduct her and yet they acted as if all was normal! She absently rubbed her wrist, steaming and ranting inside her head. It was red and sore where the cuff had rubbed. Maurits got out a first aid kit and knelt by her again.

"I am sorry. They were instructed to bring you, without injury." He tenderly applied some ointment and a bandage.

She studied them as they played their card game. They were attractive, well dressed, well mannered and kind, and yet they dealt with undesirables to illegally achieve their end. They were obviously educated. Dutch, which they spoke to each other, was most likely their native language. They also spoke Italian with their hirelings, of which she understood very little, and English to her, which they spoke very well. Could they really be who they said they were? Maurits noticed her watching them.

"Can I get something for you, a drink, some biscuits perhaps?"

"You seem like decent men. How can you do this to me? You tear me from my home, my life, my things!"

They put the cards down and turned their full attention to her.

"What home? What life? What things? You live alone. You have no family there. Have you left behind anything that can not be replaced?"

She really didn't have much.

"My mother's doily." She looked away, chewing her bottom lip. After her mother's funeral Anna had gone to her room and refused to come out any more than was necessary to survive. When she finally returned to normal routines, her mother's things were all boxed and removed from the home. The doily her mother had made and given her was the only thing she truly regretted losing.

"Just because I don't have much, doesn't mean you have the right to take me away from it. How can you live with yourselves? Have you no conscience?"

"As we tried to explain before, our country desperately needs a strong alliance with the Netherlands. Your marriage to our King's son, Prince Charles, could provide that alliance."

"But I am American!"

"Your father was the only son of Prince Alexander and the only grandson of King William III of the Royal House of Orange."

My father, grandson of a king? She never knew her father. She knew very little about any of her family. Maybe this is how it's done in Europe, but she wasn't raised with the notion of marrying whomever she was told.

"You'll have to find someone else."

"You have no siblings or cousins on your father's side. Your only living relatives are the queen and her daughter, Juliana, who is heir to her throne."

"Why doesn't he marry the daughter, heir to the throne? Wouldn't she make a stronger alliance than a relative they've never met?"

"His Royal Highness, Prince Charles would become a useless decoration at her side—in her country. Yes, it would form a powerful alliance, but his strong leadership is needed at home. You, however, would be given to him and his country."

They waited for further questions, as she sat, eyebrows furrowed, internalizing this information. When no more questions came, they returned to their game.

"It is quite a long trip to New York. You really should find something to occupy yourself."

They leaned their elbows on their knees and played on the floor in between. Anna knelt on the floor to join them. They had to teach her the rules as she had not played before.

What a sheltered life she led up until now. She had very little social life or experience with the world. She smiled when she thought of Aunt Josephine's reaction. If she were to see her now, sitting on the floor playing Rummy with a couple of strangers!

She picked up the game quickly and found it an enjoyable pastime. Two hours had gone by pleasantly when suddenly the craft jerked violently. She tumbled off her knees, on to the floor and into Diederik's leg. She clutched at him just below the knee holding tightly as she waited to crash to the ground, and their death. Diederik stroked her hair gently as he reassured her that they were safe and turbulence was normal. Once she felt quite sure it was over, she carefully lowered herself to lie on the floor, holding her stomach. Maurits rummaged through a bin of supplies and found a couple of blankets. He rolled one and placed it under her head as Diederik covered her with the other.

"A little motion sickness, you will be alright."

When she woke up they were nearly there. They encouraged her to get up in her seat for the descent and landing.

When they landed, the pilot was busy fueling and checking the mechanics of the airplane. Diederik was busy talking to airport officials, while Maurits kept watch over Anna.

"May I please use the restroom before we start again? And maybe get something to eat?"

He stood and locked the handcuff back on to her wrist and then to his own wrist.

"I don't know anyone in New York and it's a long walk to Chicago. Do you really need this?"

"I can not take any chances."

She took his hand, pulling her sleeve over the cuff to hide it as much as possible. It was 2:00 a.m. and was still dark. Very few people were there, but it was still so embarrassing for her. There was a little hot dog stand, but it was closed. She reminded him that she needed to use the restroom.

"Are you coming in with me?" she quipped.

He unlocked her wrist and waited by the door. A narrow window stood open just above the end stall. She stepped quietly on the toilet and hoisted herself up and through the window. Staying to the back of the buildings, she cut her way back to the main road, using the occasional headlights as her guide.

An empty taxi was parked at the side of the road. Maybe she could hide inside until the driver came back, or at least until Diederik and Maurits left. She tried the back door, it was unlocked. She slipped in and pulled the door shut behind her. Just as she laid her weary head on the stiff woven upholstery, the driver groggily sat up from his nap on the front seat. He strained his bleary eyes to focus on the horizontal mass of feminine fabric, hair and fruity essence that had crawled onto his back seat. She slowly sat up, smiling sheepishly.

"So...where to?"

"Grand Central Station?"

She didn't relax until she had purchased her ticket to Chicago and was on the train nestled in her sleeping berth. Finally, the gentle rhythm of the train lulled her to sleep.

Chapter 4

Brussels, Belgium
May 1930

Dark clouds billowed and rumbled as they gathered in the sky outside his window, threatening to unleash their contents on the unusually thirsty land below, as top officials gathered in the Belgian Royal Office where Charles sat watching the storm move in. His polo game that afternoon would most likely be canceled, but that was one of the least of his concerns. He was preparing one of his perfectly articulated speeches for parliament and didn't have the time or desire to listen to the Elite Guard give their report. As the incoming storm would bring much needed moisture to his country; even more importantly, the outcome of this meeting could bring life renewing hope to his people. He would accept the negative personal effects from both without complaint.

He knew without looking at him, that Geoffrey was waiting for his complete attention before he began. This was his moment to gloat. In their youth, Charles usually won, whether it was athletics or academic, but Geoffrey was nearly always a close second. Now, with Geoffrey engaged to the girl of his dreams, he was finally on top, and was enjoying the information he had to present.

Charles refused to look him in the eyes; he would not play this childish game. It did not matter who was better or happier, only that they both gave their best effort in all that was required of them. Geoffrey's continual show of emotion was a sign of weakness. Any task is better accomplished when emotion is set aside. He lifted his chin, burying his own sentiments more deeply. This attitude became a habit for Charles, making it hard for everyone around him to discern his feelings, but making him a very effective leader. So his habit kicked in and he let Geoffrey proceed with the account of their findings of the past months.

"We feel we have found a suitable connection with the Netherlands." Geoffrey stepped to the large slate board hanging on the wall and began drawing out the lineage. "William III of the House of Orange—Nassau had three sons, all dying young, supposedly leaving the House of Orange extinct in the male line." He wrote the names of the three sons, under King William's at the top and center. "Willem Alexander Karel Hendrik Frederik, the third son; called Alexander, incidentally;" he stated as he underlined the second name of the third son "had asked for permission to marry the Princess Friederike of Hannover. This union was approved by parliament but denied by his father. After the death of his mother, King William's first wife Sophie, Alexander withdrew from his father." He wrote Friederike's name next to Alexander's name on the board.

"We have discovered that while traveling in Germany, he secretly married Friederike. Due to poor health and political pressure, he returned home where he died at age 38. When Friederike found herself alone and "with child" from a marriage that was not formally recognized, she fled to England where she was accepted by Queen Victoria, who had extensive German ancestry herself."

When Geoffrey turned from the board to relate the details, Charles was looking out the window again. King Albert and eight others, including three members of the Elite Guard, seemed comfortable enough as they all sat around the back side of a large conference table facing Geoffrey, listening intently, some taking notes. The supple black leather loosely stretched over the thick padding of the heavy mahogany chair where he sat, was not enough to make Charles comfortable while this particular topic was being discussed.

Had his thoughts returned to the speech he was preparing for parliament? Or was he thinking about the woman he was to marry? Because Charles had never met this woman, the subject of their meeting this morning, he could not be in love with, or even remotely attracted to her; but he should at least be curious to know who she was and where she was from!

Geoffrey went on "After Alexander's death in 1879, Friederike returned to Germany and married the Dutch baron William Charles Reginald van Tuyll van Serooskerken, leaving her young son, Nicolaas, to be raised in Queen Victoria's court." He placed Nicolaas' name under Alexander and Friederike.

It wasn't that Charles didn't care who they had found so much as it didn't make a difference in his decision. He would do whatever he had to do to secure his country. Political unions were as old as time and those Heads of State joined in such relationships were quite often on the surface only, their personal lives unaffected. But marriage was sacred to him and he had no intention of keeping a mistress on the side. He accepted his fate and anticipated that she would accept hers.

"Nicolaas was 27 when he married Camila." Geoffrey continued. "They were happy for a time until they learned of certain groups in the Netherlands searching for a true male heir to the throne from the House of Orange."

Charles absently turned his attention to the large map of Europe hanging on the wall adjacent to the slate board that held the attention of the others. They were happy for a time? He laughed humorlessly to himself. Was happiness ever permanent for anyone with royal responsibility? This efficient room with its immaculately clean tile floor, adequate lighting and ample furnishings where Charles spent so much of his time; was closing in now, suffocating him. Just outside his window beckoned trees, the horizon, the sky. His escape was only temporary and only in his imagination, for his integrity and loyalty to his country and people bound him more firmly than any shackles could.

"Because of the rise of opposing groups, they feared for their safety and the safety of their unborn child, should it be a son. Nicolaas took his wife and quietly disappeared." Geoffrey kept an eye on Charles as he wrote Camila's name next to Nicolaas.

"We just recently discovered that they fled to America. They settled in Chicago, but Nicolaas died before the child was born. Camila lived there with a close friend, Josephine Hendrikson, until 1927, when she died. Until recently, Josephine kept the child, a daughter. This child, Anna Elisabeth, born in 1912, is now 18 and living alone in an apartment on the south side of Chicago." He drew a large circle around Anna's name directly beneath Nicolaas and Camila.

Geoffrey shot Charles a crooked smile. He knew Charles was not anxious for this arrangement to take place and taunted him mercilessly. "She may have royal blood in her veins, but she will have American soil under her fingernails." he had teased Charles this morning on their way to this very meeting. "You think you are a patriot now, but wait until you see her face. You will turn tail and run." None of them had ever seen this Anna that they had spent many hours researching and paper chasing to learn of her existence, but that didn't dissuade Geoffrey from the friendly banter that was common between them.

They stared at each other for only a moment, but Geoffrey could see it, and he knew Charles too well. Charles would do whatever was expected of him and so he continued, "She lives in Chicago. That is in America."

Growing tired of the subject, Charles replied, laying down his pen and looking Geoffrey directly in the eyes, "Very well, bring her here and I will do my part."

That was the Charles everyone knew, responsible, dedicated to his country and efficient; and at the moment he was not in the mood for fun and games.

Knowing that Charles would never do it, Geoffrey tried anyway, "Perhaps you should go there personally. Court her, and bring her back with you?" He had a little sting of regret when Charles' piercing eyes seared through his, but it swiftly left when his eyebrows lifted.

Charles' reply was calm, controlled, and almost mocking, "I suppose I will fly to America and pretend to be in love with her? Sweep her off her feet?" His eyes narrowed, "I do not want to marry her...I am willing to marry her; and I will not lie to her. Do not put all of our efforts at risk." Charles let him think about this before continuing, "Offer her whatever is necessary, convince her, bring her back, your work is to get her here...and I will do my part."

As Geoffrey and the others left, Charles turned to his work. He was no longer thinking about the novel, Mein Kampf, written by the Führer of the National Socialist Party, Adolf Hitler, and the trouble it had caused in the five years since its emergence and how he would address it in Parliament. He was preoccupied with how Geoffrey would accomplish his assignment. Geoffrey would see that the task was accomplished whatever it required. It was his methods that concerned Charles at times.

Geoffrey had been trying to prove himself since they were twelve years old. Charles and Geoffrey could point to the same incident as a defining moment in their lives, but each came away with a different definition. Geoffrey vowed never to allow fear to stop him again. Charles vowed never to allow emotion to determine his course of action again.

Some friends of Leopold, Charles' older brother, gave Charles and Geoffrey a challenge. If they succeeded, they would be included in this prestigious group of older boys. The boys kept taunting and chiding them. Geoffrey ran away, afraid to face the danger and inevitable punishment. Charles knew the punishment would be severe, but that was a price he was willing to pay.

Charles had passed the test as far as the boys were concerned, but failed miserably according to his father. His father's opinion of him was paramount in Charles' mind.

The look in the untamed stallion's eyes, as he put a bullet between them, would haunt Charles forever. The disappointment in his father's eyes, he determined, would never be present again when he looked at his second son.

It began to rain. A few drops tapped on the window, summoning Charles to refocus on his speech. Only the weather understood how he felt at that moment.

Chapter 5

When the train pulled into Pittsburgh it was 10:00 a.m. As Anna stepped off the train she watched a flock of geese heading southward. She could barely see their silhouettes against the glaring August sun. Pittsburgh seemed like a reasonable retreat to her. The smell of factory was in the air and the bustle of city life on the streets. She could walk for miles and no one would think twice about her. It shouldn't be hard to blend in here.

She had all day to find a place to live and hopefully a place to work.

The first thing she needed was a new purse. It was inconvenient to have to find a restroom every time she needed money from her garter.

When Anna exited the busy train station her eyes were drawn to the huge smoke stacks off to the west. Her eyes burned from the sent of brimstone, but she marveled at the site of the huge billows of smoke. She headed east and wandered through the city. Not knowing how, she found herself standing outside of a department store.

There was a stream of people coming out and she waited for an opportunity to duck inside. Once inside she didn't look around much. She just went straight to the purses, found the cheapest one, made one little stop at the perfume counter to freshen up with the testers, and was on her way.

Once she had her purse, the next immediate need was food. There was a café across the street. There was a sign in the window "room for rent." When she finished eating, she asked about the room. The owner seemed in a bit of a panic as the lunch crowd began filling his café.

"The name's Henry." He stuck out his hand to her with a quick nod. "Look, if you'll start now, you can have the room and the dishwasher job!"

Being times of depression, jobs were hard to come by. There was no "Help Wanted" sign. She suspected the dishwashing job had come available 20 minutes ago when a young man stormed out of the café just as she was walking in! She put on an apron and jumped right in. By 3:00 things were slowing down a bit. The cook took a break and stepped over to her.

"Hi, my name is Jack. I haven't seen you around before. Where are you from?"

She dried her hands and reached out to shake.

"I'm Anna." She hesitated, not sure how much information she wanted to give out. "Chicago." She turned back to the sink; she was almost finished and wanted to get her hands out of the water before they turned wrinkly.

"So, how long have you been in Pittsburgh?"

She looked at the clock above the door, "About 5 hours."

"Wow! Well, it's nice to have you here."

Anna liked the idea of living above where she worked. It wasn't so frightening walking home from work at night! And it was easy to get to work on time each morning.

Today Jack was coming in early to take her sight seeing before work. They both had the evening shift, so they would have several hours together.

Anna sat on the front steps, waiting for Jack, when she heard a noise. She followed the sound around the corner on the alley side of the café, behind the garbage cans. It was a small tabby kitten. He was injured and frightened. He scratched her as she picked him up, but she spoke soothingly and stroked him gently. She took him inside and cleaned him up. She was giving him a bowl of warm milk when Jack came in looking for her.

Henry gave her a box with an old blanket to keep him in. "You'd better tend to your own wound there, before you get an infection." He picked up her hand and rotated it to look at the scratch on her arm. Anna had never had a father to care for her. Henry was different than Enzo. He was skinny, leathery, but still nice. Robust or quiet, male protection was...nice.

"He's a little tiger, isn't he?!" He grinned at the kitten's miniature ferocity as it clung to his finger and gnawed at it.

Tiger went with Anna and Jack sight seeing that day. They began at the Duquesne Station where they hopped aboard a wooden car to ride the incline to the top of Coal Hill. A great view of the city center, nestled in the fork of the Ohio River, opened to their view as they slowly ascended through the trees. They drank in the fresh air as they rose above the bustling, billowing industrial center across the river below.

She found Pittsburg an interesting place to live. There were so many interesting things to see and so many bridges! Jack told her he would take her to a picnic spot that he knew of, across a covered bridge, on their next day off.

It was nice to have a friend. Anna was surprised to learn that Jack was barely 17. He was nearly a year younger than she was and a good ten inches taller. She should have guessed at his youth because of his carefree attitude; still unsullied by the hard times and lack of bright future. He wasn't looking for a serious relationship, which suited Anna. She wasn't looking for anything permanent yet either. She avoided talking about her past or plans for the future. She saw Jack almost every day at work and she enjoyed his company immensely.

She still had difficulty trusting anyone and still caught herself looking over her shoulder a lot. Too much Chicago imbedded into her psyche. Maybe that was one of her attractions to Jack, his boyish, trusting nature. She hoped it would rub off on her and she would be able to relax and settle in more permanently.

"The Yankees are in town. They play the Pirates today at Forbes Field. Do you want to go?"

"Who are the Yankees and the Pirates and where is Forbes Field?"

"Are you kidding?! Babe Ruth?! Baseball?!"

"That sounds familiar."

"OK, we're going for sure. You'll love it!"

Fans streamed through the majestic multiple arches into the stadium where they would load up with hotdogs, popcorn and sodas before making their way up the wide ramps to take their seats. Anna had never had a hot dog before, which was very odd coming from Chicago. Hot dogs were not Josephine's style, and she hadn't been on her own long enough to encounter that experience. Tiger was healing well and getting stronger, but Anna was still protective and liked to take him with her whenever she could. He liked baseball and hot dogs too! After their stop at the concession stand Jack fed Tiger bits of one of his hotdogs while Anna squirted ketchup and mustard on hers.

"Ya gotta have lots of this stuff too." Jack informed her as he piled onions and relish on top. He handed Tiger to Anna and gathered up their food and drinks. This was a place to escape the cares of the world, poverty, hunger, lack of employment and the ravages of war. This was a happy place to be, win or lose, and smiling fans poured in to cheer their team and witness the famous Babe Ruth.

"Run!" Anna yelled. "He might have made it. Why didn't he run?" She folded her arms, obviously the only disgusted fan in the stadium. Baseball, she learned, is a lazy sport. The fans were laid back as well as the players. If the batter didn't hit the ball far enough to easily get to first base, he didn't even try. Jack just smiled at her enthusiasm. The sun, though dropping further south in the sky, was bright and warm. A cool breeze occasionally tempered its heat as they kicked back to enjoy a relaxing afternoon.

Tiger curled up on Jack's lap for a nap, but tired of being wakened every time Jack jumped up to cheer. He finally moved over to Anna's lap. Her cheering was less exuberant as she had found crowd watching to be as exciting as the game. The Yankees were up to bat and the home team was giving one of their players an especially hard time. The crowd started booing him as he swung his bat and scuffed his feet before taking the mound. The men in the dugout started throwing things onto the plate. The batter confidently pointed at center field before hitting the ball squarely to center field for a home run! The crowd went wild cheering for the man they had been cheering against. He took off his cap and waved to the crowd as he rounded third base.

"Wow, he's pretty good."

"Pretty good? Are you kidding? That is Babe Ruth. He's amazing."

***

This was beginning to feel like the kind of town in which she could put down roots. She was feeling comfortable at work now. Henry had hired a young boy as dishwasher and put her out front to take orders. She was familiar with waiting tables and knew what was expected of her. She was making a few friends and was glad her mistake at the train station had brought her to Pittsburg. She was getting to know the "regulars" and made them feel at home.

A couple of policemen came in she hadn't seen before. They sat down and she took their order. The round one with bushy brows and mustache wanted the steak and potatoes special with blueberry pie for dessert. The tall thin one with the hooked nose and deep-set, dark eyes ordered meat loaf and vegetables. She stuck their orders on the nail by the griddle and went to the next table. She could feel their eyes on her, but couldn't make out what they were saying.

She dropped a bundle of silverware as she set the meatloaf in front of the hawk-looking man, and the one that looked like a walrus groaned as he bent to pick it up.

"I'm sorry." She took the bundle and stuck it in her pocket "I'll get you another."

"That's quite alright ma'am." He rubbed his tongue across his teeth. "What's your name, ma'am? We was just tryin to figure where we know you from. You look right familiar." He rolled back in his seat eyeing her.

"I'm Anna. Sorry, I'm new in town. I haven't been here long enough to commit any crimes!" she laughed.

"You're new eh? Where you from?" Officer Walrus did all the talking while Officer Hawk studied every move she made. She slopped the coffee as she filled their mugs. She had never seen these two before today, they were law officers and they were both wearing wedding rings. Why all the questions? They didn't have the social interest in her that she was accustomed to receiving from men. She grabbed a towel to mop up the spill and a clean bundle of silverware behind the counter.

"I'm really sorry, I don't know what's wrong with me today. Is there anything else I can get for you?"

"You could answer his question." Hawkman's eyes bored right through her. She knocked over his water as she reached for the wet towel. Jack stepped out from the kitchen and took the towel from her.

"I've got it; take a break." He motioned to the back with his head and bent to wipe up the floor.

"It's not a problem, we hope you like Pittsburg, ma'am." The Walrus smiled and picked up his fork.

Anna was folding napkins and stacking them when Jack came back to the kitchen.

"What was that all about?" He picked up his big wooden spoon and stirred the mashed potatoes.

"Are they gone yet?"

"No." He turned and watched her frustration with the toppling stacks of napkins. He stepped over to her and divided the napkins into shorter stacks.

"What's wrong? This isn't the first time men have taken an interest in you. It has never bothered you before."

"I know, I just, I don't know…they're different."

"You're not in trouble with the law, are you?" he asked half teasing. "Why are you here? I mean, you just show up one day, alone, with no past…"

She smiled, "You wouldn't believe me if I told you."

"Try me."

She hardly believed it herself; how could she expect anyone else to. "Alright, how about this? I am running from the law. I've committed some heinous crime. Murder, yes, bank robbery and murder! And I am hiding out under cover as a waitress." He leaned back against the counter and folded his arms, smiling.

"Or maybe I am a princess from a far away land. They are trying to kidnap me and force me to marry some horrible prince against my will."

"Alright, I get it; it's none of my business."

"Or perhaps I've just run away from a bad situation at home." She shrugged and went back to folding.

"You don't strike me as the murdering type. If you were, I think they would have arrested you instead of just watching you. The runaway story is much too boring. I like the princess story." He made a sweeping bow.

"Your Highness, what you need is a night out on the town. You're off in an hour and I'm off at 4:00. I'll be back to pick you up at 6:00."

* * *

Jack was taking her to the symphony at Carnegie Music Hall tonight. She had heard wonderful things about both the Hall and the Symphony and was glad to have a reason to dress up. Her lifestyle didn't have a lot of elegance or culture in it any more. She spent all afternoon shopping for a new dress to wear. She could hardly wait for Jack to arrive and their evening to begin.

She wasn't disappointed, the Music Hall was gorgeous. With its elegant architecture and rich red and gold colors, she was delighted. Then the music started…she was in heaven with Mozart, Strauss and Bartok. Seeing her complete rapture made it worth sitting through the evening for Jack, who much preferred baseball.

* * *

Anna had lived in Pittsburg long enough to know her way around. She was just starting to feel at home when things began to make her uneasy again. She just couldn't shake the feeling that she was being watched. Why was she still so paranoid? She was more comfortable going places with Jack, but he wasn't always available.

There was a little market just down the street. She usually went there rather than walk the distance alone to the larger market.

"Hello Jim." She called as she headed for the dairy case, the bell above the door jingling again as she let it swing shut.

"What can I get for you today, Anna?" Jim, the store owner, called back without looking up from his books.

"Nothing, I'll get it. I just need some milk and butter." The bell rang again and she heard footsteps to the counter behind her and then they stopped. She picked up a carton of milk, a block of butter and a wedge of cheese wrapped in waxed paper. She couldn't really afford the cheese, she tried to live on what she made at the café and keep her "other money" for emergencies, but it smelled so good and it had been so long since she had toasted cheese on rye. The bell rang again and a bunch of noisy boys came tussling in to buy licorice sticks and gum.

Anna gathered the cheese into her arms with the milk and butter and started for the bread aisle when she nearly dropped everything on the floor. Officer "Hawkman" was watching her while pretending to look at some canned goods. Her pulse quickened. Was he following her? Of course not, he just needed groceries the same as everyone else. "Officer Goldstein" his shiny badge read. He put the can of beans back on the shelf and tipped his head as she went around him to the bread bins.

"Good evening, Miss Frederik." His predatory deep eyes pierced her again. How did he know her last name? She stumbled to the front and dumped her items on the counter. The Walrus was just coming out of the back room; he saw her and started toward the front. She dug through her purse for the exact change and dropped it into Jim's outstretched hand. She glanced back as she slipped out the door with her bag of groceries; they were coming down the aisle toward the door.

What do they want with me? I haven't done anything wrong. They aren't trying to arrest me or they would have done it already. Why would they follow me? They want to know where I live? I can't go home. She stepped down onto the sidewalk. The door opened behind her. What now? She couldn't outrun them. They obviously aren't going to try anything in public. Pretend like you dropped something and go back into the store. She looked over her bag and around behind her.

"Excuse me." She smiled and ducked between them, back into the store. She went to the rear and peeked back to the front. She could see them out the front window. Now she was stuck; there was no back way out and they were guarding the front. She should have bolted down the nearest alley when she had the chance.

The bell jingled, it was Mrs. Williams. Anna picked up various canned goods and read the labels, trying not to look suspicious. The bell rang twice more.

"Hello dear, how are you today?" Oh, how dear old Mrs. Williams made her jump. "Didn't mean to surprise you dear."

"I'm fine, and you?" Anna put her hand to her heart as if to calm it.

"Oh, I've been better. I have a cough that just won't give up and my joints are paining me again." She added a bottle of tonic to her basket with the camphor and menthol rub.

"I'm sorry to hear that." They were gone. It must have been her imagination. It was ridiculous to think policemen would be following her. But why did they make the effort to find out her name?

"I suppose it's part of getting old." She laughed and started for the dairy case. Anna turned to wish her well and saw the Walrus at the back of the store again. What was he doing snooping around back there? Was he looking for a back entrance? He turned and saw her. She whirled and headed down the nearest aisle to the front. Just get outside and around the corner out of sight, then figure out where to go from there. When she got to the front of the store, Goldstein was standing by the door. What now? She backed up and picked up a jar of pickles, returned it and worked her way back down the aisle, becoming very interested in the various relishes and olives. How long could she stall this way? She went around the end to the next aisle and worked her way slowly back to the front. Walrus was keeping his distance behind her; Goldstein remained at the front door.

Mrs. Williams was just paying for her groceries. She was struggling to wrap her arms around the two large bags. Yes! That will do.

"Mrs. Williams, let me help you with those." Anna rushed forward and picked up one of the bags. "I'll walk you home."

Goldstein smiled and held the door for them.

"I don't know how I would have gotten these home without your help."

"Don't mention it." A quick glance back revealed both men were out of the store now.

"Why, I can hardly walk anymore, I'm getting so stiff."

Their shoes clacked softly at a distant slow pace.

"My daughter is coming next week. I just have to be well by then. She has three very active children you know."

"Oh my." Anna replied, only half listening. Don't turn and look; if they think you suspect them, they may not keep their distance.

"Little Billy has always got a ball in his hands, bouncing it, tossing it. Why, he nearly knocked Harold right off the fireplace mantle!"

"No!"

The clacking grew louder and faster paced. It was difficult to focus on the conversation.

"Who is Harold?"

"My late husband."

This got her attention! Anna stopped and turned to face her.

"He's in an urn on the mantle. A beautiful black marble urn." She laughed merrily. "Oh, the look on your face!" She nearly dropped her groceries for giggling.

"Good evening ladies. Allow us to assist you." Walrus took the bag from Mrs. Williams while Goldstein took both bags from Anna before she could protest. "We're going your way.

"Mrs. Williams…is it?" Goldstein asked nodding to her.

"Oh yes, yes, that's me, Margaret Williams. Margie, my Harold used to call me. That's my late husband, Harold you know…"

"Yes, Mrs. Williams, have you lived in the area long?" He cut in to finish his question.

"Oh my, yes, I've lived here all my life. Seventy four years that'll be next month. Seen a lot of change in those years, I'll tell you that." She shook her finger at him to emphasize her point.

Goldstein lifted his knee to reposition the bags higher in his arms.

"Anna, how about you, how long have you lived in the area?"

"Not nearly as long as Mrs. Williams." She evaded his probing. "And you, Officer Goldstein and…" She leaned around to see the Walrus' badge. "Officer Novak, how long have both of you lived in Pittsburg?"

Novak wheezed, most out of breath. Goldstein held her with his trenchant gaze. His right eye twitched and one corner of his mouth lifted in a possible smile.

"Long enough to know when something is amiss. What brings you to our corner of the world?"

Anna's purse slipped off her shoulder and fell to the ground as she tripped on an unleveled section of the walkway. She slowly gathered her lip color, brush and coin purse and stuffed them back inside. She hoped to think of some way to change the subject by the time she stood up. If she could get Mrs. Williams talking again; she could take the conversation in so many directions.

"Mrs. Williams, in seventy four years, you have witnessed a lot of progress. What do you think of automobile travel? Do you think you will ever drive one?" She avoided eye contact with Goldstein but could feel his biting glare boring into the side of her head as Mrs. Williams went on about the evils of automobiles.

"Well, here we are." She announced abruptly to Anna's relief, and reached for her bag from Officer Novak. Anna turned to Officer Goldstein for the other two bags.

"Thank you for your kind assistance."

He resisted.

"We will be happy to see you safely home as well, Miss Frederik. How much further to your place?" He grinned.

"This one is Mrs. Williams' bag." She stated pulling one bag from him and positioning it on her hip. She then wrapped her free arm around her own bag and pulled it away. "We've taken enough of your time, gentlemen. I'm sure you have more important things to do than carry groceries." She smiled triumphantly and headed up the walk to the front door.

Once inside, she looked out the front window. The officers were walking slowly across the street. She took the groceries into the kitchen and set them on the counter by the sink. There was a door behind the table leading straight out the back. She made her excuses when Mrs. Williams invited her to stay for a tall lemonade and slipped out the back.

* * *

Anna slammed the refrigerator door shut and leaned against it with her arms folded. She didn't get rye bread. What right did they have to deprive her of toasted cheese on rye? She hadn't broken any laws. She paced the small kitchen area a couple of times arguing with herself about whether she dared to go back and get the rye bread. It was just a coincidence; they were just overly friendly policemen...overly nosey. Were they studying her or was she being paranoid? American policemen wouldn't be in on the Belgian plot, would they?

She clicked on the radio Jack gave her. It was very old and she had to turn it just the right direction to get reception. She propped it with a book at just the right angle and dropped on to her bed. She would get the rye tomorrow morning before work.

* * *

Jack had gone to visit his brother for a few days and wouldn't be coming in to work, which meant she could expect another boring day. There would be no baseball game or concert for her tonight. She grabbed her purse and keys, locked the door and started down the stairs. She could smell bacon cooking and hear the voices of the breakfast patrons in the café below. She wasn't on duty until lunch today and had time to go to the market first.

She decided a slice of onion would go nicely on her toasted cheese on rye. She went to the produce at the back of the market. As she sorted through the onions, movement to her left caught her eye. She looked up and there he stood, gently tossing an apple in his hand, leaning against the wooden bin. Diederik smiled and winked at her. Nearly a month of sending her picture out to police departments and checking on leads had finally paid off. The generous reward they had offered helped as well.

She felt like the wind had been knocked from her. She stumbled backward, franticly looking around for an escape. He just stood there calmly shaking his head as if to say "It's no use, we've got you." Maurits was out front and there was no back door. His calm, confident, smug demeanor made her panic all the more. She put her hand out to catch herself and knocked an onion to the floor. Diederik swept it up and placed it back in the bin behind her as he leaned close and spoke in a low voice.

"Don't make this difficult. We can walk out together and not draw attention, or I can throw you over my shoulder and carry you out. Do not mistake my dignity for weakness. You are coming with me."

She saw no other options, so she went quietly to the front of the store, though her heart was pounding wildly. She could bolt. How far could she get before he caught her? Would he chase her down in public? He said he would throw her over his shoulder, but would he really? This wasn't a dark street in Chicago, surely he couldn't force her to go with him here, in front of people that knew her. Jim was at the front helping a customer.

"Jim, help me, I'm being abducted!" She dashed to the counter. Diederik stepped calmly to the counter beside her, taking her arm.

"Anna, please, it is time to come home and work things out." He turned to the store owner. "We have been so worried, searching for her this last month. We were so relieved when the police notified us that she was here." He put his arm around her shoulders and gave her a brotherly squeeze.

"We wondered how a girl like her could just show up all by herself, with absolutely nothing. We kind of thought she might be a runaway. We've all sort of watched out for her. She's a good girl, don't be too hard on her." He nodded his approval to Diederik and flashed Anna a condescending wink and smile. Diederik shook hands with Jim and thanked him for taking care of Anna before he bustled her out the door with her mouth hanging open in complete astonishment.

Diederik got in the back of the car with her while Maurits drove. He quickly locked a cuff over her right wrist and then to his left.

"I can't believe you got away with that! He has known me for nearly a month now and you walk in off the street and he believes you!"

"It was easy; we look too respectable for anyone to suspect us of anything underhanded. You look too respectable to be out on the streets by yourself. I warned you not to draw attention to yourself."

She leaned back and tried to fold her arms, dragging Diederik's hand across her lap. He jerked it back to the space between them. She couldn't even pout properly! If she was to take advantage of opportunities, she must first get her wrist free.

She leaned toward his window, pointing at various bridges and sights as she stuck her right hand in his left pocket. No key. She leaned further across pointing excitedly with her right hand, clumsily dragging his left hand along, trying to cause enough confusion to cover her left hand in his right pocket. She had it! Just in time, as he gently pushed her back to her side of the car.

"Would you like to see a baseball game while you are here? There are so many things I can show you if we stay a few days. When will you ever have the chance again?"

"So that you will have more time to escape? I think not."

"You know I will escape again anyway, why not have some fun first?!"

The looks they gave her drove her to sit back in silence. It was enough distraction though, the cuff was unlocked and they were coming to a busy intersection. Just as they came to a stop to let a mother and her two small children cross, Anna clipped the cuff to his door handle and jumped out her door.

"Sorry, you had your chance. We could have had a great time here."

By the time Maurits could pull the car over to the side of the road and get out to chase her, she had caught a ride going the other direction and was out of sight. They spent the next 15 minutes trying to pick the lock before they saw the tip of the key between the seat cushions. As Maurits stuck his fingers between the cushions to grab it, it dropped behind the seat. They spent the next 10 minutes getting it out.

They decided that if she remained in town, they would eventually find her. So they went directly to the train station to cover that option first.

They showed her picture to the men selling the tickets. Luck was smiling on them. Not only did one recognize her, but he remembered the destination she had purchased. New York! They supposed she would have gone back to Chicago. She was a clever girl. Her train was leaving in five minutes. Diederik quickly bought a ticket and ran for the train. Maurits would meet him at the next stop with the car.

The sights of Pittsburgh rolled past, slowly picking up speed. Sadness settled over Anna for the things she probably would never do and the people she would never see again. Would she ever be normal? Would she ever be able to stay in one place and develop permanent relationships? What would become of Tiger? She convinced herself that he needed her, but he was pretty independent now that his leg was well. Jack would look after him if he still needed anything.

Jack. He was the closest friend she had had in a long time, and she hadn't even known him for a full month. What would he think when she came up missing? Would he care? Would he search for her? Jim would surely tell Henry and he would most likely tell Jack that her brother had found her and taken her home. She couldn't circle around and return to

Pittsburg now; that bridge had been burned. She didn't have any serious or permanent ties to Pittsburg, but she wasn't anxious to move on.

She looked over the stops on her ticket. Where should she get off next? They were out of the city and the countryside flashed by outside her window. She was so deep in her thoughts as she stared out the window, she barely realized someone had taken the seat beside her. She looked back at her ticket in her lap and then noticed Diederik's shiny black shoes and jerked up to see him sitting beside her. Her heart did a back flip and landed with a thud at the bottom of her stomach. How was he able to keep doing this? Was he a magician? She shut her eyes and breathed deeply to regain her composure.

"You enjoy instilling fear in me don't you? What will your King say if I die of heart failure?"

His smile betrayed the fact that he did enjoy her reaction. If he didn't have such attractive boyish features, she might be seriously frightened.

"Just as you enjoy causing me so much trouble." He pulled the necklace he had given her from his inside pocket.

"The money you have been living on is about half of what it cost me to buy it back." He closed the box and replaced it in his inside breast pocket.

"When will you tire of this cat and mouse game? We have other responsibilities in our homeland. We should have returned long ago."

"Then return. When will you realize that I am not going with you?"

"We are getting off at the next stop. Maurits will meet us there with the car. It may take him longer to get there, however, but make no mistake, you will be with me."

"You know you really missed out on a lot of fun in Pittsburgh. You should have let me show you around, take you to the symphony and a baseball game. The next time you find me, wherever that next city is, you should let me show you around. By the time you find me, I will try to have some fun things planned for us to do," she said playfully.

"I am not playing your little game and there will not be a next time."

He was getting angry so she decided she had better stop teasing him.

"Excuse me, I need to use the restroom."

"No!"

"What are you worried about? Do you think I will climb out the window going this speed?" She laughed as she slid past him, "I think you are worried that I am better at cat and mouse than you are!"

He stood and followed her. He had no intention of losing her again. When they pulled into the station, she was still in the restroom. She decided to stay until the train left this station. This is where Maurits would come for them, but he wouldn't be here yet. Diederik wouldn't be able to get word to him to go on to the next station. She didn't know how to get away from Diederik, but this would definitely confuse his plans.

Diederik was getting anxious to get off the train and knocked impatiently.

"Come out at once or I will be forced to come in after you." He hissed after a large group of people had gone past.

"I'll scream."

"You can't stay in there forever. I am not getting off this train without you."

He had come to the end of his patience and was about to go in to get her, when a woman came down the aisle and stopped next to him.

"This is the women's restroom, sir."

"Yes…I a" He spoke to the door. "Anna, dear, come out please. A line is forming." His face felt pink and he knocked again.

"I'm very sorry, I'm not feeling well." She moaned and the woman sent Diedrik to the dining car for some peppermint tea.

Once the train was moving again fast enough that she was sure Diederik wouldn't grab her and jump off, she opened the door and stepped out into the aisle. Diederik glared at her as he handed her the cup of tea. The woman slipped into the ladies room and Anna hid a smirk behind her cup as she sipped the warm tea.

"We have an hour until the next stop." She smiled. "Let's go to the dining car and get something to eat." She put her arm through his and started down the aisle, pretending not to notice his extreme indignation.

She was out of ideas when they pulled into the next station and he wasn't letting her out of his grasp. It would take some time to get word to Maurits of their new location, then they would have to wait for him to get there. She stayed on watch for any opportunity that might arise.

Diederik was better at the game than she had expected. He bought return tickets and they got directly on a train that would be back where Maurits would be waiting for them, about the time he would get there!

She spent the time asking him questions about his family, flirting and trying to develop a friendship. She hoped that if he got to know her as a person, not just as an assignment, maybe he would be more inclined to help her in her cause of freedom. He was not unkind, but he was not talkative either. He gave her very little information. He was a patriot to his country and he had no intention of letting himself be dissuaded from his cause.

When they got off the train, Maurits was waiting and very relieved to see them. When they weren't there waiting for him, he was worried that something had gone wrong.

"Nothing I could not handle." He snapped, then he shot her a triumphant wink and put her firmly into the car. "Maurits, get in here. It is my turn to drive. And do not let her get away!"

Chapter 6

The ride to New York was surprisingly pleasant. Anna had resigned herself to the idea of relocating and was making the best of the situation. These men were polite and attentive to her needs. They were so reserved and proper that she relished giving them a hard time. She could tell that beneath their discomfort, they enjoyed the idea that she was flirting with them.

They were very cautious every time they stopped to refuel, stretch their legs or to use the restrooms. They bought food to eat in the car while driving. No opportunity for escape presented itself.

"You just don't give up, do you? Why are you are so determined when you know you can't win?" Anna marveled at their persistence.

"Why are you so determined to not help us?" Diederik became serious. "Are you so selfish you can not think of the needs of others? What is so important here that you can not leave, even to help an entire nation?"

That stung. She stopped teasing as she thought about their cause. She needed a cause, a purpose for living. She wanted so much to be needed and loved, but the thought of living in marriage with a Henry VIII or a Napoleon was so repulsive.

After reflection she replied. "I will go and serve your people, but I will not marry a man I don't love."

"The way you can serve our people is through a political marriage, a union with the right country would bring much needed protection."

"Then, what if I marry both of you? The two of you should equal a prince!"

The look of horror she exacted from them let her know her humor was not appreciated.

"Are you implying that you love both of us?"

She sat back and smiled, enjoying the discomfort she was causing them.

"Well I must admit, you are starting to grow on me."

They became very serious and rode in silence for a while. The next time they stopped to stretch, she headed for a rocky area off to the side of the road. She wedged the spiked heel of her shoe between some rocks and snapped it off. She pretended to be upset about it and convinced them that she would need a new pair before they began their trip across the Atlantic Ocean. Diederik agreed to drop Anna and Maurits off at Macy's while he contacted the pilot.

She found some cute little black pumps with a rhinestone buckle. They purchased them and started back through the store.

"Oh, look at this dress. I only have the dress I'm wearing. Every time I "relocate" I have to start over on my wardrobe. May I try it on?"

"No," he said firmly. "I have no intention of letting you go anywhere without me. If you know your size, you may purchase it, but you will not try it on."

She was running out of time. She saw a security guard looking her way. She gave him a suspicious look and quickly put her hand in her pocket. She grabbed Maurits arm.

"Let's go then." She hurried him toward the door.

The security guard intercepted them.

"You're going to have to come with me, Ma'am." He took her by the arm and guided her to the security office.

Maurits glared at her. She gave him an innocent "What's going on" look.

"Do something. Help me." She mouthed.

Maurits had to wait outside the office while they questioned her and searched her pockets. They found nothing, of course and she acted very offended by their unfounded accusation.

"What is this all about?! I just bought these shoes here and now I'm treated like this? I've never been so humiliated in my life!"

Actually she was more humiliated when some men had waited for her at her apartment in Chicago and one of them threw her over his shoulder and stuffed her in the back of their car, especially since she had brought this on herself intentionally. But she had no intention of correcting herself.

When they apologized and asked what they could do to make it up to her, she asked if they had a back entrance, as she had no intention of humiliating herself further by walking through their store after this. They offered to get the gentleman she was with.

"No, I won't embarrass him by letting him be seen with me now." She wrote him a note and asked them to wait 15 minutes, and then give it to him.

"He will be upset at first, but he will understand my reasons." They agreed and she slipped quietly out the private entrance.

Maurits was pacing nervously when they finally gave him her note. His worst fears were confirmed as he read the note.

Dear Maurits,

Thank you for a lovely day. I couldn't possibly leave my country forever without seeing New York! I wish we could all three see it together. Maybe we shall see each other again, if not here, perhaps in California. I hear it is pleasant there this time of year. I am sorry to cause you difficulty, but I will not marry some spoiled, rich royal just because he thinks I should. I am sure you feel you must give him his way and gratify his every whim, but I do not. He can find someone else.

Sincerely,

Anna

Diederik and Maurits spent the rest of the day hiring two dozen men to search New York City and to follow the rail line to California, checking every town in between. They returned to Belgium to report to the King.

Albert, King of the Belgians, Leopold, Charles, Geoffrey and other government officials sat in the Royal Office listening intently as Diederik and Maurits reported in detail the events of their assignment in America.

"We feel that inappropriate feelings are developing and request to be taken off this assignment. We recommend that reinforcements from the Elite Guard be sent over. We also recommend that His Royal Highness, Prince Charles, be there personally to meet Anna and reassure her that ours is a cause she can believe in."

Maurits read the note Anna had left for him at Macy's. It shed some light on why she was so adamantly opposed to their offer. Charles reluctantly agreed to go—after she was found again. He would spare only the time that was absolutely necessary.

Charles was mildly amused that Anna thought she was being brought on a whim, to satisfy his spoiled, royal desires. She couldn't be further from the truth.

The last fifteen years had not dimmed his commitment to remove his personal feelings and desires from his decision making process. He had lasted a good three seconds on the back of one of his father's new stallions. Charles was thrown into the wooden gate to the small pen where he was kept separate from the other horses. The gate gave way, probably saving his life, and he scrambled through, kicking it shut with his foot. He escaped with some scrapes and pretty intense bruises. The beautiful animal was not so lucky. He thrashed around wildly, terrified by the firecrackers set off by the older boys, nearly severing one of his front legs between the slats of the fence.

His father had required him to end the suffering of this prized animal.

"There are times when taking a life is necessary; but it never should be taken lightly. Your acceptance has come at a very high price. You can not just live for the moment; you must learn to think ahead to future consequences." This was advice he would not soon forget. "Doing what is right in the face of peer pressure requires a great deal of courage…You have a great deal of courage…do not allow it to become misguided."

He would have preferred some form of corporal punishment, but this had a much more profound impact on his life. He would not run from peer pressure as Geoffrey had, but he would not give in to it either. He would look it squarely in the eyes, turn and walk away from it. Never again would his emotions rule him.

The praise and acceptance of these older boys, which had been of supreme importance to him, began to sour in his stomach. The memory of this incident seared his conscience even more when the word spread of his bravery. The older boys clapped him on the back congratulating him for his heroics. It was almost more than he could bear when Johanna walked up to him and kissed him on the cheek, right in front of Geoffrey. The attention only intensified the guilt. Geoffrey was so jealous he wouldn't speak to Charles for nearly two weeks.

He continually found examples of good men being destroyed by yielding their judgment to the desires of their hearts.

Bringing Anna to Belgium was a result of Charles yielding only to the good of his people.

Chapter 7

Anna stared out the window as the landscape became a blur of yellow, orange and red. Surprisingly, she missed her two companions. She was tired of being a new stranger in town. She desperately wanted someone familiar, someone to need her and love her. Would she ever belong anywhere, to anyone? Tears started to trickle down her cheeks as loneliness surrounded her. She was finished with traveling, uprooting, and starting over. The next stop was New Haven, Connecticut. That would be her new home, her permanent home. She would develop relationships firm enough that someone would care if she came up missing again.

New Haven was a charming little city, especially in autumn. Anna planned to work and save her money until she could be a student at Yale University. Until then, she spent her extra time in the library, reading, studying and learning everything she could.

She met Thomas there. He was a law student at Yale and a stimulating companion. They enjoyed walks up the path to the top of East Rock overlooking the town. The autumn colors were spectacular, the crisp air invigorating and their conversations were enlightening. Thomas was very intelligent and knowledgeable. He was more mature than Jack. She struggled to decide if that was a good thing. He was also more possessive and overbearing.

Thomas took Anna to her first American football game. There was more action in football than in baseball. She didn't know all the rules or catch all the intricacies of the various plays, but she understood the general idea and joined in the spirit of the game. New Haven was steeped in tradition and joining in was expected.

New Haven was founded in 1638, it was nearly 300 years old. There were so many historical places to see. George Washington had been in this very city. Nathan Hale attended Yale University and had lived at Connecticut Hall. There was a statue of him out front at the corner of the building.

Lighthouse Point was one of Anna's favorite places. She and her friends, Barbara, Sally Jo and Margaret, occasionally went out to Lighthouse Point for picnics. She loved walking along the shore. Sometimes she would go there by herself with a book and spend an entire day reading.

Occasionally, when she was in the library reading, she would find herself reading about Belgium. She was annoyed with herself today. She didn't miss them any more. For all she knew, Diederik and Maurits could have wives and children back in Belgium. She had friends now. And she was going to the Harvest Ball with Thomas tonight. She loved New Haven. She liked working for Frank Pepe at The Spot, he was good to her. He was so much like Enzo, back in Chicago. Frank always talks about moving his pizzeria to Wooster Street. He has big plans of expanding. He wants her to move to the new place when he opens it.

She had covered a lot of ground and met a lot of people in the last few months. She still looked over her shoulder occasionally, but she noticed it wasn't so much out of fear, as it was hope. Why was she still struggling with her past? How could she long for the very people she was hiding from? She became very irritated with herself, put the book away and left the library. She needed to be with friends right now.

Anna stood behind Sally Jo, brushing her hair while Barbara painted Margaret's nails. They laughed and teased each other, until the topic of marriage was brought up. Barbara was engaged and the others hoped their boyfriends would become fiancés soon. They assured Anna that in time Thomas would come to that point as well. That thought hit her like a sand storm. She felt flushed with anxiety.

"But we hardly know each other."

"Don't act so surprised, surely you know how he feels about you."

"You're not just leading him on are you?"

"Well I, I'm not sure." She looked at the floor. He was fun to be with sometimes, but marriage! They all looked on reprovingly, waiting for her explanation.

"I don't know how I feel about him." Visions and scenarios jumped at her, none of which really tempted her.

"Don't be foolish, he is from a prominent family, he will be a very successful lawyer. You are lucky to have him."

She quietly put on her gown and Margaret buttoned her up the back. "Shall I brush out your hair?"

She pulled on her stockings, straightened the seams up the back and buckled on her heels.

"Anna," Margaret leaned over her shoulder. "Would you like me to brush out your hair and pin it up?" She laughed at Anna's far away look.

"Oh, yes. I'm sorry." She shook her head and tried to laugh.

When the young men arrived to pick them up for the dance, Barbara's mother insisted on a photograph of each couple and then the entire group. While Sally Jo and her beaux were being posed, Thomas pulled Anna aside.

"Do you have other shoes?"

"Not here with me. Why?"

"I don't like the shoes you have on. We'll have to swing by your place to change." She opened her mouth to protest but he wrapped his arm around her and hurried her over to pose for the group shot.

She was still irritated when they finally made it to the ball. He hadn't liked any of her shoes and she ended up wearing the original shoes she had intended, arriving 30 minutes late.

One of Thomas' old girlfriends found him and decided to reminisce extensively. Anna, tired of waiting on the outside of their conversation, joined Margaret and Sally Jo at the punch bowl. When Thomas noticed, he caught her attention and pointed at the floor beside him, nodding to her. She turned her back to him, fuming. Did he think she was his trained puppy? He treated her like she was one of his many possessions. She was becoming more convinced of her feelings for Thomas and they didn't include marriage.

"Excuse me, I think I'll go...powder my nose or something." She slipped out a side door and walked home.

Flowers were delivered to her at work the next day with a note explaining that she needn't be jealous of an old girlfriend. Norbert, the newest employee, watched curiously as she read the note gave a short laugh and tossed the flowers in the waste barrel.

"You don't like roses?"

"I love roses. I just don't like Thomas anymore."

"Then you are available for a movie tonight? *Animal Crackers* is playing at the Madison."

A good Marx Brothers comedy sounded appealing.

"Yes, I guess I am." Norbert was cute. She felt drawn to him. She wasn't sure if it was his foreign accent or that he was new in town and struggling to make friends. Maybe she was just subconsciously looking for someone to edge Thomas out of her life. Whatever the reason, they soon became good friends. He seemed to enjoy being with her, but he didn't push a serious relationship the way Thomas did. He didn't talk about himself much, which was a welcome change. She didn't want to divulge her past either, so she avoided asking questions that might lead to divulging her own recent past. They just kept it light and friendly. All she knew was that he was from New York.

Norbert gradually became Anna's only friend. The friends she had made were all friends of Thomas. The more she avoided Thomas, the more uncomfortable she felt around his friends. They questioned her about Norbert and how she felt about Thomas. They kept pressuring her to make a commitment to Thomas. The truth was, she was not in love with Thomas and he seemed to be more in love with himself than anyone else. His accomplishments and plans for the future were his favorite topics. He did have a lot to be proud of and he was interesting at first, but she couldn't envision spending the rest of her life with him. She didn't dream about spending the rest of her life with Norbert either, but the good part was she didn't have to. He didn't expect any commitment from her.

Anna strolled down the sidewalk toward the Madison movie house, looking in the windows along the way. Warm cinnamon aroma drifted out of the bakery as a tray of puffy frosting smeared buns was placed in the window. A smart little wool skirt and jacket with fur collar caught her eye in the next window; until she noticed the head was still attached to the fur!

"Ugh!"

"Anna?"

She whirled around. It was Margaret.

"You don't have to pretend you don't know me." She laughed derisively. "Where have you been hiding? We never see you anymore."

Norbert called to her from across the street and Anna waved back.

"It's good to see you again Margaret." She was honestly sad to lose Margaret's friendship.

Norbert loped over to where they stood. **"We need to hurry, the movie will be starting soon."** Anna and Norbert spent an increasing amount of time together and they enjoyed a movie on the rare occasion when they both had an evening off work.

Margaret's eyes narrowed and she sliced him what could barely be construed as a smile.

"Norbert, this is Margaret." Anna introduced. He smiled and held out his hand to her.

"He's cute. Are you babysitting, Anna?" She took his hand and laughed lightly. "I'll tell Thomas 'Hello' for you." She flounced away.

"Don't mind her." Anna took his arm and pulled him toward the theater.

All Quiet on the Western Front had earned rave reviews and Anna had hoped to see it some day. She was excited to learn that it was the movie now playing, but after watching it she was somewhat depressed as they slowly left the theater.

"War is horrible. They were all so excited to go off and become heroes and they ended up dying." She flipped her collar up and jerked her coat tighter around her. "Why do we have wars? Everyone should just refuse to fight." Norbert walked quietly with his hands in his pockets, allowing Anna to continue to vent. "Let the generals declare their wars, if they don't have anyone to fight for them, see where it gets them." She wagged her finger at no one in particular.

"So, Margaret was right." Thomas stepped directly in front of Norbert, feet spread and arms folded. "What do you think you're doing?"

"Thomas?!"

"Stay out of this, Anna. Go wait over there." Thomas motioned to a bench with his head.

"What is this all about? What do you want?" Anna was practically screaming.

"I said wait over there." Thomas pointed and then clenched his fists.

"Anna, do as he says. Please." Norbert put his hand on her shoulder and asked gently.

"Get your hands off her." Thomas bellowed and Anna stepped back.

"I'm not going to fight you." Norbert remained relaxed. "Anna is old enough to make her own decisions."

"You had better mind your own business and stop messing up my life." Thomas glared.

"I am not..." Norbert took a blow to the side of his face. Anna leaped forward but was assaulted with Thomas' putrid breath.

"You've been drinking!" She fell back. "No wonder you're making such a fool of yourself."

Norbert stood taught, his jaw clenched and muscles pulsing, but made no move to defend himself. Thomas drew back to take another swing and Anna grabbed his arm.

"Stop it. Leave him alone." He shoved her hard and she stumbled back into a gathering crowd. Norbert blocked one blow but took another to the ribs before two men grabbed Thomas and sent him on his way.

"Are you alright?" Anna dabbed at his lip with her handkerchief. "I'm so sorry."

"Why did you break up with him? He seems like such a great guy." He teased as he put out his arm for her and led her away from the dispersing crowd.

"Why didn't you hit him back? If anyone deserves it, it's him."

"What about your lecture about everyone refusing to fight?" He smiled again. "He is bigger than me." He shrugged and moved on.

"How about an ice cream soda?" He guided her into the drug store and seated her at the ice cream counter. She watched him while he read the flavors to her and ordered. His lip bruised and starting to swell marred his innocent boyish face. Margaret had asked her if she was babysitting. She was only trying to insult him and make her go back to Thomas, but Norbert did look quite young.

"How old are you?" she asked as he handed her the cherry soda.

"Twenty two." He cocked an eyebrow. Where did this line of questioning come from?

"Really? I would have guessed 18, 19 at the oldest."

"Oh?" He stirred his chocolate soda with the straw and drank.

"You seem so carefree. You just go to work…you're not in school…you have no one to care for except yourself. What are your plans for your future? What will you do with your life?"

He swallowed and smiled. "How about you, what are your plans? Were it not for your youthful appearance, I would suppose you to be about 30 years of age. You seem to have life all figured out."

Ugh. She didn't want to get into her life or plans for the future.

"Well sonny, get me my cane. It's time we were heading home; it's way past my bedtime." She answered in a shaky voice as she stood to leave.

"I meant it as a compliment. This will have to do, you have no cane." He held his arm for her. "We will take it slow."

"Where are you from?"

"I've come from New York." More questions?

"No, before that."

He wrinkled his brow.

"Your accent, where are your people from?"

He smiled and pointed straight up.

"Heaven?" She laughed. "I believe it. I love your accent, I could listen to you talk all night."

"All night?! I wouldn't be from Heaven if I kept you out all night." He winked and offered her his arm again, this time she took it.

* * *

She showed him all the historical places around town that she had learned about, explaining the significance of each building and monument. She looked forward to meeting him each morning before work to take him on a tour. On their day off they hiked up East Rock and had a picnic on the grass near the Soldiers and Sailors Monument commemorating those that had given their lives in battle. She read the plaque to him as he stretched out, leaning on one elbow.

"I have been thinking about that movie...about the Great War. I admire those willing to give their lives in the battle for freedom." He looked up at the monument, then at her. "Of course it is best to peacefully work out agreements if possible, but sometimes war is unavoidable."

She gave a short laugh remembering Thomas and his determination to fight Norbert.

"Would you give your life for the freedom of others?" He rolled over to his back and shielded his eyes from the sun.

"It's hard to say, not being in that situation. I hope that I would...and you?"

"Yes, I would do whatever I had to do. Giving your life for others does not always mean dieing for them; sometimes it means living a life that maybe you would not choose, for the good of others." He jumped up anxious to change the subject. "Would you like to play catch? I brought a football." He pawed through their lunch basket and pulled out a football.

She remained sitting on the grass, stacking and rearranging the acorns she had gathered within sitting reach. He was afraid to fight Thomas, but he claims he would give his life for others? Norbert was definitely more fun to be with than Thomas, but this was the first serious conversation they had ever had and it lasted less than five minutes. That, of course, was as much her fault as his. She avoided any conversation that might lead to disclosing her own situation.

"I am highly offended that you prefer a pile of acorns to me." He smiled, tossing his ball and catching it. She smiled and held her hand out for him to pull her to her feet. After each throw, he shortened the distance between them. "You throw like a girl!"

"Oh Really!?" She stood with her hands on her hips and a defiant look on her face. With a twinkle in his eye he ignored her pretense of being offended. He placed the ball in her hand with her fingers on the stitching.

"Now cock your hand back behind your head and put a little spin on it as you fire it off."

He stood behind her helping her get it just right. With his left hand on her shoulder and his right hand on hers, he showed her the correct form for a perfect throw.

She loved being able to flirt with him without him taking it too seriously. But sometimes, she wished he would take her bait just a little. She wouldn't mind a little noncommittal contact once in awhile. She lowered her arm and turned to face him.

"So, you've never noticed that I am a girl? I guess that's why you've never tried to hold my hand." Uncomfortable with this exchange and her close proximity, he snatched the ball from her and loped across the grassy park.

"Just because you are a girl doesn't mean you have to throw like one." He smiled, firing a perfect spiral right into her arms.

It was a warm afternoon for late autumn, perfect for their leisurely stroll back to town. A patchwork of red, gold and deep orange maple and oak leaves spread on the ground before them. A muted sparkle twinkled across their path as the leaves above fluttered in the gentle breeze, casting alternating light and shadow. Occasionally, a break in the trees afforded a sweeping view of the landscape below. Tufts of varied autumn colors dotted the countryside while whiffs of juniper and pine danced on the breeze.

"Would you like to go to New York sometime?"

She cocked her head to the side and narrowed her eyes. Of course, she would love to go, but what exactly was he proposing?

"I will need to go there sometime soon. I thought you might like to go with me. The Empire State Building is near completion. It is quite a sight to behold. We could go to Times Square and maybe a Broadway play."

"I would love to go, but I don't think it would be appropriate."

"We could stay in separate hotel rooms, separate hotels if you like! And I would have people in New York, we would not be alone."

She thought about that. "I would like that very much. Thank you."

Anna was surprised at how much she trusted Norbert after knowing him for such a short time. She felt so safe with him. He was always protective of her and attentive to her needs. He never rejected her advances, but he never made any himself. She slipped her hand into his as they walked.

"Tell me about New York."

"Well, I haven't studied the history of New York as extensively as you have New Haven. I am afraid I won't be a very good tour guide. Perhaps you should study about New York at the library and you can teach me."

A small bushy squirrel dashed across the path in front of them and behind a nearby tree. They crept closer to watch it but it scampered away. He placed her hand at the bend of his elbow and held it there with his other hand as they continued on.

She realized that New York was probably the last place she should go especially since she was getting those feelings of being watched again. Diederik and Maurits had most likely hired people to find her and they were possibly closing in. New York was the place they kept hauling her back to, each time they found her. She didn't know how they planned to cross the ocean, but New York seemed to be the launching place. All they would have to do is follow her there and close in.

She considered telling Norbert of the possible dangers, but it was all so unbelievable. She decided to tell him only if trouble showed. He was strong and quick, and could probably figure their way out of trouble. And she really wanted to see New York!

Several days had passed since Norbert had invited her to go to New York with him. He hadn't mentioned it again since, although they had spent time together nearly every day. They had just spent the morning on The Green. She explained to Norbert how the Green had been the cemetery for the first 150 years of the settlement. Later they moved the headstones to the new cemetery, but the bodies remained beneath the Green. He seemed to enjoy learning the history of New Haven. She knew quite a lot about the area considering the short time she had lived there. She spent a lot of time reading about it.

They had lost track of the time and were nearly late for work. They had to run to make it on time. When they burst through the door, Frank called to Norbert. "Bert, you have a telegram waiting for you. Go pick it up. The telegraph office will be closed when you get off tonight." He turned and ran out the door.

After work Norbert told Anna that he had gotten word from his people and needed to go to New York tomorrow!

"I asked Frank if we could have a few days off. He said it would be fine. Pack your things!"

Chapter 8

The next morning they got a later start than Norbert had hoped. Anna was having a hard time deciding what to pack.

"Take everything, that way you don't have to decide." He smiled but with a frustrated edge to his voice. She quickly threw everything she could fit into her bags so as not to try his patience any further.

They stopped at Louis' Lunch for a quick hamburger to-go and got on the road by about 11:00.

It was beautiful weather for this time of year and she was so excited to finally have the chance to see New York.

They wound through colorful maple groves, pumpkin patches and apple orchards. Norbert stopped at a little roadside stand and bought some fresh pressed cider. Life couldn't get much better than this! There was a crisp chill in the air that sent a thrill down her spine as she filled her lungs with the scents of autumn. She loved the change of seasons and this season in this part of the country was beyond reality.

When they got back in the car Norbert turned on the heater and Anna snuggled close to him, drawing her knees up onto the wide bench seat. She rested her head on his shoulder and she could feel him tense up as she wrapped her hands around his arm. Was he really that shy? If he didn't like her, why did he invite her to come with him? She decided he could just get used to it, she wasn't moving away from him.

They pulled into the next filling station they came to. As Norbert got out of the car pulling his wallet from his back pocket, the telegram fell out onto the seat. He didn't notice. He shut the door and went to find a telephone while the attendant filled the tank. Her curiosity overcame her and she picked it up and read it.

"We are in New York stop

Proceed as planned stop"

She quickly put it back on the seat and looked out the window, pretending not to notice it. Her mind started to race, what could it mean? It could mean anything. She was just being paranoid again. But the last time she felt paranoid and started suspecting that she was being watched; she was being watched. Who was he meeting in New York and what was their plan? The autumn chill seeped through her skin and soured in her stomach. He said he had people in New York, she assumed he meant family. Whoever this was, just arrived there. Why had he invited her? Was he really "from" New York or did he just land there on his way from Belgium? By the time Norbert got back in the car, her face was moist and her heart was pounding.

"What is wrong? You look pale!"

"Oh Bert, I'm not feeling well. Please take me home. We can go to New York some other time."

The telegram lay folded on the seat. Had she seen it?

"Maybe you have a bit of motion sickness. Would you like to get out and walk around?"

"No, please just take me home."

He started the engine and slowly pulled out onto the road again.

"Bert, you're going the wrong way, please turn around."

"Roll down your window. The fresh air will make you feel better." He replied flatly without looking at her. "I can't wait until later. I have to go to New York today." He began clenching his jaw stubbornly, still refusing to look at her.

"Why?"

"I have business there."

The more he refused to go back, the more nervous she got.

"Please," She pulled up onto her knees, facing him, taking his arm in her hands. "Please take me back now." She begged with increasing intensity.

He bit his lip as he struggled with his decision. If he told her, the trip would be more difficult. She already knows. She must have seen the telegram. Why else would she be acting like this? Once he vocally confirms what she already suspects, things will get rough. You can handle this, you are in the Elite Guard, you are a trained professional. He looked into her big, frightened eyes as she continued to plead with him.

"No," he said firmly and looked straight ahead again, his jaw jutting forward in determination.

She sat back and closed her eyes as tears started to stream down her face.

"How could you do this? I trusted you." She bent her face to her knees and openly sobbed.

For a long time, he didn't know what to say. How could doing the right thing feel so rotten?

"Why are you so opposed to this? He is wealthy, but he is not spoiled, and he is not marrying you because he wants to. He has never met you. He is doing what is necessary for his people, to ensure their freedom. He is a good man...You will have a good life. Please don't be so upset about this. It is a good thing to do."

"I am not upset about being captured again. I will escape again, like I always do. I'm hurt because I thought you were my friend. I trusted you. When you told me the fun things we would do in New York, you just said it to trap me. You knew I wanted to see New York. You never had any intention of showing me those places."

"I will talk to His Royal Highness when we get there. Perhaps he will show you some of the sights before returning."

"Don't bother yourself, I will not go to your country or marry your prince. I will escape again and I will see New York myself."

"You won't escape again," he said flatly. He pressed his lips together, the muscles in his neck pulsing with anger. He was angry that he had to do this to her, but more than that he was angry that he had allowed himself to care; he knew better.

"You see the car ahead of us and five cars behind us?" She hadn't paid any attention to the other cars on the road until now. They were spread out far enough as not to be visible at the same time except on long straight stretches of road; but they were all the same dark grayish black color and shape.

"They are all Belgian Elite Guard." Each sentence was halted and deliberate, letting each statement sink in before the next.

"We have spent the last two months checking towns along the train route from New York to California. When I found you, I wired them and they began gathering in New Haven. The telegram I received yesterday let us know that His Highness had arrived in New York and it was time to bring you in." He looked directly into her eyes as he narrowed his own.

"You won't get past them." It was very obvious that he didn't enjoy delivering this information to her, but he wanted her to know how futile her efforts would be.

"Trying to escape again would be a waste of everyone's time and effort, especially yours."

He rolled down the window partially and let a red streamer fly out, then rolled the end of it into the window.

"What is that for?"

"They have been keeping a distance. That is to let them know that you are aware of what is happening and to be on alert." The mysterious dark cars shortened the gaps between them causing tightness in Anna's chest as they closed in. They're just men, civilized men, not ax murderers, she told herself. They're not going to hurt me.

The next time they stopped at a station to fill, the six cars pulled in a large circle around them. The men got out, four per car, and stood ready until they finished fueling. She searched the faces of the men in the circle around them for Diederik or Maurits. They were all serious, dignified, clean shaven revealing sturdy chiseled features with short military haircuts, but neither Diederik nor Maurits were among them. When they finished refueling they pulled up to a small market and parked under a nearby tree.

Norbert got out and went inside. He was glad for a break from being with Anna. This was a very emotionally difficult assignment. He grabbed two sodas from an ice chest and got in line at the register. He cared about Anna and he didn't want to hurt her. Why couldn't she just give Charles a chance? She was rejecting him without even meeting him. He felt guilty and was blaming her for his own sour attitude.

When Anna got out and started toward the store the circle of men around their car tightened. Only half of the men surrounded her, as the other half were refueling the other cars and buying snacks in the market.

"Excuse me," she said with some irritation as she tried to go between them, but they tightened shoulder to shoulder and would not let her get past them.

"Let me through please. I'm just going inside." She insisted, eyes narrowed and brows furrowed incredulously.

This prison wall of solid muscle and determination glared at her menacingly. Don't even try it; the unspoken threat hung heavily in the air between them. They had spent so much time and effort obtaining her that they weren't going to let her get away again. She backed up against the car just as Norbert came back. He slipped through the circle of men, handing one of them the two drinks he had just purchased.

"What are you doing, Anna?" It was more of a statement of accusation than a question.

"Norbert! Don't let them treat me like this." She cried as she went to him. He took her by the upper arm with his left hand as he opened the car door with his right and put her brusquely back in the car. He got their drinks and got in the driver's seat.

"I told you trying to get away again would be a waste of time," he said handing her one of the drinks.

"No, thank you." She looked away.

"Stop pouting, Anna, and take the drink," he said impatiently. She took the drink, rolled down the window and threw it out smashing it against a rock at the feet of one of the men as he jumped out of the way. Norbert ground his teeth as he backed up and started to pull out to the road again.

"Why are you acting like such a child?" He hissed, not hiding his frustration.

"If I am not allowed to use the restroom, I am not going to continue to drink."

"Is that what this is all about?" His frustration climbed to exasperation. "Why didn't you just say so?"

"Why didn't I just publicly announce to 24 men that I need to use the restroom? You figure that out." She leaned back staring straight ahead, legs and arms crossed with lips pressed into a tight line.

He whirled the car around to the same parking place as before, just as the other cars were pulling around to enter the road. He got out and informed them in Dutch of the change in plans as 18 of the men got out of their cars to form a circle around the entire market. The other six parked their cars and joined the circle watching particularly for back doors and windows.

Norbert opened her door as she timidly stepped out.

"You are making this as humiliating as you possibly can, aren't you?"

"I am just doing what I have to do. Now go do what you have to do." Irritation was still evident in his tone.

She took her time in the restroom. She slowly washed her hands and dried them thoroughly. Then she leaned against the wall between the door and the sink. Why was Norbert treating her like this? She was the victim here.

He was standing outside the door. He felt bad for embarrassing her and regained his composure. When he heard the water turn off, he figured she should be coming out soon. When she didn't, he became concerned.

"Anna, are you alright?...Come out now."

"No, Bert. I told you, I'm not going with you."

"Anna, the market is surrounded. You can not get away. Please stop this foolishness."

"I'm in no hurry."

Curiosity overcame the owner of the market and he came peeking around the corner at them. Norbert explained that she was of royal European descent and they were taking her to Europe by order of their king. Being such a small town, this was extreme excitement for him.

"Are ya gonna break the door down!" He rubbed his hands together excitedly. Norbert cringed at the idea.

"Not if I can get her out otherwise." He pleaded and coaxed until he could see that it was no use.

"How much will a new lock cost you?"

"Bout a dallar fifty, meby two."

"How much for a new door?"

"Not more'n ten dallars. Heck, don't worry bout it, just do what ya gotta do! I'll pay fer it maself." He grinned, hooking his thumbs in his suspenders.

Norbert held the doorknob to keep the door from flying into Anna, should she be behind the door and put his shoulder firmly into the door, splintering the door and casing. When he saw Anna standing off to the side, he tossed the door and grabbed her upper arm. He pulled her firmly out to the car and told her to get in while he went back to pay for the damage. The circle of men closed tightly around her and the car.

"You think because you are bigger and stronger than me you can intimidate me?" She breathed out threateningly, adrenaline beginning to surge through her veins. She marched up to Sebastiaan and grabbed his lapels.

"You can't just do this to me!" She tried to sound powerful. He smiled at the other men in disbelief that this little wisp of a girl thought she could manhandle him. She quickly slipped her hand inside his coat and snatched his gun from its holster. She backed up hastily waving the gun at them and ordering them to get in their cars. They were all smiling. A couple of them were laughing out loud. Sebastiaan was no longer smiling. He grabbed her arm as she desperately tried to fire into the ground to scare him back. Nothing happened, as she knew nothing about safety levers, cocking a pistol or anything but squeezing the trigger. He pulled his gun from her hand.

"You obviously don't know how to use a firearm. Now get back into the car before someone gets hurt."

Thoroughly humiliated, she picked up a good sized stick, fallen from the tree above.

"Well I do know how to use this, so just back away from me or someone will definitely get hurt." She held the stick up and tried to look as daunting as possible.

They were all the more amused that she thought she could take on 24 physically conditioned men—with a one inch diameter stick!

Not wanting to further embarrass her, they just held their perimeter as Norbert joined them.

She was so angry and frustrated that she took a backhand swing at Norbert as he strode up to her to end the standoff. Her weapon broke on his shoulder to about a twelve inch stub. He caught her arm before she could strike again and held her while she fell on his chest pounding with her other fist.

"How could you do this to me? How could you be so cruel, so heartless? You have all these friends to back you up...I don't have anyone! No family, no friends, no one. I haven't been allowed to stay in one place long enough to make any real friends." Her fury sank hopelessly to misery.

"I thought you were my friend. I thought you would protect me...and you turn out to be one that I need protecting from." She broke down and sobbed, dropping her stick and burying her face in his embrace. His heart melted as her small frame shook in his arms.

He held her until she pulled back wiping her eyes and sniffing. He handed her his handkerchief and asked her to get in the car to finish their discussion. Sebastiaan stopped him. "I will trade cars with you...Inappropriate emotions seem to have developed between you."

"She is not finished yelling at me." He half smiled as he gently helped her into the car and shut the door.

"It's alright, I have it coming. I knew when I accepted this assignment there would be risks."

"You did what you had to do. If she knew who you were, she would have run before backup could have gotten there."

His earlier lack of patience with her behavior had only fanned the flames of her resentment for him. He needed to put this fire out before it was out of control.

"It will be better if she gets out her frustrations before we get to New York. She can be very pleasant when she doesn't feel trapped. Their relationship will have a better start if she is in a better mood when she meets His Royal Highness."

They finally got on the road again. Anna stared down at her hands in her lap. She felt horrible about how she had acted. How could she let herself get so far out of control?

"Go ahead, get it out of your system. I deceived you. You have every right to be angry with me."

"I'm sorry Bert. I don't know why I behaved so badly." She replied softly, her emotions still very near the surface.

"Because I betrayed your friendship. You have a valid reason to hate me."

"I don't hate you. I care for you very much. I hoped you were more than just a friend to me. That's why it hurts so much that I am just an assignment to you."

Norbert struggled with how to react to that. He had tried hard to not let more depth into their relationship than necessary. Obviously there were more emotions on both sides than he had planned.

"I think I would prefer to stop and get you a stick." He glanced quickly in her direction. "That hurt much less than this."

"I'm not trying to hurt you, Bert." She answered tenderly, still unable to look at him.

"Nor I you, but the pain is there none the less." He choked back emotions of his own. "You are not in love with me. You don't know me. You are merely in love with the idea of being in love with me. You want someone to care about you, to watch over you and protect you. You want me to be your knight in shining armor, to rescue you and ride into the sunset to live happily ever after. That is a fairytale; it is not real life."

"Can you honestly tell me you don't have feelings for me?"

"Of course not. I have spent nearly every day with you for the past month. Of course I have feelings for you. But I am not in love with you. I do not allow myself that privilege. I would not allow my personal feelings to affect my allegiance to my king, my prince or my country." He looked at her now with pleading eyes.

"Please give His Highness a chance. Just meet him, get to know him…with an open mind."

Give His Highness a chance? Why should she trust any of them? She wasn't set on a serious relationship with Norbert, but she had always felt safe with him and had hoped for his protection going to New York. She never suspected that she might need protection from him. He had tricked her. How could she rely on anything he said, ever? And yet, even now, she wasn't afraid of him. Somehow she felt she could still trust him.

What options did she have? Could she get to know this prince and still reject him if she chose? Would she be allowed to return home if things didn't work out between them? Perhaps he wouldn't want her after he met her. That was certainly a possibility since she had no idea how to act around royalty. Hopefully she wouldn't get herself beheaded!

"If you promise to always be my friend." She took his hand in hers. "I'm afraid to go there alone. I don't know what to do, how to act, what to say. Please say you'll always be nearby."

Norbert took a deep breath to procrastinate his rejection.

"I can not make that promise." He squeezed her hand and returned it to the steering wheel. "A relationship between us will not be encouraged."

Norbert forced his eyes forward, his jaw clenching in rhythm with knuckles alternating white and red as he drove, his lips tightening in silent conversation with himself.

How difficult all of this must have been for him. He had to get to know her to make sure she was the right person. Then he had to keep watch over her until everyone could get word, pay those they had hired to help, and join him in New Haven. He had to build a close enough relationship so that she would trust him, but not "too close," as she was to marry his prince. Anger washed away like a tide slowly retreating down the beach. He was just doing his job. He didn't mean to hurt her. But he had, and she felt so alone. Norbert wasn't really her friend, just a dedicated patriot to his country. Tears welled in her eyes again, spilled and trickled slowly down her cheeks.

They had to refuel once more before they reached New York. Norbert finished first and waited with Anna outside while the others finished and went inside. They walked around a bit stretching their legs. He arched his back and rotated his shoulders in the awkward silence. She kicked at a small rock with her toe. She followed it kicking it again until it rolled into a patch of dandelions where she studied a ladybug without really seeing it. Conversation would never be the same again between them. She was buried in thought when four burly young men ambled over looking for trouble. Norbert ignored them until the tall gangly one began taunting Anna.

"Look at the city girl. Ain't she a purdy little thing?"

"Leave her alone." He commanded.

"Look at the purdy boy here with her." He smiled revealing three gold and two missing teeth. The one in the red plaid flannel shirt shoved Norbert.

"Are you tellin' us what to do?" He glared menacingly.

"We are not looking for any trouble. Just go on your way." Norbert straightened as he evaluated their position.

"She's too purdy for you." The dentally deficient one said as he rubbed a lock of her hair between his fingers. She pulled away and he grabbed her arm as the other three closed in around Norbert.

"Leave us alone or you will regret it." Norbert tried to sidestep the three stooges and get to Anna. She looked nervously toward the market, hoping the others would come out before Norbert got hurt. The middle stooge with a bushy face lunged at Norbert swinging his chunky fist. Norbert caught his arm by the wrist with his left hand and snapped it with his right. He shoved him into the man to his right, the one with the plaid shirt, knocking them both to the ground giving him time to deal with the large keg shaped man on his left. As this one kicked at him, Norbert jabbed his heal into the shin of the leg he stood on, snapping it and dropping him to the ground. The two unbroken men came at him together like twin locomotives. He stepped to the side and ducked his shoulder into the gangly one, tripping the other and sending him sprawling. His momentum carried him over Norbert's shoulder. Norbert caught him, wrapping his arm around his neck from behind. He thrashed around, helplessly dangling and unable to get his footing.

"I can add his neck to your list of broken bones," he said placing his other hand to the side of the man's head. The man in plaid, lying in the dirt, stood up and dusted himself off. He pulled the round man with the broken leg up and wrapped his arm over his shoulder. The bushy-faced man stopped moaning and got to his feet as well.

"Go on your way." Norbert motioned with his head toward the road.

The lumberjack in plaid spit into the dirt.

"She ain't worth it." He turned and hobbled off, hauling his gang with him. Norbert dropped the man he was holding and he scrambled to join the band of not-so-merry men in their retreat.

It all occurred so fast Anna had no time to process what was happening. Her jaw was still unhinged as Norbert put his arm around her and guided her back to the car. Her mind was still spinning as the procession returned to the highway.

"Where was that when Thomas bloodied your lip?"

"What…are you asking me?"

"That breaking bones and flipping over your back stuff. You could have flattened Thomas."

"I don't go around beating people up to pass the time. Thomas was angry as he thought he was losing you because of me. I can not blame him for that." He glanced at her and smiled. "Breaking his legs and throwing him to the ground might have blown my cover as well. Don't you agree?"

She rolled her eyes "Absolutely!" She looked back at the string of cars following them. "Do they all know how to fight like that?"

"Of course, that was very basic training, nothing to be so impressed with."

"What about Diederik and Maurits? Do they…"

"Yes, they are members of the Elite Guard as well."

These men, her captors, were trained weapons. She was never a threat to any of them. The only reason she had ever eluded them was because they had no intention of harming her. If that changed…

"Does…" She shook her head and looked away trying to swallow.

He glanced quickly. "Yes, he does also, but he will not hurt you."

The air field was just outside of New York City. Norbert stopped and the other cars formed a U shape around them. When three more cars pulled into their midst, the men got out and stood at attention in a circle surrounding them. The doors opened simultaneously and twelve men got out. They were all in the black dress uniform that the men in the circle were wearing, except one. He was wearing a white dress uniform, covered with badges, ribbons and gold cords. That must be "him." Anna's heart drummed out a rhythm that would have led an ancient war ship in the speediest of retreats. She squeezed her hands tightly to stop their trembles. A thousand questions sped through her mind. How should she act? What should she say? What must he think of her, causing so much trouble? Would he have her locked in chains and thrown aboard as a prisoner? How could she face him?

"Norbert, please don't make me do this." She grasped at his arm as he opened his door. "I can't do this."

He took her hand in his, gently rubbing the back with his thumb. How could he say the things in his heart?

"I would ask you to trust me, but that would be pointless." He gazed directly into her eyes now. "He won't hurt you, there is no reason to be frightened." He kissed her hand, nodded respectfully and got out.

I'm not getting out of this car; she thought as she rotated straight ahead in her seat again. Surely these men are too dignified to drag me out...I hope. Norbert shut his door, straightened and walked over to "him." The last trace of "friend" disappeared, he was a soldier. She quickly locked all the doors and tried desperately to force her breathing and heart rate to return to normal.

When Norbert reached "him" he made a formal salute, hesitantly dropped it and took his outstretched hand in a firm but cautious handshake. His demeanor suggested his simultaneous desire and hesitation to make a request. The slight angled twist of his head and narrowed eyes invited Norbert to explain.

"In order to entice her to come with me to New York, I promised her a tour of the Empire State Building, Times Square, some of the prominent sights...She wants very much to see New York."

The prince nodded "Then we shall take the time to visit these sights. We must be true to your word." He turned away but stopped as Norbert opened his mouth to speak, but closed it again.

"Is there something else?"

"She is still quite determined not to leave her homeland."

"You have had trouble with her today?" He smiled. "You are much later than I expected."

"Yes...She took Sebastiaan's gun."

He glanced in her direction, at Sebastiaan and back to Norbert in disbelief.

"She mostly just waved it around ordering them to get in their cars and let her go. She tried to fire it into the ground to scare Sebastiaan when he took it back from her, but she never released the safety or even cocked it." He rushed on to explain. "She is not a serious threat, I just wanted to warn you to be on constant alert."

"Thank you, we will take the entire guard with us then." He studied Norbert.

The other men were smiling as they stood at attention, mission accomplished, heads high. Norbert was looking down, troubled, volumes yet to be disclosed.

"There is more." He stated rather than questioned.

"Yes." Norbert looked up with a slight glisten to his eyes. "I request to remain with the crew preparing the vessel."

Charles eyes narrowed with concern. "Is there something you have to tell me?" His look was deeply penetrating, anxious and yet compassionate.

"There is no physical contact to report…but when we return, I will be requesting a transfer to the Congo." Understanding, respect and appreciation passed between them with a look and firm grasp of hands.

"You are off duty. Go to your cabin and get some rest."

Anna watched as the man in white walked around the circle, shaking hands and speaking to each guard. He was tall and slender with broad shoulders, but not gawky or awkward. He had the masculine grace of a panther as he moved smoothly and confidently from man to man. He was not overly handsome, but there was something very attractive about him. What that "something" was, however, eluded her.

The show of deep respect from these men for their leader in white, as they saluted, bowed, and conversed with him was impressive. They didn't appear to be oppressed or afraid of him, but devoted friends. Norbert had only good to say about him. His prince was a good man, unselfish, he would marry her for the good of his country. The occasional glance in her direction made her aware of the topic of their conversation. How much were they telling him?

This icon, image of perfect manhood, the idol put on a pedestal by every other man here, the cause of her abduction, finished his final instructions to his men and strode smoothly to her car. He curiously raised an eyebrow when he tried to open the door and found it locked.

He unlocked it and got in the car with her. He had the key? How embarrassing. This wasn't part of her plan. Fear, admiration, inadequacy and confusion coursed through her; she wasn't sure what to think or feel.

"Hello," he tipped his head and put out his hand. "I am Charles. And you, of course, are Anna."

Still trembling, she put her hand in his to shake it and he lightly kissed her fingers.

"I apologize for the conditions under which we meet and to which you have been subject to for the last few months." He studied her for a moment to determine her reaction.

"I understand you would like to see some of New York City before we proceed on our journey?"

"Yes" she squeaked. She cleared her throat and nodded her head. She knew she wasn't thinking straight and wasn't sure how she should react. She swallowed hard, she could hardly speak. His voice, his accent, his demeanor, the gentle look in his eyes, the way he touched her, the overbearing majesty of his presence made even breathing difficult, thinking and moving impossible.

These emotions were not at all what she expected. He was at the center of all her problems and she planned to let him know how she really felt about this plan of his that involved her, with or without her consent. She certainly did not expect to sit here awestruck. She was angry with herself and confused at her feelings. It wasn't too late, she could still find an opportunity to get away at one of the sights.

"Where is Norbert?"

"He has requested to remain with the crew preparing the air craft…He has also requested that he be reassigned to the Belgian Congo."

His eyes narrowed lifting one brow as if he suspected that she knew why he would make such a request.

He started the engine and pulled out of the circle as the men got in their cars and followed. She pushed on her heart and held her breath in an attempt to force both to slow to a reasonable pace as she sat, not knowing what to say or expect. He noticed her nervousness and tried to calm her with noncommittal conversation.

"Would you like to see the Empire State Building first?"

Her emotions had been near the surface all day. She looked as though she might burst into tears at any minute. So he quickly went on with all the information he could remember about the Empire State Building, hoping to divert her attention away from her present apprehensions. He avoided any topic that might lead to an emotional confrontation. He had been informed by his men of her attitude toward him and her determination to not cooperate. He hoped to break the ice somewhat and calm her fears if possible. He wasn't sure just how to do that in the short time they had, but above all he intended to bring her back with him. If he couldn't convince her here and now, then he would have to do it back at home. He wasn't accustomed to failure or giving up.

Anna wasn't very impressive in appearance. Her eyes were red and swollen and she looked overall like she'd had a rough day. From the report of his men, she had. This changed nothing as far as Charles was concerned. A lack of physical attraction would make it easier to keep his heart in check and prevent his emotions from ruling him.

When they stopped most of the men spread out and surrounded from a distance, inconspicuously standing guard. He had gone to great lengths to obtain her and had extensive precautionary security. Yet he treated her with respect and gallantry.

She quietly studied him as he talked freely, enjoying each stop they made. He was attractive and confident, but not arrogant. He was concerned and attentive to those around him. Occasionally he spoke in Dutch to his men; they would laugh and return conversation. He would then go on with more travelogue information. She didn't realize that he was gleaning information from them to keep their conversation going. One of his men even went around the corner to read a plaque with dates and trivia about the building's construction and relayed the information back to him.

While Charles, Anna and three guardsmen stood in line at the Empire State Building, waiting for the elevator to go to the top, some young ruffians walked by looking for trouble. They heard their foreign speech and started baiting the guardsmen, calling them Krauts, trying to start a fight. Anna backed against the wall and braced herself for another fight;

any one of the guards could have taken the entire group alone. But the guardsmen tried to ignore them, not wanting to create an international incident.

Charles turned to the young trouble-makers and looked directly in their eyes. It wasn't a menacing or threatening look, but it was piercing. He could have summoned a dozen men from the perimeter of the building to intimidate them, but it wasn't necessary. They apologized and quickly left.

They strolled through Central Park past the Boat House, along the east edge of the lake. They past a row of small paddle boats stacked against the fence until spring. They rounded a curve in the path and a large pavilion came into view. A statue of an angel stood in the middle of an empty fountain at the center of the pavilion. A massive stone staircase flanked each side of a multi arched bridge that stood as a backdrop.

They came upon a young mother who was trying to quiet her infant in the carriage while struggling with her toddler that was crying, tired and wanted to be carried. Charles went to one knee and pulled a coin from the toddler's ear, then made it disappear and reappear. He handed the boy the coin and gently picked him up.

"How much farther do you have to go?" he asked the mother.

"I'm meeting my husband at the west entrance, near the Natural History Museum."

"I have a niece just about his age." He laid the child's head on his shoulder and whispered a story to him as they walked. He was sound asleep when they reached the gate and his father. The young mother was very grateful for the assistance; and when he saw Anna take Charles' arm, the father was grateful as well.

How could she not trust someone so kind and gentle? He was as comfortable with a small child as he was giving orders to a company of grown men or even ruling an entire country.

Their final stop was Times Square. The bustle of shoppers and vendors, the smell of hot dogs and chestnuts roasting was exhilarating. They came upon a young lad that was struggling to get his share of the shoe shine business, as he was the smallest and obviously the youngest.

Although you could see your reflection in his shoes, Charles stopped and asked him for a shine. He talked with the lad while he polished and shined. He learned that the boy's father had died and left his mother, himself and three younger brothers. He was now the man of the house, at age 9.

Why was he so at ease getting his shoes shined rather than keeping close watch over her? Her fear of him had subsided, she was quite at ease with him. He didn't seem to be the monster she had expected. In fact she enjoyed being with him. He was considerate, interesting and attractive. If they had more time to get to know each other, perhaps there could be some romance. But time was not on her side and if she was to take advantage of any opportunity, now was her chance. It was rather careless of him to leave her open like this; perhaps he isn't as intelligent as he looks. She began slowly backing away toward a crowd of people.

He clapped his hands and almost instantly 24 guardsmen appeared from every direction, four stood shoulder to shoulder directly behind her. When his shoes were finished he stepped over to Anna and took her hand, placing it on his arm. He quietly gave Sebastiaan the money and instructions to have all their shoes shined and to inform him when they were ready to leave.

Charles took Anna to a street vendor and purchased a bowl of soup for her. The warm soup felt good in her empty stomach on this chilled autumn evening. He sat quietly while she ate. He was relaxed and yet acutely aware of everything around them, patient but not lackadaisical.

When Sebastiaan came with the news that all shines were finished and the boy was paid, Charles turned to Anna. "Is there anything else you would like to see now? It is getting late."

"California?" She replied with a crooked smile.

"It is time to go." He announced, smiling at her attempt at humor.

When they returned to the air field, a crew of men had the Zeppelin fired up and ready to go. It was a magnificent airship, custom made for the King of the Belgians at the factory in Germany. It had 15 deluxe cabins and two grand suits. The gondola was luxurious from end to end.

It was dusk when she got out of the car and stood staring up at the massive airship before her. Men scurried about busily loading crates and untying ropes, doing their jobs to prepare for this adventure.

The reality of leaving America, possibly forever, set in. Her eyes swept the landscape around her, darting wildly like a cornered asp, coiled and ready to spring while searching for a route of escape. But there was none. She would be flying over the ocean, with this group of people she didn't know, in this contraption. It was too overwhelming.

She turned to Charles trembling, "I'm sorry, but I can't do this. Please understand."

Charles turned to one of his men and nodded to him, the guard walked quickly away. As he stood silently looking at her, she became very self conscious. She felt so selfish. He had gone to so much trouble and expense for the benefit of his people. He was willing to marry someone he didn't love.

"It's not that I don't want to help. If there were some way…" She didn't know what to say. She didn't want to be selfish, but this was asking too much.

The guard returned shortly and Charles turned to Anna "I don't want to force you. I would like you to do this of your own will." He took a deep breath and let it out slowly.

"Do you understand how important this is for our country, for our people?" His gaze was penetrating, hypnotic. "Will you do this for the good of many lives?"

"Yes…I want to help…but I don't…it's not that…" Her eyes darted about, her throat swelling shut, wringing her hands, she couldn't seem to finish her thoughts.

"Then you agree." He nodded to the guard behind her; who then held a cloth over her face and everything went black.

Some time passed, an hour, a week? Forcing heavy lids apart, the sparkle of a million diamonds shot needles at her weak eyes. Squeezing her eyes tight again she fought through dense fog. A low gentle rumble lulled her back to sleep. She was standing in Josephine's dining room staring up at her brilliant chandelier. Her mother stood smiling with arms outstretched to her. She tried to go to her but it was like running through water and she faded before Anna could reach her. She was floating and swirling. Where would she be lying in clouded comfort under a chandelier? She fingered and grasped, straining to solve her quandary. A feather bed beneath her and a down comforter atop.

"Mmm." She snuggled deeper into the soft warm sanctuary.

Images swirled in her mind. She was standing in a grassy meadow. Norbert was holding a football cocking his arm to throw. When she caught the football, it changed into a large tankard of cold cider. Her throat was parched and she gulped it down. She kept drinking and drinking but to no avail. She ran through pumpkin patches looking for more cider until she was lost and alone. There was a bright light ahead, she ran to it. She ran into a clearing and stood before a huge zeppelin protected by men in uniform and the man in white! She sat bolt upright her eyes wide, the fog cleared and her heart pounding.

A young girl sitting in a chair reading jumped up, dumping her book to the floor. She picked it up, laid it on a gleaming, intricately carved rosewood dresser and exited quickly. She was, no doubt, informing the captors that her charge was finally awake. A drop of cold sweat trickled down her face. She was on her way to Belgium. She clutched at her nightgown; where were her clothes? How did she...? She jumped up and threw open the closet doors. Her clothes were neatly hung and her shoes lined up at the bottom. Her purse was on the nightstand by the bed.

She was surrounded with elegance. The soft muted greens, peach and rose of the coverlet complimented the green and gold trim and accents on the walls.

Her feet had never felt carpet so soft as she padded around the room snooping, still trying to convince herself she wasn't dreaming. Her personal belongings were in the drawers and on the dresser. Her mother's doily was spread on the top of the dresser with an elegantly handwritten note. She gratefully held it close and dropped onto the bed to read the note.

"I apologize for any inconvenience to you and thank you for your cooperation. The sacrifices you have made and continue to make are very much appreciated." It was signed simply "Charles." How did he know? How did he get it? She carefully folded it and tucked it into an inner pocket of her purse. With all of his personal importance and responsibility, her doily must have seemed so insignificant to him and yet meant so much to her. His effort to obtain it and return it to her was impressive. She had misjudged him to some degree at least, if not entirely.

The young girl returned and introduced herself as Adelheid and informed her that lunch would be served in the dinning room in one hour. She had slept right through breakfast. Adelheid turned and went into the next room. Anna could hear water running as the girl drew a bath for her.

After she had bathed and dressed, Adelheid showed her to the dinning room. When she entered, all the men there stood and bowed to her. These men, who a few hours ago were her captors, were bowing to her, their future princess.

Having experienced so many unexplainable emotions in the last 24 hours, it was surprising there were still new sensations left to be felt. What was she to do now? She hadn't been raised as royalty. They were all standing there looking at her. She swallowed hard. Could she turn and run back to her room?

She was about to do just that when Charles entered from across the room. All eyes turned to him, they bowed to him now, he tipped his head slightly as he raised his hand to them and they went about their business. Would she ever learn all the protocol? What was she doing here?

Charles crossed the room and put out his arm to her. Somewhat relieved, she took it and he seated her. He kept his face unreadable as he took in her much improved appearance today.

After lunch, he took her for a brief tour of the air craft. The cabins the men occupied were at one end of the craft. Her suite was at the other, with a conference room in between. The dining room was directly above the conference room with windows on all sides and sliding glass doors leading out to open decks above the sleeping cabins. They walked along the deck that ran all the way around the outside of the gondola, connecting the two large decks on each end of the dining room. A sturdy railing ran along the outside of the entire oval deck.

White crested waves chopped and splashed below. A wisp of cloud passed beneath them, shrouding the three dolphins that leaped from the water playfully chasing after them, lending perspective to the distance between them and the churning water below. They were about as high as the Macy's rooftop. However, with nothing but water in every direction, it was difficult to tell if they were barely above the water or miles above.

Anna shivered in the stiff breeze. Charles put his coat around her shoulders and held it there. It felt natural to be there with his arm around her and yet she didn't feel comfortable asking him the questions to which she so longed for the answers. How did he feel about this arrangement? What did he think of her? What exactly did he expect of her? Did he realize that she still had the option of not cooperating?

She had developed an attraction to Belgium and its people over these last few months, but she still wasn't sure she could marry this man. He was definitely no Henry VIII and she was impressed with what she had seen of him so far, but she barely knew him. Hopefully there would be time to get to know him well before she would be pressured into a wedding. What was his family like? How would they treat her? An endless barrage of questions swirled about in her mind.

"Diederik explained to you our situation. What do you think of this…arrangement?" His dark eyes penetrated her as if he could read her thoughts. How could she even begin to tell him what she thought of all this? Could she pour her heart out to him without looking like a fool? She tried to talk but too many thoughts came at once and stuck in her throat. He was so intimidatingly perfect! She closed her eyes and let her breath out in an attempt to regain her composure.

"It is too cold out here for you. Let's go inside." He could tell she was as uncomfortable with the weather as she was with the conversation. He politely changed the subject when they got inside.

"Are you familiar with Belgium?"

"A little, I read about your country while I was in New Haven."

He smiled, pleased that she was interested.

"Would you like to know more?"

"Yes!" Her eyes lit up. Then, feeling embarrassed at her own enthusiasm, she forced all emotion from her expression. She was more fascinated with his country than she wanted to admit.

He led her to the conference room where he pulled out books and maps to show her. He showed her a picture of the beautiful Grote Market where she would reside. He told her stories of each place as he showed her pictures of various buildings, parks and the beautiful landscape of his country.

When he had to leave to meet with his men, he gave her some books to take back to her room. She poured over them, learning all she could.

Early the next morning, she was awakened by a tramping noise above her. She dressed quickly and hurried up to the dining room. The men were all out running laps around the deck. When they reached the largest deck at the back end, they dropped and did pushups. Then they resumed their laps. How could they be awake this early and out in the cold exercising! They were all crazy, she muttered to herself as she went back to bed. As she laid there listening to their endless tromping, her irritation turned into admiration. She hopped out of bed and began preparing herself for the day.

She liked watching Charles interact with his men and she was anxious to learn more about these people and their country. She was impressed with them and was no longer so opposed to becoming one of them, under the right circumstances of course.

Chapter 9

The sun struggled to hold its position in the heavens as it sunk deeper into the horizon. A final burst of glory, crimson and gold, sprayed the western sky and then slowly faded to a deep indigo, echoing thin streaks of shimmering ginger off the underside of the low hanging clouds in the distance. A large harvest moon traded places in the sky as the sun succumbed to the night. Glittering diamonds sparkled brilliantly on the horizons but were obstructed from view directly above by the huge lumbering zeppelin.

A sprinkling of light appeared below as sea gave way to land. A bright spot in the midst of lesser lights drew nearer until it was directly below. A bustle of activity went on in the large plaza and then faded in the distance as they dropped in altitude just outside of the city.

It was late in the evening when they landed at the Belgian military airport. Charles led Anna to a car that was waiting to take her and Adelheid to the Town Hall in Brussels. He rode in the car at the front of their entourage.

They wound through narrow cobbled streets and Anna started to doze when the brightly lit plaza she had seen from the air opened before them. It was as though the entire plaza was on fire with the glow of the glorious gothic structures surrounding them. She bent and angled herself in various contortions to see the plaza from every window. They rolled to a stop in front of the tallest of the structures and Anna jumped out for a better view.

Charles dismissed the guards and they dispersed to their various homes. Their mission was accomplished and the guards on duty here at the Town Hall could handle any security issues that might arise. Anna turned and circled, still gaping at the magnificent square.

"Come this way please." Charles offered his arm.

"What is this place?" Anna backed away from the Town Hall to get a full view of the lofty tower blazing above. "I've never seen anything like this. It's gorgeous."

"This is your new home." Charles answered, pleased with her appraisal.

"I get to live up there?!"

"Well, not up there, actually, you will live in one of the guild houses to the side." He motioned to the ornate gothic and baroque styled apartments on both sides of the central towering Hall. She slowly turned again taking it all in.

"Anna, the king awaits."

"The king?!" She snapped back to reality. "Now? Here? Why?" She began pulling up the straggler hairs, whipped down by the salt breeze, and tucking them back into the clip on the back of her head.

"My parents want to meet you. Do not worry, you look adequate. It has been a long journey, no one expects you to look otherwise." He motioned her toward the massive doors under the central arch.

"Oh, no, please." She shook her head even as she walked toward the entrance, straightening her skirt and jacket lapels. Adequate, I look adequate? I am to meet the king looking adequate?

"What am I supposed to say?"

"You do not need to say anything, just listen…and smile." His teeth flashed with a smile of his own as he turned to pull open the door.

"But, what do I call him?" She ran her fingers over her buttons unconsciously making sure they were all done up.

"Do not speak to him unless he addresses you first. In that event, 'Your Majesty' will do." He held his hand in motion for her to enter with the slightest air of impatience. "We have arrived much later than was expected. They have been waiting at dinner for us for quite some time." He held his arm for her once again.

"We're going to eat with them?" She took his arm with her right hand and fidgeted with her buttons again with her left.

"There is no cause for nervousness. Your manners are quite good...for an American." He smiled again.

"Oh, thank you. I feel quite at ease now." She rolled her eyes.

"And we have no dungeon to throw you in if they are not."

A nervous laugh stole from her lips.

Everyone in the dinning hall stood when they entered and Charles led Anna directly to the head of the table to meet his parents first. This was more than just his parents waiting for dinner. There were probably thirty people here! Hold your head up, good posture, don't stumble.

Charles made the introduction and walked away as soon as she let go of his arm to give her hand to the king. "I'm pleased to meet you, sir...Your Majesty." He kissed her hand and she turned abruptly to follow Charles.

"Anna" She turned back to the king. Her eyes darted nervously between Charles and his father while she pulled at her buttons and tried to swallow.

"Did you find your travel accommodations satisfactory?" Charles father smiled reassuringly while his mother raised a brow and turned to talk with the woman next to her. Anna caught something about Leopold and love match, a privilege her second son did not enjoy. It seems the queen was as opposed to this arrangement as Anna had been.

"Yes, sir, thank you s...Your Majesty." She clasped her hands together to hold them still.

"You have not been in Belgium long enough to form an opinion yet. I hope you will find it agreeable as well."

"Oh yes, it's beautiful here." Her bottom button popped off in her hand and her face flushed. It could have been worse. At least it wasn't positioned where she would be exposed. She quickly slipped the button in her pocket and folded her arms over the position of the missing button. "What I have seen of it, of course, it is dark and I haven't been here long, as you said, but what I have seen..." She took a deep breath. She was floundering, sinking.

"Charles, Geoffrey can wait. Finish your introductions and take Anna to her seat. She must be exhausted." The king smiled compassionately and nodded to her. Was she supposed to bow now? She smiled weakly. He thinks she looks exhausted. Or was he merely dismissing her before she lost more buttons? Where did Charles go? She searched the room. He was coming back around to her side of the table. Her knees felt soft.

Leopold and Astrid, Geoffrey and Adeline, on around the table they went. She tried to remember everyone she met, but her mind was in a whirl and not much could stick.

* * *

The chatter of distant voices below in the square replaced the hum of the zeppelin, pulling Anna from pleasant dreams to reality. Pittsburg, New Haven, New York, soaring over the ocean and the magnificent town square were not just a dream. It had all actually happened. It was an exciting and yet terrifying reality. She really was in a foreign land and the only people she knew here, she had known for only the three days trip across the ocean or had met only last evening.

Adelheid, the young girl that had cared for her on the trip over, was her personal lady-in-waiting now. Her English was limited, but she was very attentive. She seemed quite anxious to improve her English, so Anna patiently helped her improve her speaking skills in return for guided tours of the town square. There was so much to see and learn. There was so much history just in this town square alone.

Anna was to reside in The Rose, one of the guild houses in the Grand Place or de Grote market, until she and Charles were married. He resided with his family at the Royal Palace. Each of the guild houses was unique in architecture and origin. Side by side bordering the massive town square, they fanned out from the magnificent Town Hall. She felt like a child in a candy store; she hardly knew where to begin. Each new day held the promise of an unbelievable adventure!

She had only seen Charles a few times since she had dinner with him and his family the evening she had arrived. He was usually passing through the main entry of the town hall when she happened to see him, or in his office during important meetings. He was always with other men, and usually hurrying off to something important. He always stopped and bowed slightly to her as he passed.

One day, Anna and Adelheid were passing through the foyer when they overheard Charles in his office. Anna could see him pacing back and forth, hands clasped behind his back, in front of a starched line of soldiers, stiff and serious.

"What is going on?" She whispered. He wasn't yelling or threatening but he was definitely not pleased.

"Some of the men were drinking on duty last night." Adelheid whispered back. "I suppose this has something to do with that incident."

"Discipline is doing what you are supposed to be doing, when you are supposed to be doing it." None of the men flinched or made a sound. "Make yourself do the right thing until it becomes a habit, until it is part of your character." Chins were held high and backs were straight, but their eyes betrayed their regret. "Force yourself, if you must, until making right choices is woven into the very fabric of your being." Charles' tone was firm and even.

She had become quite familiar with this Elite Guard. Discipline set them apart. Ivan the Terrible, who began to rule Russia at age 16, built his nation into a vast and powerful empire. He took the title of Tsar for himself; he was feared and therefore respected. Until, through selfish and unwise choices, he caused his empire to crumble. He killed his only son and heir to the throne in a fit of anger. Unlike many of wealth and privilege, Charles was disciplined and he expected it of his men. He didn't just give good advice and flowery speeches, he lived what he taught. He was the pillar of strength upon which these men stood, building the lofty framework of the Elite Guard. These were some of the new recruits. They would not make this mistake again.

After a week Anna had seen most of the town square, but there were some areas of the town hall she had not yet explored. Adelheid seemed so superstitious. Whenever she started to enter the main, center tower of the Town Hall, the crowning jewel of the Town Square or de Grote market, Adelheid backed away and begged her not to go there. She always looked so frightened. But today Anna made up her mind, ghosts or not she would explore the tower. If she got in trouble for it, at least she would get to see Charles.

Taking an entire week to personally bring Anna to Belgium had set Charles back. He had been so busy catching up since their return that they hadn't spoken for days. She decided any encounter with him was better than nothing. He never lost his temper, so what did she have to lose?

Off she went. She slipped through the main doors. The large ornately carved double doors squeaked slightly as Adelheid hurried through trying to catch her.

"No, madam. No we can not go there!"

"It's alright, you wait here." She whispered, and then she whisked around the corner and started up a large stone spiral staircase. There were several doors along the way. She planned to check out every one of them, but first she was going to the top. She was getting tired and out of breath when she finally reached a point where the staircase narrowed. There was a doorway that led out to a long balcony that called to her, but she kept going up. Her legs felt weak when she finally reached the top. When she stepped out onto the small circular balcony she nearly collapsed.

The view was breathtaking. She didn't realize how high she had climbed. The narrow balcony circled all the way around the tower. She could see for miles in every direction. She could see the town square below with crowds of people and the various museums, government buildings and parks spreading out across town.

She went around toward the back side of the tower and didn't hear Charles coming up the stairs. When she turned to go back, there he was, standing with his perfect posture and uprightness, watching her as she drank in the majesty of the world around her.

He was so hard to read. Was he irritated that he had to stop what he was doing and come all the way up here to retrieve her, or was he amused? He had the look of an adult watching a child doing something she shouldn't, but was too young to know better. He would deal with this situation with complete patience and maturity.

"This is so amazing!" She turned back to take it in. "Is all of this yours?"

He stepped over behind her and put his left hand on her left shoulder, bending over until his sight was level with hers, pointing out with his right hand, the various landmarks denoting the borders of the land, far in the distance.

"There is much beauty in this land, but there are many dangers as well." He straightened slowly with a distant look in his eyes.

"The wolves are circling about us," he said softly as he stared off to the east where Germany loomed. After the massive destruction of the Great War, Germany could take years licking its wounds and recovering from the devastation. Or it could become as a wounded wild animal, lashing out, irrationally attacking anything in its path. Circumstances suggested the latter.

"Our servants know where it is safe for you and where it is not. You must allow them to guide you." A reprimanding look replaced any amusement.

"Why are you not with Adelheid?"

"I think she was afraid of ghosts or something! I told her to wait for me below."

"This is a very old tower, it is not safe. You must not come up here again." He put out his arm for her and she took it, scanning every detail of the masterpiece that lay in a panorama beneath her. Just as they started to duck through the doorway to descend the narrow staircase, she turned back for one last breath. It was as if she had just discovered a rare artistic treasure, only to be forced to turn it over to the authorities, relinquishing all hope of seeing it again.

She gently ran her fingers over the smooth stones as they descended. Charles had grown up with old castles and obviously didn't appreciate their beauty. When they came to the first arched wooden door, she stopped.

"What is in here?"

"Nothing important, just old rooms."

"Please, let me see." She had such longing in her eyes. "How can you live here and not explore every inch?!" What secrets lay hidden behind this door? What human dramas unfolded, what historical events took place here? She ran her hand down the grain of the wood, willing it to share its quiet observances.

"I don't have the keys with me. I'll bring you back sometime. Why don't you explore the shops in the market place? They are much safer."

Chapter 10

Charles had Anna moved to the Chateau de Laeken. He felt she would be more comfortable there. There were gardens, greenhouses and stables to capture her interest and hopefully keep her out of trouble. Charles had his dealings transferred to the office there where he could do much of his work and keep watch over Anna.

Anna stepped through the large double door main entrance into the circular foyer, capped by a great dome. Off to the right, Charles was busy filing boxes of papers and organizing his things in the new office. She followed the servants up the wide marble staircase to her left that swept up to an oak railed balcony on the second floor, circling the perimeter of the foyer below and the dome above.

While servants hung her clothes, filled her dresser drawers and unpacked her personal items, she wandered about trying to get a feel for her new surroundings. She circled the upper floor and meandered down through the foyer. Paintings of past and current monarchs, wives and children hung on the walls. Massive marble pillars supported the balcony above. An immense Ming vase stood on a richly carved mahogany base at the back of the foyer. Shimmering gold bordered the intricately detailed red and black dragon and lotus blossom design. The colors were so vivid and the rich varying textures so tempting. She reached up to touch the glittering enamel scales of the dragon.

"Would you like a guided tour?" She jerked her hand back and turned, heat rising from her neck and flushing her cheeks.

"I wasn't...I wouldn't have...yes. Please."

"This way." Charles strode down the hallway through the north wing. He stopped and waited, holding the door open to the dining room. She skittered to a stop and straightened her skirt.

"If you wouldn't mind waiting here for me, I'll go find better shoes for running."

"I apologize for my mmm" *afleiding, tempo van het leven*. He waved his hand in circles as he searched for the English words. "preoccupation and pace of life." He still had several boxes to sort and organize and his subconscious kept rushing him back to that task.

She peeked inside the light blue room with a long mahogany table and matching chairs.

"This is your dining room. Meals are served at 7:30, 12:00 and 6:30. If, for some reason, you can not make it to the dining room at the appointed time, merely send Adelheid to notify the kitchen people and they will bring a meal to your room."

He clasped his hands behind his back and continued down the hall. His stride was still lengthy, but he slowed his pace with great exaggeration. He grinned as he watched her take three steps to one of his own.

"Your legs are longer than mine." She giggled and took his arm.

They passed three doors and stopped at the conservatory.

"Do you play?" He motioned to the piano inside.

"Some." She blushed.

"Will you play for me?"

"I should practice first, it's been awhile since I've had access to a piano." She ran her fingers lightly across the keys of the glistening ebony Steinway grand that stood in the center of the small room.

"You may practice here anytime that it is unoccupied." That would be soon. She longed to hear and feel this beautiful instrument. She couldn't resist playing a short excerpt from Fur Elise.

"Please continue."

"I don't remember the rest."

"You will find more of Beethoven's work as well as many others in the cabinet." He motioned to a large oak cabinet on the wall opposite the door.

Next they entered the library. The entire room was surrounded with bookshelves from ceiling to floor. A long table and chairs stood in the center.

"Do you read?"

"Of course I read." She was offended.

"Of course. I meant do you read for pleasure? There are a few novels written in English. The books are arranged by topic, not by language, but if you search carefully you should find something of interest."

She scanned several titles for something she recognized. There was one just out of her reach. She had never heard of it, but it had an English title. When she stretched she could barely brush the bottom edge of the book. Charles pulled it from the shelf and handed it to her.

"There are a few English editions of Sir Arthur Conan Doyle's Sherlock Holmes. Would you like to see one?"

"Oh yes, I love mysteries."

He rolled the ladder to the middle section and climbed up to reach the third shelf from the top. "Have you read The Hound of Baskervilles?"

"Yes, that is the one with the phantom hound that kills the Baskerville heirs." She recounted in a sinister voice.

"Yes, it is. How about *The Adventure of the Musgrave Ritual?*"

"Is that the one that ends with a bit of a treasure hunt?"

"Yes, the ritual, which also leads to the solution of the mystery."

"Do you have *The Adventure of the Speckled Band?* I started reading that one, but never finished."

"Yes, here it is, but it is in Dutch." He pulled it from the shelf and descended to the floor. "I'll translate it for you. We cannot leave you hanging in the middle of a mystery." He smiled and pulled out a chair for her.

An issue of the newspaper, La France, lay open on the table next to a pad of paper.

"What is this? It is dated 1895?" She inquired. He pointed to a Magic Squares number puzzle in the center of the page.

"Let me show you." He slid the pad of paper in front of her and opened it to the puzzle he had drawn. It was a graph of nine squares by nine squares with a number randomly filled in to a few of the squares, identical to the one in the newspaper.

"I discovered these puzzles in the issues of some French newspapers. They were in a box at the back of an old storage area, undisturbed since the Great War. I copy them on paper to solve them. That way they can be solved more than once." He handed her a pencil.

"You must have one of each digit from one to nine in each row, column and diagonally across the puzzle."

"That sounds easy enough." She began filling in numbers and Charles waited patiently for her to discover her folly. After a few rows she realized she could not finish the puzzle correctly.

"I guess I'm not very good with numbers." She pushed the paper away and Charles put it back in front of her.

"It is not a matter of mathematics. It requires deductive reasoning, like solving a mystery." He winked. "Come now my little Sherlock, do not give up so easily." He erased the numbers she had written in.

"How do you do it? I don't understand." She stared at the puzzle again.

"Look at the clues. If there is already a nine in this row, this row and this one, the nine for this column cannot go in any of those squares. There are already numbers in the other squares of this column, so the nine must go there." He pointed as he spoke. She became excited as she discovered some of the correct numbers and impressed with his reasoning as he showed her some of his tricks to figuring out the rest.

"I am sorry, I have kept you too long. You will miss dinner if I keep you any longer." He stood and offered her his arm.

"If you go to the end of this hall and turn left," he explained as they left the library. "It will lead to the Orangerie. Beyond and to your right is the Grand Jardin." He motioned with his hand. "Perhaps you will spend some time there tomorrow."

"Another tour tomorrow?" She brightened.

"I have meetings all day tomorrow." He apologized.

He led her back to the dining room, bowed and turned to leave.

"You're not coming in with me?"

"I must have the office in order before morning." He bowed again and she leaned against the wall watching him as he disappeared down the hall and across the foyer. He's handsome, he's intelligent, he's…she sighed, wonderful and he's going to be mine.

She rolled off the wall and entered the dining room. A group of girls was already seated, laughing and talking together. She slipped into an empty seat at the other end of the table without understanding a single word they said. A slender, stylish blonde girl stood and approached Anna.

"You must be Anna, from America?"

"Yes."

"I am Stephanie of Windisch-Graetz." Anna looked puzzled. Was that supposed to mean something to her? Had they met before?

"I am a cousin." Stephanie clarified. "Welcome to Chateau de Laeken."

"Thank you. It is very nice to meet you." Anna smiled. "Are you living here or just visiting?"

Stephanie cocked her head to the side and bit her lip. "Yes."

Anna waited for more. Yes she lives here or yes she is visiting?

"Welcome to Belgie." Stephanie smiled again. Her English vocabulary was not extensive. Anna's Dutch vocabulary consisted of about four or five words.

"Dank u." Thank you. Anna smiled back.

Stephanie brightened. "Ik ben zo blij u het Nederlands spreekt. Ik spreek zeer Engels niet." Anna's strangled look stopped her excited outburst. "You do not speak Dutch?"

"Very little." Anna held up her thumb and forefinger pinched, almost touching. Stephanie smiled and returned to her seat. She and her companions resumed laughing and talking together. They were not unkind, but Anna was not a part of their group. It would have been better had Charles been there to translate.

* * *

Anna slept late and went in search of Adelheid next door. She was not there. The voices of a large group of men drifted out of the office as she hurried across the foyer. A servant pushed a cart with silver domed plates and stopped outside the office door. Anna frowned. Charles would not be in the dining room today.

She peeked inside the dining room to see if Adelheid was there. Stephanie's brothers Franz, Ernst and Rudolf had arrived earlier that morning and were seated there with her and her friends. She quickly turned to leave.

"Miss Anna." Stephanie called to her. "Please, my brothers would like much to meet you." They all stood and bowed as Stephanie introduced each of them. After a bit of small talk and strained conversation, due to a limited common language, Anna excused herself and continued her search for Adelheid.

She finally found Adelheid in the kitchen, eating with the staff. She refused to eat in the dining room with Anna, claiming she was not allowed to do so, so Anna decided to join them.

Adelheid was happy for the move to Chateau de Laeken as her father lived in quarters there. He was the chief of kitchen staff. She and Anna often stopped at the kitchen for a visit and snack between explorations. Anna much preferred the kitchen and its inhabitants to the formal dining room.

Adelheid's mother, Jayani died bringing her into this world. Jayani, born in India, came to Belgium with her family in her teens. She worked in the kitchen with Nico after they were married, until her passing. She brought a lot of Indian influence into that kitchen. Nico still used many of the various curries and spices in his cooking. Anna grew to love the pungent aroma drifting down the hallway from the kitchen on "curry days."

Adelheid had grown up in the service of the royal family. Nico raised her as best he could with the entire staff taking her under their wings. Now with Anna and Adelheid becoming fast friends and Anna with no parents of her own or royal responsibility to keep her busy, she spent much of her time with the staff and they had somewhat adopted her as well.

When she wasn't in the kitchen, Anna was exploring and finding her way around or in the library studying the history of Belgium and particularly the palace where she now resided. Charles had only shown her a small fraction of the rooms in this spacious palace. There were ballrooms, dining halls, nooks and private rooms that were locked. This royal residence was much newer than the Town Hall, but still very historical. It had been owned, for a short time, by Napoleon.

Charles was in meetings most of the time or away on business, which left Anna with a lot of time for exploring and studying. He was returning one day, as Anna came down the stairs with a large heavy atlas. He left his group and carried it back to the library with her, but returned immediately to the office. He could be so chivalrous and yet so infuriatingly unavailable.

Chapter 11

The greenhouses were an exceptionally pleasant place to spend the day as the weather chilled. The different greenhouses with their fountains, statuary, and tunneled pathways under a wide variety of rare tropical plants, ferns, fruit trees and flowers, kept Anna and Adelheid busy for days. Adelheid took Anna to the greenhouse with tropical fruit trees. They sat on a bench drinking in the warm tropical air on a cold November morning.

"I suppose you would rather be in the stables smelling animals than here with the perfume of orange and almond?" Anna teased as she noticed Adelheid's distant gaze.

"What do you mean?" She blushed.

"I mean Hans is out at the stables right now." She smiled knowingly. "I've noticed the way you look at him and I've noticed the way he looks at you!"

Her color deepened. Wishing to divert the attention from herself she questioned Anna "How does it feel to know you will marry a prince?"

Now it was Anna's turn to blush. "I think he is wonderful." She smiled as she thought about him, the way he carried himself with such nobility, his air of confidence and the way he handled every situation with wisdom and patience.

"I just wish I knew how he felt about me. He is so hard to understand. I haven't known him long enough really. Sometimes I think he is too perfect to be real. Is he just putting on a show?"

"Oh no, Madam. He is a very good person. He has always been kind to me. He is kind to everyone. He has very much respect."

They picked some oranges and took them to the kitchen for juice.

Anna thoroughly enjoyed their explorations of the greenhouses, but the more Anna thought about Charles the more she decided plants, no matter how beautiful, can't replace male companionship. They do enhance it however. She decided that a stroll through the gardens in the greenhouses would be even better with Charles.

Anna stood at the doorway of the office, waiting for the men inside to notice her, not wanting to interrupt. His Majesty the king, Charles, Leopold, and two others Anna didn't recognize, were bent over the desk discussing something in Dutch. They saw her, and Charles straightened.

"What may I do for you?" He was wearing his mask of formal propriety that made him so hard to read.

"I was just wondering if you might have some free time today to go for a walk in the greenhouses."

He exhaled deeply and looked around at the others.

"Where is Adelheid? She is familiar with the greenhouses. Or I can get you a driver, English speaking. He can take you for a tour of the city. Would you like that?" Impatience was seeping through his mask.

Why was he always putting her off? He never had time for her. She blinked away the tears.

"Never mind, you are busy." She turned and walked quickly away, hoping to get away before anyone saw her hurt and embarrassment.

Charles' father knew she wasn't there because she needed a guide for the greenhouses or because she was bored and wanted some entertainment. He looked directly at Charles. "Go to her. This can wait one hour. She is important also."

Charles found her sitting with Adelheid at the top of the wide marble staircase overlooking the path to the greenhouses.

"Adelheid, wordt u verworpen één uur." He spoke in Dutch and Adelheid quickly got up and left.

"Would you like to go for a walk now?"

"No. I know you are busy. You don't have to do this." She stated, looking away.

"I have one hour," he said sitting on the step by her, ignoring her sour attitude. "We can sit here…" He craned his neck trying to get her to look at him. "Or I can just follow you around. I am at your command for one hour," he said smiling as he finally caught her attention.

"May I show you my favorite place among the gardens of the greenhouses?" He stood and held his hand out to her.

"Alright." She hesitantly smiled back as he gently pulled her to her feet. She couldn't resist that captivating smile and twinkle in his eyes when he talked to her.

She took his hand with both of hers and leaned her head on his shoulder as they walked. Besides his elegant physical appearance, there was a strength of character and integrity that was very attractive to her. She could be in love with this man she was to marry, if he would just let her! She couldn't explain it, but there seemed to be a protective wall around him that she couldn't get through. Sometimes she could see in the window of his eyes that he cared for her, but the gate to the wall was always locked.

He led her to a small courtyard with a fountain and benches, surrounded by trees and thick green shrubs.

"This is where I used to come to read or think or just be alone." He seated her on one of the stone benches and stooped to search among the ferns growing at the base of a bushy evergreen tree.

"There was a patch of strawberries growing here at one time…aha! One lone berry survives." He bowed, holding the large, deep red berry on his extended palm.

"For you, M'lady." His eye twitched in the slightest of winks. "Perhaps that is what made this a place of preference. Strawberries have long been a favorite of mine." He explained as he sat on the bench with her.

"This is the only one?" She held it back to him but he refused it.

"Then we'll share it." She sunk her teeth into the end, slurping the juice and laughing as it dripped down her arm. She put the rest of the berry up to the leafy stem into his mouth before he could protest and caught a drop of juice on his chin with her finger. He jerked back in surprise, stood quickly and stepped over to the stone child pouring water into a small stone pond. He caught a few drops of water and wiped his chin and mouth. Was he embarrassed by the messiness, offended by her manners, or uncomfortable with her forward gesture? Surely sharing the same fruit hadn't broken any rules of intimacy. When he noticed her watching him, he looked away nervously.

"I used to consult her with any dilemma." He rubbed his hand over the smooth stone figure, squelching his nervousness under a cloak of dignity. "A young boy, in trouble, pouring out his heart...she was always a good listener."

"You were once a young boy...in trouble? I find that hard to believe. I would imagine you were born in a uniform, all stiff and proper." She giggled in spite of his injured look.

"Oh, I could climb a tree with the best of them."

"That, I would like to see!"

A small mouse scurried out from under one of the bushes. She drew her feet up on the bench and sat quietly watching. He darted about finding seeds and nibbling. Charles watched her, amused at her fascination with the little creature.

"Did you ever have a pet?" She whispered so as not to scare off their little visitor.

"We have horses and hunting hounds."

"I mean like a puppy, that you played with, that was your friend."

"The hounds were grown and trained when we received them. My friends were other boys."

"So you were never really a normal boy then, were you?" She teased. "And I don't believe you ever did anything wrong. What did you do to get in trouble? I can listen as well as your stone fountain."

This brought back memories he preferred not to recall. "Yes, but she won't tell anyone my secrets." He winked and looked at his watch. "We should get back now." He stepped toward her and held out his arm.

Just as she stood up, a snake slithered out from under a large fern and swallowed the mouse whole! She jumped at Charles crying hysterically, dancing to get away from the snake. He swept her up in his arms and carried her swiftly away as she buried her face in his neck.

"I am sorry you had to see that."

"Do you think the little mouse is dead?" she asked looking intently in his eyes.

"I'm quite sure there is nothing we can do for him now," he said, trying to keep the amusement out of his voice.

He gently set her down at a safe distance away from the snake.

"My hair clip, it must have fallen out back there." She noticed as her untamed curls cascaded down.

"I will retrieve it, you wait here."

He absently put her hair clip in his pocket while he watched the snake lying under the tree, still bulging in the middle from the mouse. What a tender hearted, delicate creature Anna was; like a little child—in the form of a woman. He actually entertained the idea of slicing open the snake and delivering the tiny fugitive mouse to her. Her large round frightened eyes, her innocence and dependence for protection made his heart squeeze within him. He found himself more attracted to her than he wished to be. Suddenly, he was irritated with his emotions. He returned to her and quickly led her back into the palace.

"Gentlemen, I am sorry for the delay," he said as he returned to the office, a bit ruffled and annoyed.

"This is not a problem. You should spend more time with her, get to know her." His father offered.

"I'd rather not," he said stiffly as he stepped over to the map trying to recall where they had left off.

"Charles, you are going to marry her. How do you expect to love a woman you hardly know?" His older brother Leopold questioned, stretching back in the pillowy softness of his chair, not so anxious to get back to work.

"Men who allow themselves to fall in love, base their decisions on whims of the heart rather than on sound rational judgment. I have no intention of yielding my heart or my judgment to any woman and I don't intend to discuss this further."

As he turned back to the map, movement at the doorway caught his eye. Anna stood there, straight, chin up, trying to bury her emotions, but failing miserably. The hurt in her eyes was unmistakable.

Charles' dark eyes searched her, trying to assess the situation. How much had she heard? Her lip quivered and she bit it. She had heard too much. What could he say? He had spoken the truth and sometimes the truth is unpleasant. The moment grew awkward and he took a deep breath to deal with it. Then her nostrils flared and eyes narrowed. She was angry. She didn't agree with his philosophy. He lifted his chin and set his jaw with determination. He hadn't meant for her to hear his plan to stay aloof, but that was still his plan.

He tipped his head politely, carefully putting on his mask, as he asked "What may I do for you?"

"You have my hair clip. May I have it, please?" She held her head high, but her voice wavered. She had not mastered the art of hiding emotion as Charles had.

He stepped over to her as he took it out of his pocket and handed it to her.

"I would like a driver after all. I won't bother you anymore," she said softly as tears welled up in her eyes.

"I will see to it immediately." He walked slowly to the guard at the main entrance while Anna turned and walked quickly away. He would not have hurt her intentionally and he wasn't sure how to smooth over this incident. Perhaps a few days sightseeing would cheer her.

"Alexandros, prepare a vehicle and tell Pier to come to me, please."

Chapter 12

Anna wanted to see all of Belgium. She had enjoyed exploring and learning about Pittsburgh, New Haven and some of New York. She would learn all she could about her new home, but mostly she wanted to get away from the palace. She was becoming very attracted to Charles. He was everything that she had loved about Norbert, only greatly multiplied, but he was determined to never fall in love with her. That was too painful to think about. So she would find something else to occupy time and immerse herself in it.

She hopped into the front seat with Pier, anxious to start their adventure. His eyes grew round and he waved his hands at her.

"No, no Madam. You must not sit here with me." He pointed to Alexandros as he stood holding the back door for her.

"I can see better up front."

"It is not appropriate. Please, get in the back."

"That's silly. Why isn't it appropriate?"

"I am your driver. I am a married man. You are fiancée to His Royal Highness, Prince Charles." He whined and she reluctantly got in the back, irritated with all the rules and restraints.

She visited the Palais du Justice as well as many gardens, parks and museums. She particularly enjoyed the Lower Town area with its labyrinth of narrow cobbled streets and medieval ambiance.

As they moved further north east, a magnificent church caught her interest. The Eglise St. Jacques-sur-Coudenburg is the Royal Parish of the Diocese of the Belgian Armed Forces. She was captivated by the beautiful religious paintings and memorials to those who gave their lives in defending their country. So many cities and countries honored their loyal dead with statues and memorials.

It seemed nice to be honored long after leaving this life; to leave a permanent mark on society for good. But the price for such honor was leaving this life early and usually in a painful violent manner. Was the reward of fame and glory worth such a price, especially when they weren't around to enjoy it? It would be nicer to be remembered for discovering or inventing something great than giving ones life for a cause. She dragged her hand across the base of an iron soldier as she read the plaque. She couldn't deny the admiration she felt. What makes a man willing to suffer and die for another?

* * *

On another outing they visited Cinquantenaire Park. This park was created in 1880 to celebrate the 50th anniversary of Belgium's independence. One of the most impressive monuments there is a massive triple arch gate with chariot and horses atop. Mosaics were still under completion on both sides of the arch. Large pavilions and halls stretched out on both sides of the glorious arch.

They ate at one of the various cafés each day and occasionally bought a trinket at one of the shops with the allowance Charles gave her to keep her occupied.

Brussels was a beautiful city with endless sights to enjoy, but they couldn't fill the hollow spot that echoed with emptiness every time she passed Charles, all efficient and urgently rushing off to save the world. His mask was thicker, less transparent since the garden incident.

Charles was going out of town this afternoon and Anna planned to send him off with an image he would not easily brush aside. She took extra time making sure every wavy curl framed her face perfectly, her lips were a glossy crimson and she wore her fitted wool skirt to accentuate her slender figure.

Her timing was ideal. Charles was just coming through the main entrance as she was gracefully descending the broad marble staircase to the spacious hall below. She stopped before she reached the bottom to send him her most dazzling smile. The look on his face made it worth all her effort. He was definitely impressed, but he quickly pulled on his mask, nodded politely to her and hurried into the main office.

Eyes stinging, Anna rushed out front to where Pier waited at the car. The hurt quickly turned to anger. Why did he have to be so stubborn? Jack or Thomas would have been putty in her hands at this point.

She avoided eye contact with Pier as she slid into the back seat where he stood holding the car door for her. Her eyes blurred, but she refused to blink hard to clear them. Anger wouldn't allow her to shed a tear. She twisted the strap on her purse so tightly it nearly snapped. Why did she have to be in this country? What difference did she make here? Would anyone even notice her absence? If she left, where would she go? She tired of being the perpetual tourist.

"Where would you like to go today, Madam?"

"A million miles from here." She mumbled.

"Pardon?"

"I don't care. You choose today."

Sensing she wasn't feeling herself today, he decided to avoid any walking tours and take her on a comprehensive motor tour of the city. Meaningless sights passed outside her window as she sat picking at a rough fingernail.

She noticed Pier was avoiding the Molenbeek municipality. She asked him to turn down Rue de Molenbeek, a street they hadn't been on before. He refused. She commanded him. He refused again. So she ordered him to stop the car. She opened the door and got in the front. She was not in any mood to be messed with.

"Please Madam, this is not proper." His eyes darted down the street and swept both sides, as if someone might see their impropriety. He didn't dare sit in a parked automobile alone with her, but he didn't want to resume their tour until she was safely in the back. He jumped out and slammed the door, opened it again and stuck his head inside.

"Madam, will you cooperate?" She glowered back with her arms folded and he shut the door again and leaned against the hood of the car. They couldn't stay here. What could he do? He could force her; he fingered the bulge his revolver made under his coat. That would not turn out well. Which would be the lesser evil of his few options? She was small enough he could easily pick her up and put her in the back, but she would likely make a fuss and draw attention and she could jump out again and get back in the front or run off. He could allow her to remain in the front and return directly to the palace...in broad daylight, in a recognizably royal car where they would certainly be noticed. He jabbed down on the fender with the bottom of his fist as he leaned away and paced the length of the car.

Why did she have to be so much trouble? She wasn't normally in such a sour mood, but she was nearly in tears this morning when she came out. Perhaps if he were more understanding she would be more agreeable. But how could he be more understanding without getting back in the car with her?! He walked around to her door and opened it. He looked down the street and licked his lips.

"I apologize for anything I have done to..."

"I'll get in the back if you promise to go where I tell you to." She snapped. What choice did he have? This was surely a better option than any of the others.

"This is not a safe part of town." He explained as he turned down the street she directed him to. It didn't look unsafe to her. They passed a small house with many children around it.

"There are young children here. How unsafe can it be?" Doleful eyes watched as they passed. "What is this place? Some of the children look too young for this to be a school and there are too many children to be just one family." She turned to watch out the back until they turned a corner.

"It is an orphanage. It is not unsafe for them, they have nothing anyone would want."

She couldn't get their image out of her mind. Their bare knobby knees showing beneath worn, faded clothing and their round cheerless eyes staring at them as they passed haunted her. She was an orphan herself. She missed the security of her mother's love, but Josephine had always provided the necessities and comforts of life. She had always lived in a home, in a safe neighborhood.

There was a small market just ahead. A roundish woman haggled prices with a man in an apron as he stacked crates of potatoes just outside the doorway.

"Pull over here." She pointed excitedly. She hopped out and purchased baskets of fruit and bread. Pier helped her load it into the car.

"What will you do with all of this? You have all the food you could possibly desire at the palace." He stated incredulously, there were servants specifically for grocery shopping and cooking. A small snack or a meal at a restaurant he could see, but baskets of food?

"We are taking it to the orphanage." She had found her cause.

The children gathered and followed them inside, watching from a safe distance, caught between fear and curiosity. After asking permission from the woman in charge, Anna knelt down next to a little blond haired girl and handed her a piece of bread.

"What is your name?" she asked, gently brushing the hair from her face and tucking it behind the little girl's ears.

"She is Karlina." Answered Marga, the woman in charge. "She no understand English." Karlina looked up and when Marga nodded her approval she smiled and quickly devoured her bread.

Anna returned to the orphanage almost every day. She held them, played with them and fed them. It wasn't long before she knew each one and developed some sort of communication with them. Adelbert, the oldest boy, watched over Jens who seemed rather pale and sickly. Anna noticed Adelbert saving half of his bread and fruit to give Jens an extra share. She gave him extra large portions so they both would have plenty. Clara and Elise, the oldest girls were protective of all the smaller children. Vanya, Edme and Carel followed them around peeking from behind their skirts.

Eventually even the little ones ventured out to get food and toys from Anna for themselves. They cheered when her car pulled up each day. They ran to meet her when she came and hugged her as she left. She was the brightest spot in their meager lives.

A man named Klaas and his wife, Hilde, started coming as well. They were kind and anxious to be her friends. Anna and Hilde talked about the children and their own families. Most of Klaas and Hilda's family were in Germany. Anna looked forward to seeing Hilde each day almost as much as she did the children.

Pier gave her so much resistance about going to the orphanage, that when Erwin offered to take her for the day, she accepted. She didn't know him well, but she saw him at the palace quite often. She assumed she could trust anyone that worked closely with the royal family.

He turned out to be a very agreeable driver. He went wherever she asked him to without any resistance at all. He was very pleasant and helpful. He seemed to approve of the assistance she gave to the poor and helpless. He was friendly to the people that worked at the orphanage, especially to Klaas. It made her uncomfortable the way Pier kept his distance from everyone there, like he looked down on them or was afraid of them.

One day as she was leaving, Klaas hesitantly asked Anna if she would post a large letter to his brother for him.

"No, never mind. I can't ask this of you."

"I am happy to help you." She smiled, taking the envelope from him.

"My brother is in a bad way and I am sending him money to help out. I am nervous sending money through the mail. The mail service for commoners isn't very reliable."

"Then I will post it personally. With my signature, perhaps it will get special consideration."

Klaas twitched nervously. "Please don't let anyone know of its contents, I can't afford to replace it."

"Of course, it is safe with me. I hope conditions improve for your brother." It felt good to be needed and loved.

Chapter 13

Charles had been out of town on business and had just returned. Pier was anxious to report Anna's activities to him and how she forced him to cooperate. He told Pier he would take care of it.

When Anna didn't come to the formal dinning hall for dinner, he went in search of her. One of the servants informed him that she was probably in the kitchen. She generally ate there with the kitchen people.

He breathed deeply to gain his composure and then went to the kitchen. He could hear them laughing and talking before he entered. When he stepped through the doorway, the room quickly silenced and all the servants bowed. Charles raised them and asked that their dinner be served in the nook by the west porch.

"Anna, come with me please." He commanded.

He gave her his arm and she hesitantly took it. She could tell he wasn't pleased and she was nervous for the ax to fall.

"You are back." She tried to sound cheerful. "Did you have a pleasant trip?"

"Yes, I waited for you in the dinning hall until I was informed that you have been taking your meals in the kitchen. Is there no one to hold your interest in the dinning room?"

"No one that misses my presence when I am not there. I spend my time with those that care about me."

He ignored her reference to his frequent absence and preoccupation. He had more important matters to discuss than where she ate and who she spent her time with while at the palace. That could come later.

He guided her into the nook and seated her. The rich heavy draperies and tapestries darkened the small, private room. The cheery glow of the fireplace sharply contrasted her mood. The look of defiance she wore told him to dispense with the small talk. How could someone so wispy and fragile looking exude such fire and determination? The emotions she extracted from him were so unfamiliar. He wasn't sure if he would rather kiss her or wring her neck! Neither was an option he would consider, so he circumspectly put on his mask and waded into the unpleasant task at hand.

"Do you recall our conversation on the tower about letting our servants guide you to safe places and away from danger?"

"Yes." she looked down, here it comes. The crackling fire that could have lent a warm, gentle ambience only echoed the anger glowing and spitting inside her. The warmth became an increasing irritation as the heat within her amplified.

The servants entered, laid out the table before them, lit the candle and then left.

"You should not have forced Pier to take you where he knew you should not go." He watched for her response.

"I don't want you to go back to the orphanage."

She didn't look up or respond.

"Do you understand?"

"No, I do not understand." She replied rising to her feet. "You bring me to your country to marry you, but I never see you. You say that your people need me, but when I find a way to truly serve some of them, you tell me to stop." She became quite animated as her temper increased.

"Anna, sit down." He commanded in his aggravatingly calm, controlled tone of voice. One of the things she admired in him most, his self discipline, irritated her beyond restraint now. Why wouldn't he show some emotion? Why was he so determined not to love her?

"The only time you bring me to this charming, romantic little room for a private candle light dinner, is to reprimand me." She leaned forward and looked into his eyes. "No, I don't understand any of this." She whirled and ran out of the room.

"Anna!" Charles called after her. He rose, dropped his napkin on his chair and went to his office.

King Albert saw the light on in the office and stepped in to investigate. "Charles, how long have you been here?"

"I don't know, 30 minutes perhaps." He replied without looking up from his work.

"I thought you left to find Anna and dine with her?"

"I told her not to go back to the orphanage and she stormed out." He laid his pen down and leaned back.

"Father, what am I to do? She is so defiant."

"She is American. Freedom, to her, is not a privilege, it is a right. You can physically capture her, but she will not be subject to you until you capture her heart."

"And how do I accomplish this without her capturing my heart and subjecting me to her?"

His father smiled at him admiringly.

"I have confidence in you, my son. You show wisdom and good judgment in all you do. You serve your people well," he lovingly patted and grasped his son's shoulder, "but remember to find some happiness for yourself as you go."

* * *

The next morning as Anna was leaving, she saw Charles in the main office with Erwin. It didn't look good for Erwin. When she climbed into the car for her daily tour with Pier, she questioned him about Erwin.

Pier smiled. "Where shall we go today, Madam?"

Her eyes narrowed, "Tell me about Erwin."

Pier took a deep breath and geared up for the unavoidable battle.

"He is being relieved of his duties. He will most likely be court marshaled."

Anna sat back, steaming as this information sunk in. How could Charles be so vindictive? This behavior was so contradictive of the man she thought she knew and was falling in love with. To crush someone simply as a show of power was so out of character for him. Had he just put up a front for her benefit?

"The market as usual." She shot at him with determination.

Pier jerked around to look at her.

"You know we can not go back there! His Royal Highness commanded us not to go there again."

"He didn't command, he said he didn't want me to go back."

His eyes narrowed, "There is no difference."

"You're right, there's not. Either way I don't see any reason not to help those children."

"No, I refuse," he said firmly. "I will take you to the shopping district," he said as he pulled out of the courtyard.

"Good idea, that will make me feel better. I will buy new clothes for myself, while the children go hungry." She spat out with contempt. As they drove on, a plan began to form in her mind.

"Pull into this market, please." She tried to put on a sweeter voice.

"What do you want here? I will not disobey orders."

"I know, I don't expect you to." Pier pulled up to the market and stopped.

"Leave the heater on. I will wait here while you go in and buy some drinks for us, if you don't mind...please?"

"What will you have?" He was relieved that she didn't try to come in and buy supplies for the children in spite of his objections.

"Any kind of juice will be fine, thank you."

He left the engine running and the heater on when he got out. As soon as he went inside, Anna climbed over the seat and put the car in gear. She had only driven once before. Norbert had once spent their entire day off, teaching her how to drive his car. It was harder than it looked and she jerked a lot at first, but she got away just as Pier came running out. He chased her down the street a short distance before he gave up.

She knew she needed to hurry. He would go back to the palace to get another car and probably Charles. She quickly bought meat and bread. Fresh fruit was no longer available, so for a special treat she purchased some dried fruit and cheese.

She realized this would probably be the last time she could come for a while. Her traveling privileges would most likely be revoked after this, but she didn't intend to let Charles win this power struggle easily.

She pulled up to the orphanage and quickly unloaded the food. She gathered the children into her arms and hugged them tightly. She was still outside when Charles, his driver and Pier pulled up and got out. She slowly stood up straight thrusting her chin up in defiance, looking Charles in the eyes as everyone else bowed. Without raising them, he strode directly to her.

"Get in the car, Anna." He commanded in a low ominous voice, his eyes piercing her to the center of her soul.

She swallowed hard.

"No." She replied firmly although she was quaking inside.

They stood looking at each other for what seemed an eternity. He wasn't sure how to handle this situation. When he gave a command, it was always followed without question. He couldn't let her set an example of public defiance, but he didn't want to use physical force with her either. His options were limited.

She braced herself, trying to look formidable, trembling, with her eyes like saucers. The feelings of desire this little matchstick of a girl lit inside him were so foreign, so confusing. How could he be so "at war" with himself, part wanting to protect her, be her champion, give her anything to make her happy, while his more coherent part knew he couldn't allow this behavior. He must win this war. These were the very emotions he went to such great lengths to avoid. He would not allow his heart to conquer his raison d'être.

Charles turned and went to Pier.

"Pier, it was your responsibility to keep Anna from coming here. And yet, here she is. Get on your knees." He pulled his revolver and put it to the back of his head.

Anna screamed and leapt to his side, grabbing his arm.

"No! It was not his fault. I tricked him. Don't do this." She looked desperately into his eyes.

He looked back at her, his face as stone and eyes as steel.

"Get in the car."

"No, please, you can not do this." She begged holding his arm tightly.

"Do you swear to me you will not come back here?"

She took a deep breath and exhaled as deeply.

"I will get in the car now," she promised in a low voice for only Charles to hear, "but I swear to you, if you kill him, I will leave and you will never see me again." She breathed out with such intensity it left her quavering. She dropped his arm and got into the car.

Charles called out orders in Dutch to Bartel, the other driver. Bartel got in the car and drove her back to the palace. Instead of dropping her off at the front entrance and returning the car to the garage, he got out and walked with her.

"This is not necessary, I can get myself inside." She told him, not hiding her irritation.

"I am just following orders, Madam."

"And what exactly are your orders?" Her eyes narrowed dangerously as she folded her arms.

He remained respectful and calm but his demeanor switched to "on guard stance."

"To take you to your room."

"And what if I don't want to go to my room just now?"

"Then I will have to use force." Their eyes locked momentarily before he softened and altered his angle.

"Please, Madam, why do you want to make things difficult for us? Haven't you caused enough trouble with Pier?"

Her irritation with Bartel left as the sting of his question sank in.

"I will go with out causing you any trouble, if you promise to find out about Pier, and bring me word."

"Very well, Madam."

Her feet felt lead laden as she went up to her room. She took Bartel's arm to pull her up each solid marble step. What manner of man was she getting involved with? She stopped just outside her bedroom door.

"He was bluffing, wasn't he? He wouldn't really..." She looked through her open doorway to the window on the far wall and back to Bartel. "What kind of man is he?"

Of course he was bluffing, but that being the case, Bartel felt it wasn't his place to clear up that misconception.

"He is a good man," he simply answered.

"And what would happen to you if you said otherwise?" She shot back.

Again, he carefully thought out his reply, without taking his eyes from hers.

"My opinion of his brother is not so high."

"Does Leopold know of your opinion of him?"

"I do not suppose he cares much what my opinion of him is." He calmly replied, holding his hand toward her room in a gesture for her to enter.

He is a good man. That seemed to be the opinion of all those she asked. Why didn't that opinion match up with what she saw of him? Still, Bartel seemed sincere.

"Thank you." She whispered and walked to the window. The heavy door thudded shut behind her and the key clinked as he locked her door. Charles walked up the front steps below. Not far behind walked Pier, alive and unrestrained. She dropped onto the padded window seat with relief. He was bluffing. What kind of power game was he playing?

Bartel was just coming down the grand staircase when Charles entered. He glanced up the stairs and then at Bartel with a questioning look.

"She cooperated, but I had to promise to inform her of Pier's fate."

Charles turned to Pier as he came through the door.

"Pier, go to my office." He turned to Bartel.

"Tell her he is being detained."

"Detained, Sir?"

"Yes, that is all you know. He is being detained."

Charles turned abruptly and went into his office with Pier.

"I am sorry to have to use you as a pawn, Pier. You are a good, loyal man. You are free to go now."

"I suppose she will not need a driver for awhile?"

"No. You will be reassigned tomorrow."

Pier started to leave, but turned back, "Sir?"

"Yes."

"I am sorry, I should have handled this better."

"This is a new experience for all of us. I don't know what you could have done differently." He cracked a half smile. "I am just glad she didn't make a fool of me by calling my bluff."

"You would have to follow through in such a case."

"Don't be ridiculous. Your life is more important to me than my image of authority."

Pier smiled "I am glad neither was sacrificed today!"

Chapter 14

While Nico carried a tray with soup and biscuits up to Anna's room he heard muffled muttering and the alternate clacking and cushioned thumping of her pacing from oak floor to rug and back. She stopped when the key rattled in the lock.

"Your lunch, Madame." He dipped his head and placed the tray on the marble top credenza by the door.

"I don't want anything. Take it back with you."

"Yes, Madame." Sensing her mood, he picked up the tray and tried to back out quickly to avoid any confrontation.

"Nico?"

He stopped without looking up.

"What will happen to me?" She was gripping the hand carved walnut frame of the settee standing diagonal to the corner of the room facing the door. She was tense and her eyes were wet.

The staff grapevine didn't have all the details yet. He wasn't sure what she had done or what her punishment would be. It wasn't his place to discuss the situation with her, even if he did know.

"I am sorry, I do not know." He ducked his head and tried to leave again.

"I wasn't doing anything wrong!" She started toward him, but stopped when he tried to pull the door shut.

"Nico, please talk to me. Is it a crime here to help the unfortunate? Why is Charles doing this to me? Why must I stay in this country when he hates me so?" When he remained silent she turned and dropped on to the black velvet settee, burying her face in her arm. He quietly closed the door and locked it.

Charles saw Nico taking the food back to the kitchen and questioned him. Nico explained her refusal to eat.

"I suppose that is to be expected, she was very upset. Give her some time." He rubbed his thumb across a small scar under his chin as he glanced up the stairway.

"Keep me informed."

***

Nico's feet were heavy as he carried Anna's dinner up the wide marble staircase to her room. He was a soft-spoken, gentle man and he dreaded the conflict that most likely awaited him. He found her lying on top of her four poster bed, wrapped in a soft white fleecy throw, reading. Before he finished arranging the domed platters on the silver serving cart, she asked him to take it away without looking up. He felt even worse as he trudged back down to the kitchen. Not speaking to him at all was as bad as taking out her anger on him.

After each meal the next day, Nico stopped at the doorway to the office and shook his head. The next day started out the same, so Charles instructed Nico to leave the food in her room where she could smell it and possibly be tempted.

"You know what she likes. Do what you can to get her to eat." Charles was concerned for Anna's health, but he felt he had to hold his ground. He couldn't allow her to continually undermine, or as in this case, totally ignore his authority.

Anna could smell the food before Nico opened the door. She could almost taste the coconut milk with ginger and curry as the keys rattled in the lock. Nico entered and lifted the lids with a flourish, freeing billows of steam and delicious aromas.

"Badami and chicken satay?! Nico, I thought you were my friend. How could you do this to me?"

"They are your favorites, Madam." He replied with dejection. "I have worked all day on this special creation for you."

"Nico, you know I am not eating. This is torture."

"Madam, you must eat. It is not good for you to go without eating. You are so thin. It is my assignment to get you to eat. Please do not make me fail."

"You were assigned to make me eat?" Her weakening resolve got a boost of solid steel infused with fury.

"This is a matter of principle. Charles is treating me like a child; grounding me to my room. I don't care who he is, or how important he thinks he is, or how many people bow to him and give him his way; I will not be treated this way."

"Yes, Madam." Nico bowed and meekly backed out the door, locking it with all his tempting creations inside.

Anna had wondered if her stubbornness was actually affecting anyone but herself. She spent the endless boring days taking long hot baths, reading and drinking water when the hunger became unbearable. At times she regretted starting such a campaign. Pride would not allow her to eat, as that would admit Charles' victory, but she hadn't felt she could hold out much longer, until now! She no longer questioned whether her hunger strike was worth the trouble. If Charles went to such lengths as to assign Nico to the cause, he was surely taking notice.

"He cares." She sighed. But what exactly does he care about? She sat at the smooth white vanity and stared into the mirror. Shadowy circles were forming beneath her eyes. Did he care about her or just the political union she could bring...or did he just want to win this little power resistance?

He isn't so great, he doesn't care about anything but his own position and power. Why doesn't he come himself to convince me to eat? She pinched her cheeks to restore some lifelike color to her pale face. He is kind of funny looking. His eyebrows are too big for his eyes.

Why did she hurt all over? Her attempt to convince herself that she was not attracted to Charles was failing miserably. The pain in her stomach wasn't just hunger, it intensified when she thought of Charles.

As Nico brought each tempting meal, the food from the previous meal was untouched. It had been four days now and Charles decided he had to do something before she damaged her health.

Anna sat in the window seat, staring out the icy glass. She had lost weight and the cold from the frosty window penetrated deeply. She pulled the wool throw up around her shoulders and traced with her finger the delicate lacey fronds of the frost that framed her window.

The queen's car had pulled up front in the courtyard below, the king got in the back with her and they drove away. Three of the Elite Guard had come and gone. Charles and Geoffrey had left an hour ago and Charles had recently returned. He strode up the front steps with the air of confidence he always carried. Could a man's virtue make him more attractive? His inner strength, self discipline, his determination to protect his country at whatever cost to himself, made him so desirable.

But, why did he treat her with such indifference? How could she ever love a man that dealt with her this way? How could she allow herself to fall in love with a man so infuriatingly hard to figure out?

She had had few love interests in her life. Jack was never more than a friend, really, and Norbert was not what she had hoped. She had thought Charles was like Norbert, good, solid, the kind of man a girl could anchor her life to. It seemed now that he was more like Thomas, manipulative and controlling. She would not be an easy target. He might be a powerful man, but he would not win this time.

She scratched four long claw marks across the frosty window spraying icy crystals over her drawn up knees. The white became water droplets and then soaked into her gown.

There was a rattle of keys at the door before it creaked open.

"Your dinner, Madam."

"Thank you, Nico." She answered without looking. The King's car stopped in the courtyard below. He got out alone, started up the steps and the car with the Queen inside drove away.

"Anna?"

She jerked up in surprise. Charles had come in with Nico and two other servants. His thick bushy brows hooded his dark, piercing eyes as he sized her up. Her lunch tray sat on the credenza, cold and untouched.

"You must stop this foolishness and eat something at once." He firmly commanded.

She stood up slowly, without taking her eyes from his. How dare he come in here and call her foolish?

"And who will you shoot if I refuse?" Her words sliced him like daggers.

The servants looked at each other nervously. Charles dismissed them without taking his eyes off of Anna. They tumbled over each other exiting as quickly as possible. He hoped that avoiding another public power struggle would diffuse the situation somewhat. When the door closed behind him, he softened his stance.

"Why are you doing this?" He demanded, with a hint of desperation in his voice. "Why do you continually defy my authority? You have no respect for my position. Do you think I have no command over this situation?"

Even with extreme control, he had more intensity in his voice than she had ever heard before. She was so angry, any fear she felt quickly dissipated.

"You may have the power to bring me to your country. You can force me to go where you want me to go and stop going places you don't want me to go. You can force me to stay in this room, but you can not force me to live!" She breathed out vehemently as she shoved the food cart, sending dishes and food across the floor. She stood with fire in her eyes, her chest heaving. They glared at each other, neither backing down.

As she began to relax, her clenched fists softened and her breathing slowed and deepened, her shoulders slumped. She swayed and collapsed, exhausted from hunger and her passionate display of emotion.

Two strides of his long legs brought him to her side. He caught her and scooped her easily into his arms. He gently laid her on her bed and watched a moment to make sure she was breathing normally before he slipped out into the hall to find servants to clean up the mess.

Did she seriously mean to starve herself to death?! Surely she was bluffing. If she was not, what could he do about it? If she were determined to die, there was nothing he could do to stop her.

She was young, immature and over dramatizing…or, perhaps, she was playing a battle of wits. In which case he should call her bluff and leave her to herself until she learned never to start something she was not willing to finish.

Judging from what little he knew of her, she would die before she would admit defeat. In any case, how could she fulfill their purpose while taking the role of prisoner? He wouldn't force her to marry him. She hadn't been raised to fulfill her royal duty as he had.

He met Nico coming around the bottom of the staircase with a mop and pail in hand.

"I heard the dishes break, sir. I will take care of it directly."

"Yes, well, thank you Nico."

His father was in the office, busy at his desk. He looked up when Charles walked in. He could tell from the expression on Charles face that things had not gone well. He pushed back from the desk and gave him his full attention.

"She has won. I don't know what else I can do." He slumped into a chair by the door. "It was not a good plan to bring her here."

His father's eyebrows furrowed sharply, "We need her." He was surprised Charles didn't understand the importance of this relationship.

"I have heard back from Queen Wilhelmina of the Netherlands. She is very anxious to meet Anna. She wants Anna to stay with her for two months. They want to get to know her, accept her as royal family and present her to you formally with a union between our countries." His gaze softened at the disparaged look of his normally undaunted son.

"You have been trained extensively and are well prepared for your responsibilities. You are doing a very good job and I am confident you will handle this situation as well."

"None of my training has prepared me for this!" He snorted. "For her! I have not known fear since I was a child...until now." He tossed his head. "I have never known a woman like her before."

His father's calm, unyielding confidence in him smirked at Charles frustration and he smiled back halfheartedly. "You have no idea what she is really like." Charles shook his head, hardly believing Anna's behavior himself.

"I know." Charles' sense of duty reprimanded his own actions. "The mighty do not make excuses, they find a way. I will do my best."

Charles climbed slowly up the stairs and slipped quietly into her room. The servants were just leaving. He asked them to bring some fresh food.

Charles pushed the heavy, overstuffed mahogany chair across the room next to the bed and dropped wearily into its velvety softness. He leaned back, putting his hands over his face and breathed deeply. He rubbed the corners of his eyes with his fingertips as if to wipe away the weariness and frustration. He leaned forward resting his forearms on his knees, rubbing his hands together as he struggled to figure out what he would do and say.

What was this rare creature, living in their midst, posing as an innocent young woman? If he hadn't brought her here himself, he would have thought she was sent by his enemies to torture him. She could be so compassionate and tender hearted one time and so passionately impulsive and defiant another. She lay there sleeping, looking so fragile and helpless. Ha! She would take on the world, and probably win. How could anything so stubborn and untamed be so captivating? He looked back at his hands, still unclear on how to deal with her, carefully filing away his emotions for her.

Haunting images swirled in Anna's mind as it slowly rose to the surface. Had she really thrown food across the room with a threat to starve herself to death? Why did she have to be so dramatic? There was breathing and movement in the room. She forced her eyes open and drew a deeper breath. Charles ran his fingers through his hair with his head down. She was kidding herself if she thought she wasn't falling for him. How could she be so attracted to someone she was so angry with?

She closed her eyes again. Pictures filtered into her thoughts, his irritation with her stubbornness, his self-control while she made a fool of herself and his determination to fix this problem. How could she face him now? What must he think of her? How could he ever love her when she kept playing the fool? How could she possibly win his heart now? She could feel him watching her. If she pretended to be asleep, eventually he would leave.

The silence that filled the room became suffocating. What was he doing? She peeked and quickly squeezed her eyes shut again. He was studying her with curiosity. He knew she was awake. She slowly sat up, swinging her bare feet to the floor. She looked so frail and timid now.

His dark eyes probed her as his mind was still undecided on how to best handle this situation. She traced the leafy pattern in the bedside Peshawar rug with her toe, unable to meet his gaze. His eyes narrowed, as he finally broke the awkward silence.

"What is it you are trying to get me to do? What is your objective in all this?" His frustration and strained patience were more evident than he preferred.

If he would deny her his own heart, at least he should allow her the love of the children. She blurted out, "I'm sorry, I know you have power and authority over me. You win. I'll do anything you want me to." Her wide, shining eyes tried his powers of endurance. "But please," she pleaded as she dropped to her knees directly in front of him clasping his hands in hers. "Please, don't take those children away from me. They love me." She searched his eyes for some sign of hope. "They need me." Hope began to fade as his expression remained unreadable. "And I need them. Please." She bowed her head, gently placing his hands to the side of her face and holding them tightly as she cried.

His chest constricted when he realized what she must think of him, an arrogant tyrant issuing edicts and penalties just to instill proper fear in his inferiors. He pulled his hands free and cupped her face pulling it up to look at him.

"I have not restricted you from anything as a show of my power. Everything I have done has been for very good reasons." She pulled back and looked down.

"I know you do not understand our ways." He struggled with how to make her understand how serious her offence was. "House arrest was the very least I could give you for public defiance of a sovereign command!"

"You're right, I don't understand your ways. What about Erwin and Pier?" Her temper flared again.

His eyes narrowed as he studied her, deciding how much to tell her.

"Erwin could no longer be trusted." His penetrating gaze made her wish she hadn't asked. "Pier was not at fault; but he has been reassigned."

He was uncomfortable having her kneeling to him. He took her shoulders and raised her up as he stood.

"I need you for my ally not my enemy. We must secure our borders; strengthen our position within our borders. When we are stabilized, then we will work to improve conditions for everyone, including our orphans." He gently lifted her chin to look in her eyes again.

"We have heard back from The Queen of the Netherlands. She wants you to come to her for two months. She wants to get to know you…accept you as royal family and formally present you to our country—to me—with an agreement between our countries. This is what we have been hoping for. Will you do this, will you go?"

"No!" She turned away. "No, I can't." How could he put the weight of a union between their countries on her shoulders? "I don't know what to do. Can't you go make the arrangements? What if I mess things up? I don't know anything about diplomatic dealings. What if I offend them and start a war or something?!"

"If anyone could do that, it would be you!" He laughed and she jerked back with her mouth open. "I am sorry, but you can be rather…strong willed." He suppressed his smile somewhat, but he couldn't extinguish the twinkle in his eyes. "No one expects you to unite any countries. The queen will feel more a part of this agreement if she actually knows you and has some input."

She turned away again. Don't look in his eyes, those beautiful, piercing eyes. Just say no. He never said anything about going to the Netherlands in the original deal. Wasn't it enough that they expected her to marry in order to seal their agreement?

"If you would like, I could arrange some tutoring for you tomorrow." He caught her shoulders and pulled her back to face him. Her knees felt weak and her head light. She was beyond hunger and the thought of learning a whole new set of rules made her head swim. "I am asking much of you, I know. There is something else I must ask…please, eat something; get your strength back."

She smiled weakly and nodded to him, but the sadness returned. She was so attracted to him. She had been wrong about him and his motives. He was so strong, disciplined, in control, so kind and concerned with everyone but himself, but how could she live in marriage with him knowing he would never fully belong to her? She looked down at her hands, cold and loosely entwined.

"I'll go." She whispered and turned to look out the window, blinking back a tear.

"You are making all of the concessions, let me do something for you. Ask of me anything your heart desires, if it is within my power…" He thought better of his promise and added "and good judgment, I will fulfill your request."

She looked at him hopefully, then shook her head and looked down. He took her shoulders again.

"Please, I am not your enemy. I want very much to make you happy. I can not allow you to go back to the orphanage…or anywhere unsafe." Her small frame quivered as he squeezed her shoulders. "Ask me, give me a chance. I will go to the ends of the earth! Tell me what I can get for you." He pulled her chin up and drained her of all reason with his smile.

"Kiss me," she closed her eyes and whispered.

He wasn't prepared for this. He knew she wasn't asking for a kiss on her forehead or hand. She was asking him to love her, to need her, and not just to make a political alliance. She needed him to replace the children he had taken away from her, to fill the void he had created. How could he let go of years of emotional conditioning and restraint? And yet, how could he deny her this?

A tight crushing pain in his chest radiated out to his limbs, as if she physically reached inside him and pulled his heart from him. Exquisite pain pulsed through him. He wanted to protect her and make her happy and yet fear like he had never known before seized him. How could he allow himself to be so vulnerable? The protective wall around his emotions began to crumble. He looked at the ceiling and took a deep breath trying to regain control.

She felt a groan from deep within him and looked at him agonizing over her simple request. Was kissing her so repulsive? She pulled away, tears welling up in her eyes.

"Never mind, you don't…"

Part of his mind said to turn and run. If he kissed her now, his heart would be gone forever. The other part said she has sacrificed so much for you and your country. You must give her this small token. He caught her arm and pulled her back to him.

Chapter 15

Dutch lessons began right after breakfast. French lessons were followed by etiquette and protocol. Ballroom dance and a refresher course of piano came in the afternoon. It was therapeutic for her to play again. She worked very hard each day. She was anxious to prove to Charles that she wasn't just a nuisance. She wanted very much to be an asset to him and his people.

Anna walked slowly through the domed foyer on her way to her music lesson, drinking in the rich pine and cedar aromas. Servants were busy wrapping the large marble pillars and stair banisters with pine garlands. Pine and cedar boughs tied with burgundy satin ribbons hung from the upper level railings. She dearly loved the Christmas season and everything about it, the smells, the music, the twinkling lights and candles, the traditional food and treats, and especially the joyful feelings of good will. She was in especially high spirits when she met Charles, his father and Geoffrey passing through.

"Geode middag uw highness. Zal ik u baden bij diner zien?" she asked Charles, smiling pleasantly, hoping to impress him with her language skills. His reaction was not what she expected. He cocked his head to the side, eyebrows furrowed; straining to figure out what she was really trying to ask. Geoffrey attempted to suppress a smile as he put his hand on Charles shoulder.

"Well, answer her question." He smirked. "Will she?" his eyes dancing with delight at Charles discomfort.

King Albert had a strange questioning look on his face. He was quite sure she did not mean to ask Charles if she would see him bathe at dinner. Their behavior made her quite nervous. Wide-eyed and blushing, she whirled around to make a hasty exit, whisking behind the nearest pillar. She stopped only for a moment before heading for the hallway leading to her music lesson. Charles, not wanting to stunt her confidence in attempting to speak Dutch, threw Geoffrey a sharp look and went after her.

"Anna, it is alright. I am glad you are trying so hard." He took both her hands in his pulling her to face him.

"What did I just say?" Humiliation swept over her.

"I think you meant to say 'Zal ik u vanavond bij diner zien?' Will I see you this evening at dinner? Is that what you meant?"

"Yes, isn't that what I said?"

"Well," he repressed a smile. "Your grammar was incorrect for the question you asked; but it was perfect for the question you meant to ask, just one word off. I am very happy with your effort. Please, do not hesitate to speak to me in Dutch." He let a crooked smile escape.

"What did I say?" She demanded.

"It does not matter; you did not mean to say it."

"It was so bad that you can't tell me? What will your father think of me now?" She tried to turn away, but he pulled her back.

"He understands. He appreciates your efforts as much as I do." He smiled reassuringly. "Geoffrey understands as well. He just enjoys giving me a hard time." He glanced back at his father and Geoffrey waiting for him.

"I have to go now. We will practice this evening at dinner." He quickly kissed her hand, turned and strode to meet the others.

"Anna," he turned back and called to her. "Ja, zult u me vanavond bij diner zien." Yes, you will see me this evening at dinner; he clarified for anyone who might have heard the previous conversation.

She ducked her head, blushing, and headed straight for her next lesson.

She didn't initiate conversations in Dutch after that, so Charles made a point of stopping to ask her simple questions when he passed by. She made steady progress as the days passed.

With only one week until the Christmas Eve Ball, Anna was given various responsibilities using her newly learned or perfected skills. She was anxious to prove herself and wanted everything to be perfect. She put in long hours planning and arranging the food, musicians, the guest list and invitations. Her Dutch and French were still very limited but she was anxious to redeem herself in using her language skills outside the classroom.

Anna spent much of the evening receiving guests, socializing and dancing. She and Charles would not be officially engaged until after she had gone to the Netherlands, so they would not formally receive together, as a couple, until then. Charles was busy with social responsibilities of his own.

Leopold and his wife, Astrid, had put their children, little three year old Josephine-Charlotte and three month old Baudouin, to bed with stories of St. Nicholas and were just arriving at the party.

Leopold was good hearted but didn't have the best judgment in handling situations. He somehow offended one of the Walloons. Charles saw the trouble and interceded. Leopold was embarrassed that his little brother thought he should have to step in and "fix" the situation.

Leopold had too much pride, not enough self control and a hot temper; he took a swing at Charles. Charles side stepped and caught his hand raising it high in the air he called out, "His Royal Highness Prince Leopold, Heir to the Throne! We drink to your arrival."

With all eyes on him now, Leopold calmed himself and enjoyed the positive attention he received from the guests around the crowded ballroom.

Charles' younger sister, Marie Jose, and her new husband of almost a year were visiting from Italy for the holidays. She later took Charles aside and praised him for his handling of what could have been a humiliating circumstance.

"How can you treat Leo with such patience and respect when he treats you with none? You have better judgment than he and yet he is heir to the throne. Aren't you jealous of him?"

"Jealousy serves no purpose. He will be King of the Belgians...my king. Allowing him to humiliate himself only weakens his position. I forgive him and will do all I can to strengthen him."

"I will try to learn from you, Charles, in fulfilling my responsibilities in Italy."

Anna finally had a break and slipped out onto the balcony for a breath of fresh air. She leaned on the rail gazing across the lighted courtyard below. When she left Josephine's home last spring, she certainly didn't expect to be spending Christmas like this!

Charles spotted her and stepped out to make sure she was feeling alright. She turned and smiled when she saw it was Charles coming out to her. He was as attractive in a tuxedo as he was in his white military uniform. He always made her pulse quicken no matter what he wore.

"This evening has been perfectly splendid. I have been watching you. You handle yourself very well. You are ready to go to the Netherlands. I will make the necessary arrangements for the first of the new year."

Her smile faded. She turned and grasped the cold stone railing. Could she really do all that was expected of her? She was quite comfortable conversing with Charles, but the thought of going to the Netherlands without him there to smooth her lingual blunders was frightening.

"There is a full moon tonight." He put his arm around her shoulders, placing his warm hand on her arm, squeezing gently. "And two more while you are away." He lifted her chin as he gazed into her wide eyes. "If we are both looking at the same moon at the same time, perhaps you won't feel so far away."

She nodded. No words would come. She had only a heart full of wishes. How she longed for him to feel the way she felt for him. Her heart was his for the taking. Surely he felt something, more than duty for her.

"Look at the shadows cast from the trees in the gardens from the moonlight. It looks like a painting." The scene had an eerie beauty in the pale light with undisturbed snow hanging thickly from the branches.

Anna leaned her head on his chest enjoying his warmth as the night chill set in.

"Have you saved a waltz for me?"

"Of course," she beamed.

He held out his hand and she lightly placed hers on top. Goosebumps tingled down her arms as he led her inside and swept her onto the dance floor with his warm hand on the small of her back. One-two-three one-two-three they dipped and turned, gliding around the room to Braham's Waltz. Charles scanned the room and expertly guided their "ship" as they sailed between and around the other swaying and twirling couples.

As they pulled along side Geoffrey and his new wife, Geoffrey elbowed Charles and tipped his head toward the refreshment table.

"Yes, I know." Charles rolled his eyes. "I am on guard," he said through his teeth and glided off, away from the refreshment table.

What was that all about?" Anna quizzed.

"Nothing, you needn't worry." He scanned the room again.

"I wasn't worried, but now I am. What are you on guard against?"

"You see the young men at the refreshment table?" He turned so Anna faced the table. "Those are Stephanie's brothers."

"Yes, I have met them. I thought they left."

"They are back."

"Is that a problem?" She watched them with an eye on Charles' expression. "They seemed very friendly and well behaved."

"Yes, perhaps a little too friendly." He circled to the far corner of the room as the brothers found partners and entered the dance floor.

"What do you mean?" She laughed. "How can one be too friendly?"

"Franz, the tall one with the red cravat, over there." He turned so she could see him. "He is…impressed with you." His sweet cinnamon breath tickled her ear as he bent to whisper. She jerked back to look in his face. Was he joking with her?

"He doesn't even know me. We met only once."

"He is coming this way." He spun her and glided back to the center of the room. "He is quite determined to dance with you."

"I have danced with several young men this evening. Was I not supposed to dance with anyone but you?"

"No, no, I have been dancing as well. I just do not want you dancing with him."

"Are you jealous?" She laughed, her eyes twinkling with delight.

"Jealous?" He snorted. "It is for your benefit that I keep you away from him. I am protecting you from a vulture." The three brothers began closing in from all sides as Charles twirled her off the floor and they ducked out the side door into the hallway.

"Why are they here?" The music softened as they walked down the long hallway.

"I suppose they have nothing better to do. They drift from one place to another, looking for new prey."

"How do they live? Don't they have responsibilities?"

"Some of royal birth, think that it is alright to take a donation from the state without earning it. Franz, in particular, adds to that income by his relationships with wealthy women."

"I am not wealthy. I have nothing. Why would he be interested in me?"

"He has many relationships, not all are for money." He offered his arm as they started up the stairs.

Ugh, what a horrible man, she thought. Then she remembered her responsibilities. "I must go back. I won't dance, I promise. There is still so much to do."

"You have done enough. They will finish here without you." He walked her up to her room and paused at her door. "Thank you for all you have done and for all you will do. Your cooperation and effort mean very much to me." He smiled, knowing how delighted she would be with his little surprise.

"I have a Christmas gift for you. I have arranged for Christmas dinner, toys and warm clothing to be delivered to your orphanage tomorrow."

She wrapped her arms around his neck.

"Thank you." she whispered.

Chapter 16

Adelheid and two guardsmen boarded the train with Anna, who was off again to a new land and new adventure. She shuddered with tingles of anxiety and anticipation coursing down her spine as they set off for the Netherlands.

Anna pulled her wraps tighter around her shoulders to keep out the chill as the snow swept landscape blew past her window. Ice crystals had painted their delicate lace patterns around the edges of the window and her breath came in steamy puffs. This was the first run of the day for this particular train and it would take awhile to warm it up, but the memory of Charles' face, when he bid her farewell, warmed her. She was certain she detected a touch of longing in his expression.

Noordeinde Palace, Anna had read, was originally a farm house, converted into a palace in the early seventeenth century. She found this hard to believe when they arrived there. Its massive stately elegance was impressive. Anna was taken to her rooms and allowed to rest and freshen up before a festive dinner that night.

The Queen was a welcome delight. She was stern and strict, and yet so motherly. She was very perceptive and aware of all that she had stewardship over. She was a take-charge kind of person, very confident and in control. Nothing got past her, and yet she was so compassionate and sensitive to the feelings and personal struggles of everyone around her.

Some of Juliana's friends had extended their stay after the holidays at the Queen's request. Elise Bentinck and Elisabeth van Hardenbroek had been friends of Juliana since childhood. Juliana had made some friends while visiting in France that came for the holidays, most of which had already returned home. Armand had a particular interest in Elise. He and a few of his friends, all from important, wealthy families, stayed on.

They were all waiting in the dinning room to meet the newest guest, when Anna was brought in and introduced. The queen was called away on urgent business and asked Elise to finish the personal introductions. Elisabeth was first.

"Hello, ben ik gelukkig om u te ontmoeten." Anna said as confidently as she could muster. Fernand, from France, stepped up to be introduced next. She swallowed hard as she forced her brain to switch from Dutch to French.

"Bonjour, je suis heureux de vous rencontrer." She smiled, not so confidently.

"Madame bonsoir. J'espère que vous apprécierez votre sejour ici dans les Pays Bas. Nous ferons tout quoi que nous bidon pour rendre votre temps ici aussi plaisant comme possible. Y a-t-il quelque chose que je peux faire pour toi maintenant?"

Fernand spoke too rapidly for her to grasp everything he said. She understood "good evening" and by the inflection in his voice and the look on his face, he had asked her a question, but she had no idea what he had asked. Her brows knit together above her wide nervous eyes as she tried to figure out what to say. He winked and threw her a condescending smile.

"Do you mind if we speak English? I am sure my English is better than your French."

"Do you mind if we don't speak at all. I'm sure my French is much better than your manners." Anna could feel the heat rising from her neck. Elise grabbed her arm and pushed her away, leaving Fernand with a curious look on his face. He was not accustomed to Anna's adverse reaction to his "charm."

"Don't mind him; he is just teasing you. He teases all the girls." She pulled Anna towards Damien and Patrick.

"Does everyone here speak English?" Anna whispered to Elise.

"Yes, Dutch, French, English, German and the French boys speak some Italian as well." Anna suddenly felt quite out of her league.

"This is Damien and this is Patrick." Elise smiled, pointing to each respectively. "They are much nicer than Fernand!" She laughed as she smiled back at Fernand. They obviously all knew each other well and were accustomed to teasing.

"I am pleased to meet you." She smiled weakly holding her hand out to each. She was glad she no longer had to pretend to speak Dutch or French, but she held no enthusiasm for meeting the rest of this group.

Anna took the seat next to Elise and quietly observed everyone else, commenting only when etiquette demanded. She tried to avoid any eye contact with Fernand, but she could feel his penetrating gaze on her and looked up. He was sitting across the table and to Anna's left, surrounded with female attention. They prattled on with an occasional comment of encouragement from Fernand, unaware of his lack of real interest. She felt like an outsider and was already uncomfortable in this situation, but Fernand's piercing scrutiny of her was so unsettling that she dropped her fork on the floor. A smirk crept across Fernand's lips, betraying his pure pleasure at his ability to affect her so. She quickly pushed her chair back and stood, attempting to smile.

"Please, excuse me, I'm not feeling well. It has been a very long day." It wasn't hard to be convincing as she was shaky and flushed. She barely reached the hallway before hot tears filled her eyes. How she missed Belgium…and Charles.

A blizzard in the night kept them house bound most of the next day, playing cards in the parlor. Anna was careful to join only the groups Fernand was not a part of. She found most of this gathering of friends to be quite friendly and accepting of her. Occasionally Fernand stood, walked around the room or looked out the window and joined another group. Eventually he came to the small table where Anna, Elise and Armand sat playing Rummy. Patrick had just left to get a drink.

"Do you mind if I join you? Armand? Elise?" He looked at each as he spoke their name.

"Of course not." They both agreed.

"Anna, is it alright with you?" He queried with a certain smugness. She put on her most plastic smile and replied with sugary sweetness.

"Certainly, take a seat." She motioned to the vacant seat opposite her as she slid her own chair back and stood.

"I have been sitting much too long. I think I'll walk awhile. Patrick may have my seat when he returns." She didn't look back as she swished out the door and down the hall.

Turning the corner, large oil paintings in massive mahogany frames hanging on the wall down a short hallway leading to some sort of conference room, loomed above. There were gold plates at the bottom on which their names were engraved. King William III of the House of Orange—Nassau and Willem Nicolaas Alexander Frederik Karel Hendrik were two names she now recognized. Here were her grandfather and great-grandfather. She stood in awe that she should meet them here and now. Nicolaas with his neatly trimmed hair, beard and mustache sat with dignity and a look of benevolence.

In contrast, his father, Anna's great-grandfather King William III, had a wild, unkempt, demanding look about him. It was still so hard to believe that she had royal relatives. She had lived most of her life never knowing they existed.

There they sat on the wall, painted into their thrones all regal and important, generation after generation, fathers and sons. What would they think of her, so small and insignificant, coming here now to claim some right to unite two nations through marriage?

She stared into their eyes trying to imagine what it might have been like to come before them in person. Would they recognize her as their granddaughter or turn her away as some imposter from an unrecognized relationship? Would they be kind or harsh? Would she be included in family traditions and holiday gatherings?

"You didn't get far on your walk." Fernand's voice pulled her from her distant imaginings.

"I suppose winning every game was too boring, so you decided to come out here to find new ways to further humiliate me?" she asked without looking away from her grandfather.

"You judge me severely, Madam." He declared with a look of injury.

"I suppose you have come to apologize then?" She replied sarcastically, turning her gaze on him.

"I have nothing to apologize for. I suppose you think I should grovel before you because of the noble blood flowing through your veins from these majestic beings hanging on the walls of this royal palace?" He waved his hand contemptuously at the paintings she stood admiring.

"I never knew there were paintings of my relatives on royal walls until less than a year ago." She looked back at the painting. Who does Fernand think he is attacking me? I never asked to come here; I am here only because the queen demands it.

"As soon as you learn of your majestic heritage, you come here hoping to lay claim to magnificence, through no effort of your own. I suppose, as you look into their faces, that you think they owe you because you exist?" Fernand sneered.

"Actually, I was thinking how much this one looks like my father." She replied softly. "Well, he looks like the only picture I've ever seen of my father. He has the same kind, gentle look about him." Her moist eyes softened Fernand's attack stance.

"You don't remember your father?"

"He died before I was born." She held her gaze on Alexander, longing for understanding and acceptance.

"Your mother sent you here?"

"My mother died three years ago."

"Then you are an orphan?"

"You say that like it gives you some reason to look down on me." She turned on him. "I suppose you think I should grovel before you because your parents are still living? It is no statement of your character or worth because your parents live any more than a statement of mine because of whose blood flows through my veins. I am who I am because of who I choose to be, not because of who I descended from, dead or alive." Her eyes were flashing now as she worked herself into a rage.

His opinion of her took a giant step up. His family had come into wealth and power after the revolution and he respected hard work and ambition more than birthright.

"It appears I have misjudged you as well. I thought you to be another silly female, come to claim your rights to position and substance, caring more about what to wear than the world's state of affairs."

"Humph," She snorted. "The world's state of affairs is precisely why I am here." Then muttering to herself, "It certainly isn't where I belong nor where I want to be."

"And why are you here?" He queried, now more curious than accusing.

"There you are, both of you! We had begun to wonder if you had finished each other off!" When Elise noticed the irritated look they each wore, she realized how close to the truth she had come.

"Oh dear, maybe we should have Peace Talks and see if we can arrive at some truce. Lunch has been served and we are discussing an outing this afternoon. The storm has lifted and we are all anxious to get out." She smiled, hoping to lift the storm that seemed to be brewing here inside the palace hallway.

"I am willing to call a truce." Fernand offered, lifting an eyebrow as he looked at Anna.

"Only if Fernand promises to behave himself." She warned.

"I was hoping this truce included you accepting my behavior." He flashed her his most dazzling, mischievous smile, Anna couldn't help laughing merrily.

"I have no problem with another world war. A truce is on my terms or not at all." Anna said as she shot Fernand a sideways smile and flounced away.

When they all decided to go ice skating, Anna planned to sit on a nearby bench and watch as she had never been ice skating, but Fernand wouldn't allow it.

"For the cause of world peace?" He smiled, holding out a pair of skates. He coaxed her out onto the ice and skated backward, holding her hands to keep her balance. He was quick to catch her when she fell. When she was confident enough to try it by herself, Fernand began to show off, skating circles around her.

"You are getting your feet under you. What do you say to a race?!" He challenged her with a twinkle in his eye.

"Oh, yes, that would be fair." She laughed.

"Come now, it is an Olympic race. The winner determines the superior nation." He took off like a shot. When he lapped her the second time, he raised his arms in triumph and cheered for himself.

"I win the gold!" He circled her again taunting her. "So, do you agree that France is better than the Netherlands?"

"Actually, you have been in the Netherlands longer than I have." She grew tired of his arrogance.

"Then France is better than Belgium, admit it." He teased, skating backward facing her. She wasn't sure if he did it so he could watch her reaction to his teasing or to continue to rub in his superior skating skills. "What would your Belgian prince think of you now, losing to France?" He smiled mischievously.

My Belgian prince? She glared at him, not amused by his little charade. What exactly does he mean by that!? She had no intention of discussing Charles with Fernand.

"France may very well be better than the Netherlands and Belgium, but America is better than all of Europe put together, which happens to be where I was born." She tossed her head and headed for the bench. She sat down and began taking off her skates. Her smug, sassy reaction amplified his interest in her. He was not accustomed to such a stubborn resistance to his charm.

"I am sorry, don't leave. I will stop teasing you." He begged with insincerity dripping from his tongue.

She wasn't really mad, just cold and bored with trying to learn to skate. So she pretended to pout as an excuse to leave. Fernand misinterpreted her pretended pouting as an attempt to get him alone and followed her as she headed for the lodge.

"I never knew Americans were such poor losers." He continued to tease.

"Perhaps Americans just spend their time on more important matters than learning to ice skate." She was getting rather irritated with his persistence in making fun of her. She headed across a dry patch of ground. Fernand, still wearing skates, was rather wobbly without the support of snow around the blades as he crossed the rocky ground.

"The French are superior at everything, but if we ever lost at anything, we could certainly admit it." He laughed as he had almost caught up with her.

She reached the snow just before him and scooped up a large handful, whirled and plowed it into his face.

"You lose. Admit that."

Her reflex reaction caught them both by surprise. He floundered for a moment before he fell flat on the ground.

She stood gaping at him, stunned at her own behavior. He smiled a menacing, undaunted smile as he clawed at the ground to pull himself upright. Anna whirled and ran for the lodge before he could get up and get his revenge. He caught her just as she hit the heavy oak door. They both tumbled over the stone threshold onto the rough wood floor planking. Laughing, he scooped her into his arms, threatening to haul her back out to the snow to finish what she had started.

"It is finished and you lost." She smiled innocently. "Admit it because now you owe me a hot cocoa!" She offered guiltily. Perhaps if she allowed him a little attention it would pacify him and make up for her rash behavior.

"I will buy you a cocoa, but I admit nothing. You cheated." He was afraid he had pushed his bravado a little too far and was relieved she would still speak to him.

Anna took a seat by the roaring fire in the massive central fireplace and put her feet up on the stone hearth to thaw them while Fernand was getting their cocoa. She looked up into the round, glossy eyes of the moose head, mounted directly above her. It was as though he looked down on her with stern disapproval. Her conscience crept down her spine with tingling guilt. She could tell Fernand was developing an attraction for her, but she wasn't sure what to do about it. She didn't encourage him; he pushed the relationship. She couldn't be rude; they were both guests of the queen. Obviously he had done some checking into her situation because he knew about her "Belgian prince." Maybe he was just trying to make up for his initial offensive treatment of her, she tried to convince herself. We're just friends, nothing more.

Evenings in the parlor with a cheery fire were common. Card games and cocoa helped pass the frosty twilight hours. Elise reached across Elisabeth, trying to hand a mug of hot cocoa to Anna. Anna didn't notice because she was watching Patrick closely as he tried to deal cards from the bottom of the deck. No one else in the circle noticed and he was pleased with himself until Elise slopped some cocoa over the top of the mug sending Elisabeth squealing from the room. He looked up and saw Anna watching him.

"Oh, I'm sorry, that was my fault." Anna apologized taking the mug from Elise. "Thank you."

She winked at Patrick letting him know his secret was safe with her.

When Fernand caught Anna's wink at Patrick, he became disinterested in the three girls; one at each shoulder and one at his knee, which hung on his every word. He hoped Anna was just trying to make him jealous, which was exactly what he was attempting with her. The girls nearest him were overly impressed with his bragging, while Anna ignored him altogether. This only fanned the flames of his desire for her.

He got up on the pretext of putting another log on the fire before he squeezed onto the cushion next to Anna and joined their card game. She smiled disarmingly at him as she peeked at his cards and whispered in his ear, "You'd better let me win." She felt a little guilty taking advantage of him, but it was just too easy.

Six sleighs were hitched up and filled with soft down comforters and fur throws one frosty afternoon, ready to take their group to the Rembrandt House. They were interesting tour guides, as they took Anna all over Amsterdam, giving her a detailed history about each stop. They all spoke English very well and they patiently helped her increase her vocabulary in their native languages as well.

Anna had managed to avoid Fernand most of the day, but on their way home Fernand made sure he had the seat next to Anna. The sun hung low in sky and was shrouded by heavy clouds. Icy air hit their faces as they dashed across a field, bells on the harnesses making a soft ching ching ching to the rhythm of the horses' gate.

Anna buried herself in an incredibly soft white fur throw. She made a little tent over her head and breathed into her hands to warm them. Fernand joined her under the fur, rubbing his hands together briskly.

"Good idea." He breathed slowly into his hands cupped over his face to warm his cheeks. "Next best thing to a roaring fire." He winked and she giggled. "I think I would prefer the fire."

"Let me help you." Fernand wrapped his hands around hers and blew into them. His hot peppermint breath melted the stiffness in her fingers and filled their little darkened tent. "I am hotter than any fire, madam." He growled and lunged at her. Anna could feel his lips against her jaw and she turned away. The next thing they knew, Fernand was flipping out of the sleigh backward. Luckily, he caught hold of the side of the sleigh as he fell. He lit running and pulled himself back in. Her impulsive strength surprised both of them. Anna covered her mouth in a feeble attempt to stop laughing.

"I'm sorry, are you alright?"

"Why did you push me out?" His seriousness stopped her cold.

"You tried to kiss me."

"Don't be coy with me. Surely you know how I feel about you."

"I'm sorry; I never meant to lead you on." Her feelings of guilt took a quantum leap. "I am going to marry Prince Charles of Belgium. I thought you knew."

"You are formally engaged?" He interrogated.

"Well, no."

"Then he has declared his love for you?"

She looked away as she felt her face grow hot. This was none of his business and she would not discuss it with him.

"At least give me a chance. You could be just as happy in France as you could be in Belgium."

He gently pulled her face around and saw her glistening eyes. So, her relationship with the Belgian prince was not quite what she wanted it to be. He might still have a chance, but decided not to push it just now.

Chapter 17

King Albert was in the Royal office when the mail arrived. A letter from Queen Wilhelmina was among the letters.

Your Majesty King Albert,

Your Anna is a delightful girl. With my own Juliana away at University, Anna helps to fill that void. I convinced some of Juliana's friends to stay on after the holidays to provide companionship for Anna. They have gotten along very well.

But there is a matter of concern. One of the young men has apparently taken an interest in Anna, for he has asked me to consider him as a suitor for her. I informed him of our intentions and questioned Anna concerning him. She does not return his affections as more than a friend.

I am having a ball on February 14. I suggest your son Charles be in attendance to protect your interests.

Sincerely,

Her Majesty Queen Wilhelmina

* * *

Anna was hoping for time with Charles, but never caught so much as a glimpse until the ball. He had arrived that morning and was in meetings with Parliament and the queen until the music had already started.

Elise helped Anna choose her gown for this evening. She talked her into a black chiffon gown, fitted to the hips then flared out with a sloping hemline. It was a little more dramatic than Anna would have chosen. She was drawing attention from the young men that had started to gather. Her hair was piled in a mass of curls on top of her head. She wore the emerald necklace Diederik and Maurits had given her in Chicago. It brought out the intense green of her eyes. Charles had given it to her again before the Christmas ball, with the instructions to keep it and wear it this time!

The ballroom was glowing as the light from the candelabras atop the sturdy marble columns that surrounded the room, reflected off the intricate carvings overlaid with gold leaf. The inlaid wood floor was polished to a glistening sheen, adding to the rich, golden radiance of the room.

Anna and Elisabeth chatted happily until the Queen made her entrance. Charles and the rest of the sovereigns he had been meeting with all afternoon, followed behind her. Her heart beat like the wings of a humming bird and her knees felt weak. Suddenly she was nervous to face him. She hadn't seen him for several weeks now and he stood out majestically, even among royalty. He could be so intimidating.

She stood frozen, gripping the back of a nearby chair for support, as his eyes scanned the room. He stopped when he saw Anna, smiled broadly and started toward her. Did she dare hope that he had missed her in her absence?

He was stopped several times, to greet people, on his way across the room. This gave her heart a little time to return somewhat to a normal pace. He took her hand, bowed and kissed it. His eyes sparkled as he smiled at her.

"How are you, my dear?"

She took his hand in both of hers and stepped in close to him.

"I've missed…Belgium," her eyes started to glisten and she added softly, "and you." She lowered her eyes, embarrassed to be so forward.

"You are a good ambassador for us." He went on quickly, trying to dodge a teary scene. "The Queen is very impressed with you." By his expression, she could tell he was impressed with her as well.

"I hope she will allow you to return to Belgium; I think she would like to keep you here!" A smile crept across his face as his eyes swept over her again.

"She has been very kind to me."

"Have you enjoyed your time here?" He eyed her carefully.

"Oh, yes. I've seen so many wonderful things." She replied, smiling now.

"Tell me everything, as we dance?" He took her hand and led her onto the dance floor.

The time raced by as they danced time and again. It felt good to be with him again.

Finally, Fernand decided to make his move. He introduced himself to Charles and asked if he might have one dance.

"No." Anna refused as she shook her head, her eyes darting between them.

"Please, Anna, surely you can spare one dance?"

Charles reluctantly bowed and backed up, as proper etiquette dictated; while Anna continued to shake her head. Fernand took her hand and led her out onto the floor.

"Do you know how to Tango? It is very popular in France." His dark eyes searched hers, longing for some spark of interest in him.

"No, I've never heard of it." She replied, irritated that he ignored her lack of desire to dance with him.

"I have asked the musicians to play 'Volve', just for us." He quickly showed her the basic steps and she followed him the minimum that courtesy demanded. When the music began, he swept her around the floor, masterfully guiding her about. T-A-N-GO she counted out silently. Fernand's long, lean legs marched out the dramatic steps flawlessly. His passionate gaze was hypnotic; she couldn't take her eyes from his. His hand on her back guided her across his step and dipped, pulling her back up in perfect harmony with the melody. It didn't matter that she didn't know the steps, he put her where she needed to be.

Her pulse quickened as he pulled her to his side so tightly next to his chest she could feel his heartbeat. This must have fulfilled some innate feminine desire, which she never knew existed, to be absorbed in the masculine control of a man that knew exactly what he was doing.

Goosebumps swelled as a tingling sensation coursed through her. She was not used to dancing close enough to feel her partner's hot breath on her neck. He was more attractive than she had ever noticed before. The music, the look in his eyes, his power over her, left her putty in his hands. The final chords of the song sounded as he dipped her low to the floor, his face inches from hers. She was quite breathless as Fernand returned her to Charles. She felt as though steam rose up from her neck and fevered cheeks.

"Thank you, Mademoiselle." He bowed low to her, allowing his lips to linger on her hand and strode away. Charles eyes followed Fernand as he confidently swaggered out to the balcony.

"I must learn this," he directed his gaze toward Anna, "Tango." Raising one eyebrow as he analyzed this alien feeling of jealousy.

"Yes." She panted, oh yes! She tried to quell the guilty feeling that she had just been unfaithful to Charles. It was just a dance. How could she feel such an attraction to someone so selfish, so arrogant? Now if Charles danced with her like that!...He was so nearly perfect already, if he learned to Tango, he would probably be taken up into Heaven with Enoch and his city of perfect people.

Anna felt lightheaded and took Charles arm to steady herself. She absently fanned herself with her free hand. Charles looked at her with hooded eyes. Could he feel her tremble? She dropped her hands and smiled weakly.

"You look a bit flushed and tired. Perhaps we should sit for a while?" He motioned toward two open chairs. "Have a seat. I will get you a drink."

"I'm alright," she said, regaining her composure. "Let's go for a walk, I'll show you around." She was anxious to leave before Fernand returned.

* * *

When Anna went to breakfast, Charles was not there.

"Fernand challenged Charles to a duel and of course he accepted! No honorable person would refuse." Elise became very animated with her thrilling news. "But Fernand is highly skilled in fencing." She clasped

Anna's hands in hers. "And dueling is against the law. Oh, Anna, I wish Armand would duel for me. This is so romantic." She swooned, dropping dramatically into the nearest chair.

Anna raced to the arena. She found Charles warming up.

"What are you doing?" she demanded.

"Anna, please do not attend this. This is something you won't understand." His grave expression was trimmed with impatience. He had hoped she wouldn't find out about this, at least until it was over.

"You are right, I don't. Why would you be involved in something so barbaric?" Her brows knit together over flashing eyes. She was astounded to find that what Elise had told her was true.

"Defending ones honor in a duel has been a practice for centuries. Would you have me be a coward and lose the respect of all of Europe?" Determination grounded him.

"Refusing to be a fool does not make you a coward."

He looked in her eyes with the muscle in the center of his throat pulsing the way it always did when he forced himself to control his emotions.

"Fernand claims that the affection between you gives him the right to court you." He pulled on his fencing gloves.

"What affection? We are merely friends." She tried to sound shocked, but she knew he had seen differently when Fernand danced with her last night.

"He says he has kissed you." Charles eyes darkened. He continued adjusting his straps.

"Do you believe me when I tell you he has not?!"

"Are you telling me he has not?"

"Yes! He tried, but I didn't let him. Since then I have always kept Elise or Elisabeth between us. I have never encouraged him." She answered more quietly, guilt seeping in again.

"Then I must defend your honor as well." He calmly stated.

"Is Europe a continent of fools? Either I am telling you the truth or I am not. How does the outcome of you and Fernand swinging swords at each other make me honorable?" She shot out desperately.

"It has always been accepted that if a man is to be respected and believed, he will back up his word with actions and God will defend the innocent." He had regained his control with quiet determination.

"Then it is I that should be dueling, for it is my word that needs backing up." She grasped for any argument. His determination left her knowing she was losing this battle.

"Don't be ridiculous. Now, please, don't make a scene. Go back to the palace and wait for me there."

"Wait for you there? You won't be coming back. Either Fernand wins and you are dead or you win and will be arrested. Elise told me that it is illegal to duel." Her façade of authority was crumbling and she was nearly in tears.

"My dear," Charles softened. "No wonder you are so adamantly opposed. Of course it is illegal to duel to the death. That is why we shall have rubber tips on our swords. It is only to first blood."

"First Blood?" She exploded. Was that supposed to appease her?

"Yes." He willed her to calm down with his intense gaze. "The tips prevent thrusting through to kill, but the rest of the sword is still sharp. The first to draw his opponent's blood wins."

"So he won't kill you, he will just cut your arms off?" She threw back unable to remain calm.

"What makes you so sure he will do the cutting?"

"Could you really do that? Could you actually cut a man's arm off?" The horror on her face forced him to consider how barbaric this primitive tradition was, but he felt he had no choice.

"Please, excuse me, I must finish my preparations." He bowed low to her, turned and walked back into the suite of men's rooms.

Anna took her place in the row just below the Queen. She turned and knelt before her waiting for permission to speak.

"I begged Charles not to participate in this. Won't you please stop this insanity?"

The Queen bristled at Anna's unintended offense, "Just because you don't understand something doesn't make it insanity."

"Just because something has been a tradition for centuries, doesn't make it sane."

"Is life more important than honor for Americans?"

"No, many courageous men have given their lives for the freedom and rights of their countrymen, but how can a sword fight bring honor to anyone?"

The Queen took a deep breath, "In and of itself, it can not, but it symbolizes his determination to put honor ahead of personal convenience, desire or even ahead of his own life."

Anna sunk helplessly into her seat as the duel began.

Charles and Fernand circled and stalked like two panthers, alert, watching for an opportunity to strike. They parried and lunged, exchanging conversation between themselves.

What could they be saying to each other? Fernand's eyes flashed angrily as he pulled a stroke against the stone riser under the seats, tearing the rubber tip from his sword. Charles refused to do the same.

Anna leapt to the Queen, kneeling at her feet, begging her to stop them.

"How can you sit there and allow this!"

The Queen looked at her sternly, "Remember who you are talking to."

"I'm sorry." she dropped down and she buried her face in the queen's skirts.

Charles and Fernand continued to circle, exchanging comments too low for anyone else to hear. Then Fernand caught Charles' sword against the floor and pulled his sword hard against it slicing through Charles' rubber tip. Charles found himself in the very scenario Anna had warned him of, either being dead or arrested.

He fought purely defensively while his mind raced to calculate his strategy. Fernand backed him toward the corner. Then as Fernand lunged forward, Charles side stepped and caught his arm against his hip. He spun around sending Fernand's sword flying across the floor and reversing their positions. Fernand was backed into the corner with Charles' sword point at the hollow of his throat.

Anna heard the reaction of the crowd and looked up. She wanted to look away, but the horror of what was about to happen held her like an iron fist at her throat. She twisted the queen's full skirt into a knot, but the queen didn't notice.

Fernand did not try to make any deals or plead for his life. He straightened and looked Charles in the eyes with a dark intensity.

"Finish it." He snarled.

Charles stared him down, viciously working his jaw muscles before twisting his sword with the slightest pressure, barely breaking the skin.

"First blood…it is finished." He called out without taking his eyes from Fernand's. Then he verbalized in a low voice for only Fernand to hear, what his whole person was already saying, "Stay away from Anna." Their eyes locked for a moment. Suddenly this act of honor and tradition reeked of misguided bravery. Charles turned and strode out of the arena casting his sword to the floor.

Damien, who had always been just a little jealous of Fernand, was standing near the entrance when Charles headed for the men's rooms.

"Good show my good man! You must have enjoyed that!"

"I never enjoy humiliating anyone." Charles shot back, still fighting the distasteful emotions boiling inside him, before disappearing inside.

"I had faith in your Prince Charles." The queen told Anna. "You should learn to trust him as well. He is a remarkable young man."

Anna didn't know what had happened between Charles and Fernand after she had gone to bed last night, but she certainly didn't like what had happened since then. How could this tradition be accepted? Sought out?! Elise wished for such a situation for herself.

"I don't belong here." Tears welled in her eyes before she turned to leave.

"Time goes by quickly. It won't be long until you are back in Belgium." The Queen soothed.

"I mean, I don't belong here in Europe, in royal company. I am unable to do all that is expected of me. There is so much I don't understand…don't agree with."

"Marriage is never easy, two different lives joining into one. It takes effort. But yours, I perceive, will be worth it. Actually, you are doing very well, considering your background."

Anna started back to the palace. There was just enough snow to decorate the landscape and a sufficient chill in the air to cool her temper, so she decided to walk awhile. She had had enough of people telling her what to think and feel and wanted to be alone with her thoughts.

Queen Wilhelmina found Charles in his suite organizing his things for his return home.

"You are cheating yourself." She stated in her typical, lovable flamboyance.

He gave her a puzzled look.

"She loves you, you know."

"She has told you this?" He looked hopeful. He now questioned the feelings Anna had for him, that he formerly felt quite secure in.

"I am aging, but I am still a woman. I know love when I see it."

He continued his preparations. How could she possibly know all that went on in the heart of this exasperatingly incomprehensible female?

"I believe that you could love her too, if you would allow yourself."

He stopped and looked up. She said nothing more, but her look demanded an explanation.

He stood looking at the floor while he gathered his thoughts. The emotions Anna inspired in him now only strengthened his argument that love inhibits rational thought.

"From the time I was quite young" He attempted to make her understand. "I learned that decisions are best made when emotions are kept in check. When I read of such love stories as Paris Alexandros and Helen of Troy, Marc Antony and Cleopatra, Samson and Delilah, I determined never to sacrifice my judgment to any woman."

"Anna is no Delilah. She doesn't have your understanding and knowledge of the best way to deal with each situation, but she seems, to me, to have your best interest at heart. You are not being fair to her." He knew she was right. "Ours is a difficult life. We have great responsibility. Love makes life worth the struggle."

Anna already owned a much larger portion of his heart than he was willing to admit. Part of him wanted to throw the doors open wide and let her in, but part kept a chain on the door, allowing her only to peek at his heart, teasing and torturing from without.

"Stay on a few days." It was more of a command than an invitation.

Her advice rang true to his heart. He wasn't sure why Anna would remain loyal to him over Fernand. Fernand pulled a string of hearts behind him, all eventually broken. Most women can't resist the temptation to be the one to capture the unattainable heart.

Anna deserved his love, unfettered and unrestrained. He would stay. And he would make the most of his time here.

Charles dropped to one knee and kissed the queen's hand.

"You are as wise as you are beautiful."

She tossed her head back and laughed merrily as he rose and strode out the door.

After checking everywhere he could think of that she might be, and asking everyone he thought might know where Anna could be, Charles started to feel a bit nervous for her safety. He started down the path to the stables, checking each row as he loped past.

He stopped. There she was, humming softly as she fed a scruffy looking horse a handful of corn from the bin. It had been separated from the other horses because of some chronic illness. He smiled to think how like her it was, to be helping this horse.

His emotions deepened as he stood watching her gentle tender care of this dispossessed creature. He would have accepted whom ever he needed to in order to protect his nation, but how lucky he was that she was the choice made for him.

As he started toward her, his shoes crunched in a patch of thin ice crusted over a shallow puddle. Startled, she looked up and watched him approach with guarded curiosity. He never sought her out, unless he disapproved of what she was doing and came to retrieve her.

She felt better because of her quiet stroll, but her feelings were still quite near the surface. She was not in the mood for a confrontation, but neither was she in the mood to be told what to do or how to act or what barbaric tradition to accept. She lifted her chin and squared her shoulders in an attempt to look more substantial than she really was. Whatever issues he was coming to settle with her, she just wasn't in the mood for it.

Guilt washed over him like icy water rushing down from the Ardennes Mountains. The sight of him coming made her brace for a conflict? In his attempt to protect his country from the love sick fool he was afraid of becoming, he had withheld from Anna her greatest desire, to be loved.

"What have I done to you?" He took her by the shoulders and searched her eyes. Her tough exterior was very thin and shattered with his touch. She looked down trying to blink away the tears.

"I am so sorry. I've been such a fool. You are the best thing that has ever happened to me. I should not have been so determined to run from you." He completely enveloped her in his swallowing embrace. "I will never be such a coward again." He promised, as he pulled back to look in her eyes again.

"You were afraid of me?!" She queried in disbelief.

He explained to her, as he had the queen, why he had determined never to trust his heart to a woman. It wasn't that she wasn't attractive, it was that he wouldn't allow himself to acknowledge the attraction he had to her; he wouldn't become a Samson.

"The fate of my country rests on many of the decisions I am required to make. I can not allow myself the luxury of giddy irresponsibility." He unlocked the gate to his protective wall that day and let her in, sharing some of his innermost feelings and fears. She would not betray that trust. He had given her his most vulnerable element, his Achilles' heel, his heart. She would protect it with her life. She determined he would never regret this choice.

They walked nearly a complete loop around the stables. Anna's nose and cheeks were turning rosy and her toes were getting numb.

"Would you like to go for a sleigh ride?" Anna suggested, she wanted to stay out with Charles but she was too cold to keep walking.

"If you promise not to push me out if I try to kiss you." He teased.

Her rosy cheeks deepened a shade as she ducked her head. She wondered who filled him in on those details. She was quite sure Fernand hadn't. She was relieved that he could joke about it now.

They pulled the blankets up around them and snuggled close to block the icy wind that rushed at them, as they sped over the snow covered fields. When they came to a pond, half frozen over and jeweled with sparkling frost, Charles guided their sleigh under a large willow, frosted over as well. His mood took on a serious posture.

"Anna, your coming here has helped our relationship with the Netherlands a great deal. The Queen is quite willing to form a union with Belgium," His eyes darted about nervously, which was uncommon for him. "Whether we wed or not. I know you have had your concerns about marrying me." He winced at the thought. "I just want you to be happy. Despite my desperate attempts to keep my feelings in check, I have grown to love you more than I ever thought possible. Yours is the face I want to see first every morning and last every night before I close my eyes. More than life, I want to marry you." He hesitated not sure he wanted to give her this option. "But, more than that, I want you to be happy. If you want to go back to America, I will take you there. I will take you wherever you want to go. I will buy you a home in New Y-" She put her fingers to his lips.

"Are you proposing marriage to me or trying to talk me out of it?!" She laughed as she dropped her hand from his face.

"Please, be my wife. Let me spend my life making you happy?" He begged dropping from the seat to one knee at her feet.

"You couldn't possibly make me any happier than I am right now." She beamed as she cradled his face with her hands, touching her forehead to his.

* * *

It was dark when they finally returned. They took their dinner by the fire in one of the sitting rooms.

The Queen immediately sent in a chaperone. She had been quite nervous about them being alone all afternoon, especially when no one seemed to know where they were.

Charles stayed on for three days, officially arranging their engagement and spending time with Anna. On the last night before he left, the Queen held a special dinner at which she formally announced Charles and Anna to be wed.

It had been almost two months that she had been in the Netherlands, and now that legal agreements had been made, Anna asked if she could return with Charles. Her Majesty adamantly opposed. She was strictly religious and countered that it would not be proper until the wedding. She had become like a mother to Anna and felt protective and responsible for her.

She said that the engagement should last six months to a year, but she would make an exception and reduce it to four months. Anna's heart sank. She never let go of his arm the rest of the evening. Being with Charles these last three days, engaged to him, had been incredible; how could she bare four more months without him?

Fernand and the others had returned to their homes shortly after the duel, so she didn't have to worry about awkwardness, just boredom and loneliness.

Chapter 18

King Albert received another letter from the Queen of the Netherlands. He was amused at how pleased he felt about this letter.

...I regret to inform you that I must shorten the engagement period for Anna and Charles. If I must hear Beethoven's "Pathetique" once more I shall go mad. Anna never plays anything cheerful anymore and the way she mopes around breaks my heart.

The palace was in an excited flurry as arrangements were made quickly. The wedding gown was started, but with the timetable shortened, extra people were called to that responsibility.

Yards of white satin were made into three tiered lengths for the skirt, all scooping up in the front. Underneath was a skirt of white on white brocade, which flowed out in a long train in back, with matching fitted bodice to the waist. Egyptian lace trimmed the elbow of three quarter length sleeves. Her veil of sheer organdy, with pearls embroidered into the pattern, draped lightly over her shoulders as Anna stood on a stool while three tailors pined and measured.

Others lined up to get her approval on flowers, music, pastries, colors and decorations. Every decision had to have the queen's approval as well. Sometimes Anna wished they would skip her and go directly to the queen. She would be happy with whatever was decided; she was just excited to be finally marrying Charles.

The greater burden was on Charles' end, as the civil half of the marriage would take place in the Netherlands, but the religious marriage, as well as any wedding celebrations afterward, would take place in Belgium,.

The day finally arrived. Charles and Anna rode in the State Coach to the Town Hall. Oranges tied with white satin ribbons and dangling pearls hung from the trees lining the street, in honor of the Royal House of Orange. After the civil marriage was performed they returned to the palace where a "small, intimate" celebration was held. Only the closest of friends and relatives were invited. Charles and Anna sat at the center of a long banquet table with Charles' family to their right and the rest to their left. This was her family. Most of Anna's life she had only her mother and Josephine, now she had a very large room filled with family that celebrated her royal wedding.

The day swirled in Anna's head like a dream as the royal coach took them to the port where they boarded a ship to Antwerp. She was half wed!

Leopold stood across the hallway as chaperone while Charles bid Anna good night at her cabin door. She kept hold of his hand as she leaned her back against the door and played with the ring on his third finger. He had good hands, large and strong, but soft and gentle. They were the firm hands of someone that took charge, but not spoiled. They were accustomed to hard work and service. He leaned against the door jam and made no effort to leave.

She had changed from her wedding dress into traveling clothes, but Charles still wore his white dress uniform. It was impossible to look up into his eyes without trembling. He cupped her hands in his own and squeezed. He was warm and calm. He thought her hands were shaking because they were cold? He didn't know how attractive he was.

"The dinner was very nice."

"Yes, it was." He replied smiling down at her.

Leopold folded his arms and shifted his weight to the other foot, rolling his eyes.

"And the decorations, all the fresh flowers, were…very…nice." There was a small stain on the green tweed carpet close to where Leopold stood. He shifted his weight again and looked at his watch. Charles put his finger under her chin and lifted.

"Everything was perfect." Charles nodded and gazed at her with adoration that Anna mistook for amusement. How could he be so relaxed with his older brother watching their every move? Of course she was making meaningless small talk. What else could she do? He lifted a stray lock of hair from her eyes and tucked it back in place.

"Just kiss her and let us be gone. I do not intend to stand here watching the two of you all night." Leopold said, only half joking.

"Is he still back there?" Charles asked with exaggerated annoyance for Leopold to hear, without taking his eyes from Anna. She blushed.

"Of course I am still back here."

"Leave, no one is forcing you to stay."

"You know I can not leave you two here alone."

Charles kissed her forehead and straightened to leave, but she held his hand tighter.

"Sleep well." He bowed to her and kissed her hand. "Your Highness." He added with a wink and a grin. By the time he was down the hall and turned the corner, she remembered to breathe again. She dropped into bed and the gentle waves rocked her to sleep.

It seemed she had barely closed her eyes when Adelheid knocked at her door, urging her to gather her things and prepare to disembark. All the royal family and friends traveling with them, proceeded on to Brussels by train. Anna went back to Chateau de Laeken, while Charles went to the Royal Palace. This would be her last night alone here. Tomorrow she would be fully Charles wife!

It was a beautiful day with perfect weather as Charles, adorned in his white uniform again, fully decorated with cords and medallions, arrived in a white coach, drawn by a white horse, to get Anna and proceed to the Church of Our Lady of the Sablon. The church was crowded with people, as was the street leading to it, many of whom she now recognized.

The various branches of the military were represented. She quickly searched their faces for Norbert, Diederik and Maurits. They were at the front door of the church with others of the Elite Guard, in uniform, with swords drawn forming an arch for them to pass under. Anna nodded and smiled warmly at them as she passed.

The ceremony went by like a dream, as did the dinner and the many faces of people offering their congratulations. Could this be real? The dancing began and couples swirled around them like the happy emotions swirling in her heart.

Just when she thought she could dance no longer, Charles nodded to the orchestra and smiled as a dramatic Tango tune began.

"I don't know how to Tango. I've only danced it once."

"Yes, I remember. I have practiced for both of us." He smiled again and took her in his arms.

Perspiration beaded at her hairline when the final chord was struck. He dipped her to his knee and kissed her neck. She reached up to caress his face.

"You're still here."

"Of course. Where else would I be." He looked at her strangely.

"I thought perfect people were taken up into Heaven as Enoch was." He was so very perfect at this moment. He threw his head back and laughed.

"Perhaps it is my thoughts that keep me earthbound."

"Are you thinking of another woman?" She huffed with mock dismay.

"Certainly not, when the most enchanting woman alive is in my arms and my heart forever."

"Well, we're married now. As long as your thoughts are about me, you may think whatever you like."

"I think…" He scooped her into his arms. "We have danced enough." He strode toward the main entrance, slowly enough to allow the guests to gather their rice and line up outside. They covered their heads as they were assaulted with rice and wishes for happiness. Charles placed Anna in the coach that waited to take them to a 13th century medieval Castle, complete with a tower and moat, in the charming village of Crupet. They would spend the next three days there before catching a train to Rome.

This was the happiest day of her life. She saw only goodness and light around her and could not comprehend the dark clouds gathering about, not too far in the distance.

Chapter 19

A large crowd gathered to hear The Fuhrer. Adolf Hitler was a powerful speaker and was ever increasing in popularity. He spoke of a stronger Germany, larger and more powerful than ever. In humiliated, war torn, depressed Germany, he said just what they wanted to hear.

"Without consideration of traditions and prejudices, Germany must find the courage to gather our people and their strength for an advance along the road that will lead this people from its present restricted living space to new land and soil, and hence also free it from the danger of vanishing from the earth or of serving others as a slave nation." The crowd erupted.

"Become strong again in spirit, strong in will, strong in endurance, strong to bear all sacrifices. Strength lies not in defense but in attack." He roared.

"Demoralize the enemy from within by surprise, terror, sabotage, assassination. This is the war of the future. Our strategy is to destroy the enemy from within, to conquer him through himself." The crowd cheered with every statement. He had them eating out of his hand.

"Germany is prepared to agree to any solemn pact of non-aggression, because she does not think of attacking but only acquiring security. We are all proud that through God's powerful aid, we have become once more true Germans."

He was a master at extracting the desired emotions from his listeners. He convinced them that theirs was a noble, righteous cause. He would restore them to greatness, even better than before the

World War. The self proclaimed "Wolf" would spread his doctrine across Europe, crushing anyone or anything in his path.

After the rally, Hitler met with Alfred Rosenberg, Rudolf Hess, Ernst Wollweber and Ernst Rohm.

"How is the work going, my comrades?" Hitler embraced his loyal supporters.

"Very well, we have people in France, Belgium, and Bulgaria. They are being strategically placed so as to weaken the existing governments, and collect the information you require."

"Very good, my comrades, soon we will have all of Europe for lebensraum—a greater living space!"

Chapter 20

Anna had been to many different places in the last year. She loved learning the history of every place she lived or visited. Their honeymoon was a veritable feast of historical sights.

She stood in awe beneath the massive Coliseum in Rome and pictured the gladiator events that took place there thousands of years earlier. They hiked amongst the ruins of the Forum and visited various tombs and catacombs. Even the most ancient historical buildings in America were infants compared to these treasures. These broken fragments of past civilizations seemed to whisper and moan their tales of glory and woe.

Vatican City was stunning, with all its splendor and significance. They had to move much too quickly through all the paintings and sculptures to see it all. Everywhere one looked there was some wonderful piece of art. The entire city of Rome was one large art gallery, a chapel here, an obelisk there, fountains, statues; every ceiling and wall of every chapel spoke of the artistic talent that lived and breathed within its boundaries. Even the regular buildings and cobblestone streets charmed and invited strangers from all over the world.

They found Naples to be a charming stop with its sidewalk cafes and shops. They spent hours exploring the streets of Pompeii. It was a miniature Rome with its ancient temples to the pagan gods, arenas, pillars and ruins.

Anna was stunned by the shadow cast over her heart as she gazed at the human statues caste in the cavities formed by the people that were trapped in volcanic ash as they tried to flee the city. She tried to imagine what life must have been like in the lovely city, carved into the lush green hillside, at the height of its glory.

Anna ducked through a crumbling archway into a grassy courtyard and sat by a marble pond in the center. She imagined entertaining guests there, living, laughing and dying in that ancient environment. What must it have been like when the dark cloud of volcanic ash descended over the mountainside, instantly freezing life for future viewing? Images of children stooping, faces covered, hovering in fear, waiting for the danger to pass, came to her mind. As the ominous cloud settled and passed, it took with it all life and activity with it, burying all evidence of any civilization for generations.

She clutched the lace at her throat, pressing on her heart as if to keep it from bursting. Frenzied images seared her thoughts, mothers and fathers frantically searching for their children, children crying for parents that would never come to them.

Charles pulled her up from the grassy seat and her haunting visions. He wrapped his arms around her.

"Why do you allow yourself to become victim to ancient times that you have no part in or control over?"

"I don't know." She shook her head, chasing the dark images from her mind. "It's so sad. People lived here, ate here." She ran her hand across a tiled countertop with round holes for cooking fires. "They loved their families and friends. They worked and played, until one day it all ended." She stepped outside the doorway into the stone street. Tourists wandered in and out of the roofless shops and homes. "Do you suppose some day people will read about us and care about what happened to us? Will they look at the things we left behind and wonder what our lives were like?"

"If there is a lesson that can be learned from a society, then learn it. It serves no purpose to agonize over lost cultures. What reason do we have for learning about the past if not to learn from it? Every civilization makes mistakes, we can learn from those as well as the successes. My grandfather made very poor choices concerning the Congo. I can hate him for what he did or I can learn from it." He massaged the goose flesh from her arms. "There is so much to be learned from ancient rulers, good and bad."

The sun began to sink beneath the remains of Mt. Vesuvius, casting the relics of the ancient city in a golden glow.

The view from the Eiffel Tower in Paris was breath-taking. They were able to pick out each of the places they would be visiting later.

They spent an entire day at the Louvre alone. They wandered through the various exhibits, reading about the pieces that they were interested in the most.

Anna especially loved Notre Dame. They climbed the bell tower to the very top. Anna tried every door along the way hoping to find one unlocked so they could explore all the secret places. She lingered on the balconies, adoring the gargoyles and creatures carved all around, as well as the spectacular view.

Anna's behavior reminded Charles of her desire to explore the Town Hall in Brussels. He recommitted himself to take her there when they returned home. He was charmed by her childlike exuberance for everything they saw and did. He had seen the sights they now visited, before, but never had he enjoyed them so much as he did now, with Anna. All too soon it was time to go home and return to reality and responsibility.

Chapter 21

Their honeymoon trip had been the highlight of Anna's life, but being away so long had put Charles behind in his responsibilities. She saw very little of him and she was left with large amounts of unfilled time. This seamed to be her lot in life, missing Charles. But, at least she was consoled in the knowledge of his love for her this time.

Maids and servants busied themselves polishing floors and stair banisters as Anna strolled through the main foyer of the Royal Palace. Others cleaned windows or dusted. Officials came and went, hastening about their various responsibilities. Anna stood gazing at the beautiful Ming vase in the main foyer when King Albert walked by. He stopped and explained that it had been a gift from the Orient.

"I was just thinking how much alike we are." She sighed.

He looked at her curiously.

"This vase and I, we are both gifts from other lands, but useless decorations here. We sit for countless hours with nothing to do of any real consequence."

"I am sorry you feel that way. I certainly do not consider you to be useless. You have been a blessing to us…and especially to my son. You make him so happy."

"I know our marriage has brought an alliance with the Netherlands, but I wish there was something I could do. Charles is so busy all the time and I just drift aimlessly with nothing valuable to offer."

"We are trying to build alliances wherever we can. American ambassadors are coming here in three weeks. We could use your influence."

"I am anxious to help any way I can. I don't know anything about international affairs, but I'll do whatever you want me to do." She was excited with his offer, this sounded intriguing.

"I will have tutors here tomorrow to begin instruction on international affairs and law. Thank you, I was certain you would be willing." The King smiled with his eyes. Anna was glad to have some way to help these people she had come to love.

"There is an old tower at the smelter just outside of the city that is unsafe. It needs to be replaced. I am going there now to oversee its demolition. Would you like to come along?"

"Yes, I've never seen anything like that. Thank you for rescuing me from my boredom."

Anna was dropped off at a grassy hill a safe distance away. She found a shady spot to sit and wait while His Majesty went to the sight to inspect and give his approval. When he finished, he came to sit with her and watch.

They first heard the low ominous boom of the explosion. The tower stood straight and tall for a moment, like a giant sentinel guiding people to the entrance route to the city until he swayed and collapsed to his knees and finally crumpled in a heap of rubble.

Tears welled in Anna's eyes. These emotions completely caught her off guard. She had no sentimental attachment to this old tower, but as it fell, the time and hard work it must have taken to build it and the many years of service it gave flashed through her mind.

When the king saw her reaction he was touched as well. That old tower had been there for over 100 years, a land mark from miles away and now it was gone.

"Nothing lasts forever. Things and people pass across the stage of time, some lingering, some passing quickly, some leaving a lasting impression, but nothing remains permanently. It will be rebuilt, better and stronger." He told her as he put one arm around her shoulders and handed her his handkerchief.

* * *

The dinner was well planned, as well as the seating arrangement, with American Ambassadors Frederic Mosley Sackett and Charles Gates Dawes across from Anna and Charles. Anna had studied their accomplishments and greatly admired them. Frederic Sackett had degrees from Brown University and Harvard University and had previously served as Senator. Charles Dawes had received the Nobel Peace Prize for his handling of the German Reparations and had served as Vice President, among many other great accomplishments. She was humbled to be in their presence and doubted her ability to influence them in the slightest degree. With her mere three weeks education of world events, she barely knew what they were talking about.

When Geoffrey asked what the US planed to do about the spread of communism and the Nazi attitude toward Jews in particular, Frederic responded, "The people of America are weary of war. Many feel dealings in Europe are not our concern." This attitude erased all fear and inferiority she felt.

"Not your concern! How can you say that? If a bully attacked your little brother, would you say 'It's not my concern.' and close your eyes to the abuse?" She glared back and forth between the two American guests. Frederic gasped and dropped his jaw while General Dawes leaned back and rubbed his chin with amusement.

"You are the big brother to the world! You can not ignore injustice!" She stood and leaned forward on the table. "God has given your country potentially great strength and power. More than I think you realize. You must use it to bless His people all over the world. You must not squander it on yourselves. We all have a responsibility to help those smaller or weaker than ourselves. The Nazi threat is growing and spreading across Europe. Terrible things are happening. Doing the right thing can be uncomfortable, sometimes excruciatingly painful, but it should never be avoided."

She gripped the edge of the table as her voice dropped to a low ominous level. "Do the right thing gentlemen. Make me proud to be an American."

"Madam, we are well aware of our limitations and our responsibilities!" Frederic shot back. General Dawes put a hand on his arm, and Frederic sat back.

"I'm sorry, I am inexperienced in these affairs. My comments were out of line." Anna quickly apologized and sat down, embarrassed by her impulsive outburst. She wanted to make a good impression and now she had allowed her emotions to erupt over and honest evaluation of the situation.

"Your Highness."

"Please, call me Anna."

"Anna," General Dawes continued. "I happen to agree with you heartily. Perhaps it is our common Chicago background, where injustice was rampant for many years. Corruption in the legal system made justice difficult. Some fed on the misfortunes of others. But unfortunately, it is not as simple as pulling the bully off the little brother. I am glad to know that you feel it is the responsibility of all nations to cooperate in establishing world peace."

Anna sat back and stifled her urge to say more. World peace would require much more than words. She hoped for more commitment to action, but she also knew that offending the people sent to establish peace would not help to reach that goal.

After dinner, while Charles and Albert were talking with Frederic, Anna took General Dawes aside and questioned him extensively about Chicago. She was delighted to learn of his musical experience and took him down the hall to the parlor with a baby grand piano. They played a simple duet on the piano, laughed, and chatted about jazz. She was surprised at how much she ended up enjoying the evening.

The evening wore on and eventually Charles, his father and Frederic finished their business. Charles took Frederic in search of General Dawes. They followed the sound of music and laughter down the hall.

"I see you took the better part for yourself and left your companion with the responsibility of dealing with me!" Charles teased him, glad to see the General enjoying himself with Anna. They all walked together to the front entrance where a driver was waiting to take the visitors to their suite.

Worry creased his brow as Charles put out his arm for Anna.

"This evening wasn't as successful as you had hoped, was it?" She took his arm and squeezed it.

"Not as much progress was made as I had hoped, but more than I had realistically expected." He sighed.

"I'm sorry; I should have held my tongue. I'm afraid international affairs are beyond my comprehension."

"You were wonderful. You said what they needed to hear, but I could not say it. Only a fellow American could get away with your performance tonight. Perhaps if you could give your speech to all Americans we would get the support we need. No good hearted person wants war, but sometimes it is the only way to combat evil and oppression." He took her into his arms smiling warmly. "And the only thing beyond your comprehension is how much I love you."

Chapter 22

Ivo hurried down the dark street, glancing over his shoulder once before slipping down the alley to the docks. Alfons Fictels had called a meeting with a group of dock workers he had recruited to their cause. Joop Schaap, from Rotterdam, would be at the meeting this evening. He was responsible for communist activities in the Netherlands and Belgium. Ivo was anxious to meet him and hoped Herr. Schaap would be pleased with their progress. Ernst Wollweber would be reporting his success in organizing clandestine units for shipping sabotage in Antwerp.

The clacking of his shoes against cobblestone was joined by echoing footsteps behind him. He slipped into the shadows and stood behind a stack of crates until he recognized Heinrich and Josef. They had infiltrated the local police shortly after Ivo had, two years ago.

"Good evening, meine kameraden." Ivo said, stepping out into the alley. They shook hands, clapping each other on the shoulders.

When they entered the back entrance of the warehouse, Alfons was standing in front of eleven dock workers, welcoming them to the cause. Ivo smiled as he counted the new recruits, pleased to see their numbers growing.

"Welcome, comrades." Ernst interrupted, jumping to his feet when he noticed the three newcomers.

"Shall we hear their report, before we proceed any further, so they might return to their responsibilities before they are missed?" He smiled knowingly to Alfons.

"Of course, gentlemen." He slightly bowed his head and stretched out his hand beckoning them to take the floor.

Ivo walked to the front, scrutinizing the men sitting on crates; a scruffy, rough looking bunch of men. His eyes narrowed as he looked directly into the face of each man, feeling their pain. Ivo had come from a life of poverty himself. His father lost both legs in the war and spent the rest of his short life drinking and abusing his wife and children. His mother had taken in laundry and whatever odd jobs she could to provide for her family until she took ill and passed away.

"Our day will come." Bitterness filled every word. "We will have all things in common. There will be no rich and no poor. We will no longer have to clothe and house the royal family with our own sweat and blood." His lips curled into an acidic smile.

"Our beloved Prince has provided us with an easy target, his American Princess." Sarcasm and triumph intermingled most unpleasantly.

"But Sir," One of the men sitting, rose to his feet. "She helps the poor. She is no threat to us." His commitment to this cause waned.

"Everybody dies!" Josef jumped to his feet shaking his fist. "All of the royal pigs. They pretend to care. What do they know about hunger? They all must go, every one of them."

"Sacrifices must be made." Ivo glared intensely at the men until they both humbly took their seats again. "She is the keystone that, when removed, will topple the entire royal family."

The man stood again.

"I won't be a part of any assassination." Two other men stood in agreement.

"Gentlemen, that won't be necessary." He smiled sardonically. "She will remove herself. Our plan has already been set in motion and she is cooperating, unintentionally, but flawlessly." He allowed his words to sink in.

"Make no mistake, she will be removed and she will take our adored Prince with her."

Chapter 23

Charles went to his office early to finish up his responsibilities before noon. He generally stole away whenever a break was available, seeking out Anna on his way through the palace on business, for even a glimpse or a smile, made his day brighter. He remained focused this morning, he had plans for the remainder of the day. He had intended to take Anna on this particular outing since their honeymoon trip to Paris.

Anna usually spent the early morning hours either out at the stables or in the gardens. She was given a spot in the gardens to plant and putter as she liked. The flowers she had planted in the spring were now large and blooming. The smell of the rich brown soil filled the air as she uprooted a large clump of dandelions and shook the dirt back into the garden. She carefully picked the wilting blossoms from the pansies so they would continue blooming. The sun was well up and bearing down on her. She went to the kitchen for a cold drink and to catch up on any news there.

Adelheid's cat had just given birth to another litter of kittens. Nico was promising them to some of the kitchen staff, as soon as they were weaned. He agreed to bring them with him in a few days so everyone could see them.

With limited responsibilities for herself, Anna decided to relax at the piano for awhile.

It worked as she had hoped, Charles was drawn to her. She smiled as he bent over her, gently kissing her neck. She put her hand on his cheek. He took it, kissed it as well and asked her to continue playing.

When she finished her song, she stood and turned to him. He held out both hands balled into fists.

"Choose a hand." His eyes sparkled with anticipation.

"What are you doing?" She giggled.

"Choose one." He insisted.

She put a finger to her lips and bit her fingernail in mock concentration. "What if I choose the wrong one."

"You get two chances."

"Then I choose this one." She laughed and he held out a key ring with some very old keys on it. "What are these for?"

"You will see. Come with me!" He smiled broadly.

He took her hand and they dashed out to a waiting car. They went to the Town Hall to spend the rest of the day exploring!

Some of the rooms looked like they hadn't been opened for centuries. Anna tried to imagine what it must have been like, while Charles told her tales, true and mythical, about the old tower. The tower was in desperate need of restoration and they shouldn't have been up there. When they heard the security guard coming up the stairs, Charles was nervous about how it would look for someone of his position sneaking around like a child. Anna quickly convinced him that they should hide in the closet until the guard left.

"It is even worse, to be found hiding in a closet, than snooping around!" He whispered indignantly.

"Shhhh!"

"He will know someone is here. This door is never left open." He whispered desperately.

The footsteps stopped at the doorway to the room they were in. Charles opened his mouth to say something. Anna's hand quickly found his jaw and pulled her lips over his, teasing him into submission. He slowly relaxed, surrendering to Anna's plan. The door closed, was locked and the footsteps went on up the stairs.

"Hurry, we must leave before he comes back down!" Anna said, anxious to get them out of the trouble she had gotten them into.

"Actually, I'd rather wait right here until he passes back down." He smiled as he pulled her back to him. "Being a reckless youth again isn't so bad after all!"

Chapter 24

Charles sat at his desk trying to concentrate with the smell of honeysuckle drifting in his window on the morning breeze, calling to him. Focusing on matters of state on a day like this was torture.

Charles had promised himself he would teach Anna to ride when he had the time. He had ordered a riding habit to be made for her as a surprise. It arrived from the tailor earlier that morning. He felt like a child, dancing with excitement inside. He tallied the last column of his financial summary, closed the folder and filed it.

Anna had gone to the stables about an hour previous and Charles hoped she would still be there. She enjoyed the time she spent with the animals, caring for them. She declared herself their polo team's official horse caretaker. She was brushing down the last horse when he peeked around the corner. Ebony Rose pawed the ground with pleasure. Anna softly hummed while she patiently curried her coat to a shimmering black.

He leaned easily against the door frame with a package under one arm, the other hand in his pocket. He stood quietly watching her peaceful happiness, unwilling to shatter it with the reality human conversation might bring. The world he entered when he was with her was so untouched by the political unrest he dealt with most of the time. Each tender stroke caressed the sloping curves of the animal with her delicate care. Her feminine grace was in sharp contrast to the heated arguments he constantly endured and the diplomatic juggling act required to keep good relations in place. How could he have ever been afraid of loving her? She was an anchor in his stormy sea, the calming balance that offset the challenges he faced.

If only he could freeze this moment in time. He sighed softly. The beautiful black thoroughbred mare sensed her master nearby and reared her head in his direction.

"How long have you been standing there?" Her heart skipped a beat, but not from being startled.

"Not nearly long enough." He smiled. "I have something for you." He set the package on the table next to her grooming supplies.

She carefully removed the paper and lifted a pair of cream colored trousers from the box. Underneath laid a beautiful forest green coat with short, fitted front, gold buttons and long, pleated, rounded tails in back.

"Your riding boots haven't arrived yet, but I couldn't wait. Let's go for a ride! I'll finish up here while you go put on your new clothes."

"Thank you!" She cried throwing her arms about him. She grabbed the box and hurried off.

Green was definitely her color and the cut flattered her petite figure. Astrid loaned her boots, hat and gloves when she saw Anna preparing to ride.

Charles was just tightening the final straps to the saddle on her horse. He had chosen a small mahogany Bay for her. She was less spirited and intimidating than the large Anglo-Arabian that he rode. Anna wouldn't have been able to even reach the stirrups on her.

Mounting and riding came easily to her. By noon she was quite comfortable galloping around the corral.

"It is time to test the open range!" Charles announced.

They picked up the picnic basket Charles had requested earlier and headed for de Warande.

Low hanging branches covered with vines provided a cool shaded picnic spot with some privacy. Slow moving water gurgled past in the nearby river. The scent of gardenias and lilies filled the air until Charles opened the lunch basket and the delicious aroma of roasted quail wafted out. Two chilled jars wrapped in a cloth, one of vichyssoise and another of chilled grape juice with tarts for dessert, topped off their outdoor feast.

Charles stretched out on their picnic blanket and closed his eyes while Anna repacked the lunch basket. They decided to let their food settle and to enjoy the cool, breezy seclusion, before they started back. She picked a long feathery philodendron frond and sat next to him, tickling his face with it. He wrinkled his nose and swatted at it before he realized it was his wife teasing him.

"Don't wake me. I am in the middle of an incredibly good dream."

"What are you dreaming that is more important than paying attention to me?"

A crooked smile stole across his face as he cracked one eye to peak at her. "I am in paradise and a gorgeous redhead is about to kiss me."

"Is that so?!" She rolled over and lay back; the sun twinkled dimly through the dense green leafy cover. "Well, I wouldn't want to mess up a dream like that." The knot at the back of her head hurt to lie on, so she pulled the pins from her hair, freeing her long auburn curls to spill across the blanket.

"Mess it up?" He rolled over on to his side next to her and wrapped his arms around her. "You are the best part of it!" He kissed her forehead, her nose and her chin.

She reached up and wound her finger in a lock of hair at the back of his neck. He wore his hair a little longer these days and another wavy lock fell forward to his eyes.

"How long do you suppose we could stay here before we would be found?"

He rolled to his side and rose up on his elbow, smiling curiously. "Six to eight hours I would expect."

"Mmm" She frowned. "I was hoping for a month or two at least."

He laughed out loud. "You want to hide out here for a month or two? I have a meeting at 7 o'clock this evening. I am never late or absent, they will assume something is wrong and send out a search for us. I am quite sure the hounds could find us in less than a month." He laughed again. "Do you prefer the hard ground to our featherbed?"

"Didn't you ever run away from home when you were small? I can't think of a better place to run away to than this! It's so beautiful here."

"No. I thought about it once." He looked down at the colorful pattern of the quilt and traced it with his finger without seeing it. "My sister hid from her nanny in the gardens because she had been scolded. Everyone was frantic. My mother was crying. Marie was only five years old. I was afraid I would never see her again." He looked up again. "I learned that our actions affect more than just ourselves. I could not do that to the people I love…who love me." She couldn't be serious about running away…here in the woods, but was there something more than lighthearted teasing behind this conversation? "Are you unhappy with your life here?"

"Well…no. I just don't want to have to share you so much."

His face broke into a wide deep smile. "I can't think of anything I would rather do than spend every minute of the rest of my life with you." He gathered her back into his arms and kissed her. "My life is not my own; many lives depend on my actions. I am not free to pursue my own happiness, but happiness has hunted me mercilessly this day and I surrender to it fully." He kissed her again just under her ear and followed her neck to her collarbone.

They had gone deeper into the wooded area to have their privacy than they should have. The smell of the left over game in their lunch basket attracted some wild dogs. The horses began to prance uneasily as they were first to detect their presence. The dogs crept up cautiously at first, hoping for scraps left behind. But as hunger emboldened them, they snarled and circled threateningly.

Charles leaped to his feet, scooped up Anna and placed her on his horse. He rifled through their lunch leavings, grabbed the quail carcasses and tossed them into the trees. As the dogs bounded off to pounce on their prey, he gathered their things and swung up easily behind Anna, caught the reigns of her horse and led them quickly out of the woods and danger.

Horseback picnics at Le Petit Lac became a favorite diversion through the hot summer days, but Charles was careful not to take Anna into the more forested areas.

Chapter 25

Summer drew to a close and with increasing political "emergencies," Charles had to go away quite often for business reasons, but he squeezed in an occasional polo game when he could. Anna pulled her sweater on as she hurried off to the game with him.

The grassy side lines were packed, possibly due to the flawless autumn weather, but more likely to the fact that this was the final and championship polo game. The crisp harvest breeze was invigorating as it gently stirred the colorful leaves into twirling eddies, dancing across the playing field.

Anna usually sat with Adeline, Geoffrey's wife, until this last month. They were expecting their first child now and she didn't always feel like attending. Anna was surprised to see her here today as her due date was so near, but she was happy to see her again.

"I wouldn't miss this of all games!" Adeline exclaimed. "And, I'm hoping the baby comes a little early, before Geoffrey and Charles have to go to England. Maybe if this match is exciting enough it will do the trick!"

Geoffrey pulled on his jersey with a large gold number three on the back, as he was the team captain, kissed his wife and led his horse out to the center of the field to meet the rest of the team. Sebastiaan, wearing the number two on his jersey, as he was second most experienced on the team, was walking his horse in a circle around the others. His horse was recovering from a sprain and Sebastiaan wanted to be sure he was well enough for today's game. Charles wore number one as best offensive player. He was very good and very competitive, but he had to miss some of the games for more important matters. Maurits wore number four and, of course, was their goal defender.

Maurits was filling Charles in on some of their newest strategies. Diederik was versatile and normally took their place when any of the regular players were unavailable, but he was away today. Polo was nowhere near the top of Charles list of important responsibilities and he had missed the last two games. But, from the moment he stepped onto the field, it was as though nothing else mattered. He was excited with the new tactics and was confident of their win today.

They were matched against a French team. Anna could see Fernand across the field with his team. This sport could be dangerous enough without throwing an injured male ego with something to prove into the mix. She hoped to diffuse the tension as much as possible. It had been several months since she had seen him and the others.

"Please, hold my seat for me, Adeline. I'm going to say hello to some old friends." She hurried over to the other side before the match started.

She decided to test the waters with Damien first. He was happy to see her and quickly filled her in on the others before calling them over to see her. Patrick was married and Armand was finally engaged to Elise. She congratulated them and wished them well for the match. Fernand was not overly friendly. She hoped she hadn't just made things worse, opening old wounds. Anna made her way back to her seat just as the game began.

It was an exciting, but rough, first half. Belgium had lost two horses to injuries, but they were ahead by five. Anna left Adeline to bandage the injured animals after the second chukker. She stayed to make sure they were all watered and cared for. She made it back to Adeline just as the third chukker and first half of the match ended.

The crowd poured out onto the field for the traditional divot stomping. Anna kept Adeline close to the sidelines, as she didn't look well, gently stepping on the chunks of grass chopped out by the player's mallets. There weren't as many divots where they were, but Anna was more concerned with Adeline's pale, pained face and clammy hands. Adeline grasped Anna's arm and doubled over with intense pain. She had increasing discomfort through the game, but walking around now had put her fully into labor. Anna helped her to a bench and ran for Geoffrey.

The second half of the match was delayed a bit while Adeline was helped to a waiting car and the happy couple was sent off with cheers and wishes for all to go well. Now, with Geoffrey gone, they were one player short. The rest of the team argued with the umpire that they would play short handed. The other team demanded a forfeit.

Anna knew how much this match meant to them. She could tell by the disappointment on their faces that the umpire was leaning toward forfeit. They wouldn't allow just anyone to replace Geoffrey, but she was part of their team as their horse caretaker. She had never played the game and she had watched enough to know it could be a rough sport. The idea of replacing Geoffrey herself made her nervous. How would the crowd react? She was afraid of making a fool of herself and she certainly didn't want to embarrass Charles. She knew she would get resistance from him and probably everyone else as well, but she couldn't just stand by and let the season end this way. She watched them, vacillating between giving their team the opportunity to finish the game and publicly humiliating herself. Then, she caught the triumphant glare Fernand tossed at Charles and grabbed one of Geoffrey's jerseys, the reins to his horse and walked onto the field determined to win a battle of her own.

"We have four players now. Let's play ball." She smiled at them.

"No." Charles took hold of her arm and the reins to the horse and began to take them both back to the sidelines. He liked to think of himself as open-minded, a progressive modern thinker, but there were too many issues attached to this situation.

"This is too dangerous. This is nothing like a pleasant ride for a picnic in the park. This horse is much larger and more aggressive than yours. This is a rough competitive sport."

She pulled away making her stance with hands on her hips.

"These horses know me. They might be skittish if anyone else rides them. Who else can you get to replace Geoffrey?"

His shoulders slumped as he could see she was not going to go without resistance.

"We will not replace Geoffrey. We are trying to convince the umpire to allow us to play on with three teammates. If he will not allow it, we will forfeit."

He was anxious to get her off the field without making a scene, and with heated competitive emotions pulsing through his veins he was not feeling patient enough to fight this battle with her. She wasn't intimidated by his piercing glare and she turned to get the support of his teammates.

"You think you can win this with three players? Then do it. I will stay out of the way. I'm just giving you your fourth player."

"Absolutely not, this is out of the question." Charles replied, exasperated.

"This isn't about my safety, is it? You don't think it is appropriate, because I'm a woman." She glared at him. This was definitely not a battle he wanted to fight here and now.

Maurits and Sebastiaan stepped closer to help make a decision. Charles thought they would back him up, but they wanted this win very badly.

"Let her try. If Amelia Earhart can fly an airplane across her continent, surely your American can play a simple game of polo." They chided.

He wanted to finish as much as they did and with the approval of his friends, her offer was very tempting. He finally gave in with her promise to stay out of harms way.

The other team strongly objected.

"You can't just pull someone from the crowd to be on your team."

"I am already on the team. I take care of the horses."

"You can't have a woman on your team." Fernand insisted.

"It isn't in the rules." The umpire declared. "We have never encountered this situation before.

"It's alright, I won't play. They win." Anna smiled with synthetic sweetness. "These French boys know that the only way they can win is by forfeit. At least they can admit it." She glared defiantly at Fernand, throwing down a gauntlet she knew he would not resist.

"If both teams agree, I'm going to allow it." The umpire declared.

As team captain, Fernand took the challenge. Charles lifted Anna onto Geoffrey's horse, they all mounted and the umpire threw in the ball to begin the fourth chukker.

France scored seven to Belgium's three by the final chukker. Being one man short, Belgium struggled to hold their lead.

Fernand swung a hard off-side forward, catching Charles just above his left brow with his mallet as Charles leaned out for a near-side back shot, knocking him off his mount.

Anna had her hands full keeping her mount out of the action, as he was accustomed to being in the middle of it. She gave him free rein and was soon leaping to the ground at Charles' side. He shook his head to get his eyes to focus and pulled his handkerchief from his pocket to wipe the thick moisture oozing down his face.

"Charles, you're bleeding!" Anna gasped as she grabbed the handkerchief from him and held it tenderly on the wound. A large purple lump began to swell around the cut. He pushed her hand away and pulled himself to his feet, staggering back to his horse.

As he tried to remount Anna grabbed his arm.

"Charles, you are finished. You're bleeding. You can hardly keep your balance."

"It is a head wound, they always look worse than they really are." He pressed his lips together in a hard line. "I am fine." He took his handkerchief and pressed it hard against the wound to stop the bleeding. "The worst part is Fernand scored on that cheap shot tying the game." He grabbed the reigns and mounted, still squinting his eyes and shaking his head to clear the fog.

"Charles, you need stitches. I'm not going back in. You're a player short. You'll forfeit."

He reined in his mount, considering the situation. Wanting desperately to get back into the action, his horse pranced backward and sideways, straining against the bit in her mouth. He rode back over to Anna and dismounted.

"It is just a game. The world will not come to its end if we do not finish." Charles conceded. He took her hands in his, realizing how frightening he must look all swollen and bloody. He wasn't into power struggles and Anna was definitely more important to him than this game.

"If you really don't want me to finish, I will respect your wishes." The other players were mounted and prancing around, anxious to continue the game. He gazed pleadingly into her eyes as he unintentionally squeezed her hands tighter. "But there are only three minutes left. I promise when it is over we will go to the hospital." Charles begged. "You can check on Adeline while they stitch me." He added, in an attempt to sweeten the deal.

She tenderly dabbed the cloth at the blood on his cheek and surrounding the wound as she inspected the damage, while the anxious crowd looked on. She cringed at the nasty jagged gash across his brow bone. He quickly took the cloth and pressed it on the wound again to hide it.

"It is nothing...Please?"

She reluctantly agreed. He kissed her cheek and lifted her back up on her mount to the roar of the crowd.

She wasn't following the game as she struggled to get her horse to go to the end of the field. She thought she was going to their defending goal end, but as France had just scored, they would change directions. A shout from the crowd drew her attention as the ball soared through the air and landed nearly at her feet. She lifted her mallet from her lap and tried desperately to hit the ball, but she was too short armed and couldn't reach the ground from such a tall mount. Charles and Fernand were charging directly at her.

She tried to get out of the way, but ended up nearly colliding with Fernand. His horse reared up and spun around as Charles crossed on the far side of them sending the ball to Sebastiaan who put it through the goal posts to win the game!

They were ecstatic, jumping around pounding each other on the back. Anna slid down to the ground and led her horse to the side. She couldn't understand this male attraction to pain. It seemed the more battered and bruised they were, the more they enjoyed the game.

She grabbed a handful of sugar cubes and held them out, stroking her horse while he nibbled. The other horses gathered for their reward as well while the boys continued to celebrate. She smiled and shook her head as she watched them. Evidently a close win heals all injuries. Charles didn't act like he even noticed that his head was split open and his eye was nearly swollen shut.

The other team walked out to congratulate them for their win. They all smiled and shook hands, discussing the impressive maneuvers of both teams. Anna supposed there were worse ways for men to fill that basic male need to conquer and destroy!

Chapter 26

Early morning, on the first Monday of October, Charles left for England with an absolute promise to return by Saturday. He had arranged for their trip to be delayed an extra week to give Geoffrey a little more time with his wife and new daughter, but couldn't put it off any longer.

Anna had been watching the strawberries in one of the greenhouses, hoping they would be ready by Charles' birthday. She spent the week while he was gone learning to make Belgian waffles, sampling, ordering and picking up the perfect chocolate from the chocolatier at Galleries St. Hubert, and watching the strawberries blush to perfection.

By late afternoon when Charles arrived, his birthday dinner preparations were well under way. He dashed in out of the rain through the side doors and stopped in the royal office, where his father was working, to report briefly on his activities while in England. He knew Anna was planning something because of her insistence that he return by Saturday and hoped he had made it back on time.

"Where is Anna?"

"She is most likely in the kitchen. She has been preparing your birthday surprise all week. If desire and attentive care make strawberries ripen faster, then she should have plenty." He laughed.

"So I can look forward to strawberry waffles this evening?!" He teased his father for disclosing the "surprise" although it was no secret that dessert waffles were his favorite.

"Yes, and you had better be sufficiently surprised!" He warned. "Go bathe and get out of those wet clothes. You can make your report on Monday."

When Anna heard that Charles and his entourage had returned she went in search of him. She peeked inside the office and the king looked up.

"Anna, come in."

"I didn't mean to disturb you. I'm looking for Charles; I was told he was here with you."

"He was. He went to clean up for dinner. He was quite a mess with traveling, the storm and all. How are the birthday plans coming?"

She remembered her apron and quickly took it off, wiping the flour from her hands on it. He was very kind to her, but she was still intimidated by his high station. He smiled and brushed his finger at his left cheek. When she looked confused, he rose and pulled his handkerchief from his breast pocket and wiped a smudge of flour from her cheek. She flushed and backed away.

"Would you like me to get him for you?"

"No! You're busy. I don't, it isn't, I mean, I'm not ready yet." She twisted her apron into a knot. "I just wanted to see him. If he comes back, could you have him go to the nook by the West porch? Only if he comes back, don't trouble yourself." She stammered and turned to leave.

"Anna," She swallowed hard and turned back to face him. "Are you afraid of me?"

She opened her mouth and closed it again. How was she supposed to answer that?! Yes, of course, you are KING of this country. You associate with the royalty of Europe. You make decisions of tremendous magnitude, affecting your people for generations. Your orders are followed without question. Your power and influence is felt and respected by so many.

No, of course I'm not afraid of you. You have always been so kind to me. I know that you would never hurt me. I have felt your protection, support and consideration for me many times in the short time I have known you. I have witnessed your compassion, attentive concern and sacrifice for others.

"No…" She bit her bottom lip. "I'm just…" He waited patiently for her answer. "Afraid of offending you. I'm still not comfortable…or certain, of all the protocol…I mean…" She shifted her weight, winding her apron strings around her finger.

"I am just a man, with a great responsibility." He put his warm hand on her shoulder, his dark, soft eyes melting her legs into quivering jelly. "I would like you to think of me as your father, not your king." He smiled and returned to his work.

"Yes sir. Thank you." She was glad he was too busy to observe her awkward exit.

A fire that crackled in the fireplace when Charles entered the nook, along with the soft glow of candlelight, created an inviting ambience in contrast to the pour of rain at the window.

A string quartet was tuning up and rubbing rosin on their bows. He took a seat on the small velvet divan by the fire and soon Pachelbel's Canon softly filled the small room. The calming strains wrestled the tension of the past week from his body, pulling and soothing. He leaned back stretching his long legs out into the room folding his arms and closing his eyes.

He was relieved Anna had chosen a quiet intimate dinner together rather than a large celebration of his birthday with guests and social expectations. Anna had considered a large gathering but with Charles being gone six days, she opted to keep him to herself.

When she stepped into the room, he rose and caught her in his arms, swinging her once around as she wrapped her arms around his neck. He seated her just as Nico and his crew brought in silver trays releasing aromas of cloves and endives in a rich cream soup. Poulet a la Biere with Flemish sprouts and potato tarts, delivering tantalizing scents of roast chicken, garlic and nutmeg, were savored and cleared away before Anna stood and announced dessert.

"I made it myself. Well, actually, it isn't finished. I wanted it to be fresh. Wait here while I finish making it." Her eyes danced with excitement as she made her exit.

Charles stretched out to let his dinner settle and enjoy the music. He thought it a pity she had worked so hard on dessert. He was full now and after being away for nearly a week, his thoughts were not on waffles. But he wouldn't disappoint Anna after all her efforts to surprise him.

Anna carefully poured the batter onto the waffle iron and removed it when it was a golden brown. She submerged it in the pot of melted, rich chocolate and held it over the pot until it stopped dripping and solidified, encasing the waffle in a delectable shell. She topped it with all the sliced fresh strawberries she had gathered and mounds of rich, whipped vanilla cream.

She entered the room with a towel over one arm carrying her creation on an ornate silver tray with all the pageantry as if she carried the jewels for his coronation. It was an artistic masterpiece, until a massive clap of thunder made her heart leap inside her and her precious dessert leap to the floor face down. Charles unsuccessfully lunged to catch it.

She stood with the empty plate in her hands, eyes and mouth great round circles, before dropping to her knees beside the disaster that was the culmination of all her effort and planning.

Charles picked up a fork and knife and dropped to the floor beside her. He carefully cut a square of chocolate waffle from the top and dipped it in the cream underneath.

"You don't have to eat it now." She smiled through watery eyes.

"I would kiss the ground you walk on. Why not eat the dessert you made with your own hands, from a polished floor?" He answered tucking the bite neatly into his mouth and cutting one for her. He dipped it in cream and placed a strawberry slice on top, fed her and kissed the misplaced cream from her lips.

When the last bite was savored, Charles took her towel and wiped the bottom layer of cream from the floor.

"Upside down strawberry waffles are my new favorite dessert. I have never enjoyed any dessert more." He smiled and kissed her again.

Chapter 27

Foreign pressure steadily increased. Charles found himself working late quite often. When Charles finally went in to retire, he found the light on and Anna huddled in the large chair in the corner reading. She jumped up, spilling her book onto the floor when the door opened. When she saw it was Charles she ran to him, keeping her eyes on the window as she darted across the room. He caught her in his arms and held her close. He could feel her heart pounding.

"What are you doing still awake? What is wrong?"

She was embarrassed to tell him she was afraid to go back to sleep because of a nightmare. She blushed and ducked her head. "It seemed so real! I heard a noise and went to the window. There was a large wolf with big, snarling, fangs staring in at me."

The vivid image of his large dark eyes pierced her to the center and left her cold and trembling. "He didn't move, he just stood there watching me. I was frozen, I couldn't run or scream. It was like he had some power over me. Then he smiled. It was an evil, sinister smile." She shuddered with fear just remembering the terrifying scene. "Every time I close my eyes I see him again."

"Wild dogs do not venture into town." He scanned his memory to figure out why she would have such a fear. It had been such a long time since their encounter with the wild dogs. Why would that surface now?

"Perhaps you have had too much time alone. Tomorrow we will go on an outing." He held her and whispered the details of their outing the next day. She felt safe in his arms and was finally able to sleep.

"Geoffrey," Charles called to his friend and Captain of the Elite Guard. He would be using both distinctions for the favor he would be requiring. "I need you to go to Paris for me. You will leave first thing in the morning."

"Very well, but I thought you were handling this assignment." Geoffrey started to object.

"I am taking Anna to Rochefort. We will spend the weekend at the Archaeopark of Malagne."

"That sounds very nice. I would like to take my wife on a holiday as well, but duty calls for me." The sharp edge to his tone hurt, as Charles rarely passed his responsibilities to others.

"Please try to understand, Geoffrey, I wouldn't ask if it was not important. I am worried about Anna. She seems so…fragile."

"Of course, I will prepare at once." He grasped Charles' shoulder firmly. "Do what ever you need to do." He could feel the gravity of the situation by Charles' demeanor.

"Is she with child?" he asked in a low voice.

"No, I wish it were that simple. I am afraid the political pressures I face are affecting her. She needs to get away for awhile."

"Very well, Sir, I will do all I can to ease your burden." Their eyes locked as an unspoken fear of some mental illness passed between them.

"Thank you, I knew I could count on you." He returned to making arrangements for their weekend in Wallonia.

They drove to Rochefort where they checked into a quaint little inn. The next morning they went to the Archaeopark where they hiked around the Gallo-Roman ruins. They worked their way toward an antique Gallo-Roman farm where they learned to make einkorn bread and clay pots. That afternoon they enjoyed a harvest feast of home cooked vegetables and herbs from the gardens there.

Being too full for more hiking, they stopped at the cottage by the garden of useful but unknown plants. There they learned about plants used for medicines, dyes and cord making as well as how to weave a basket; which they then filled with fruits and vegetables at the farmers market.

It was a long day filled with fresh air and physical exertion. It was the perfect remedy. Anna slept deep and peacefully that night. The sun crept over the window sill and filled their room before either of them opened their eyes. Anna snuggled into Charles' arms and kissed the underside of his chin. He mumbled something and squeezed her gently.

"Thank you for running away from home with me...even if it's just for the weekend." He smiled without opening his eyes and kissed the top of her head. They both needed this retreat.

* * *

Geoffrey would be gone the rest of the week. Charles tried to cover his responsibilities as much as he could without going too late into the night. He could always tell when Anna's wolf dream had returned because he could see the light under the door to their room as he climbed the stairs. She pretended that she wasn't tired and merely wanted to wait up for him, but he could see the fear in her eyes.

Charles sent Maurits to Switzerland in his place, so he could be with Anna for Armistice Day. They went to Flanders Fields with Leopold, Astrid and his parents. They walked somberly through the fields of wild poppies, picking bouquets of deep red blossoms and talking in hushed tones of the brave souls passed on before. A large crowd gathered for a memorial ceremony where a bugler played "Last Post" and at exactly 11 o'clock, two minutes of silence were observed in memory of those lives lost in the Great World War. The eleventh hour of the eleventh day of the eleventh month marked the anniversary of the cease fire of that war. Tears brimmed in their eyes and lumps filled their throats as "Reveille" filled the air. Every family had been touched by loss in some way or another.

More than sorrow for the past, dread for the future filled Anna's heart. Charles tried to protect her from the pressure and stress of the prevailing political and economical climate, but she knew there was cause to worry. War brought such heartache and devastation, but that seemed to be the only way the world was capable of dealing with conflicting views and problems between nations.

The air was heavy with reverence and gratitude for those willing to sacrifice their lives to protect the rights and freedoms of others, and with sorrow that such sacrifices should be necessary.

This was not the sort of day that cheered and uplifted spirits. Charles was worried what it would do to Anna, but it was an event he was obligated to participate in. After spending the day with his family and with only four days until the next holiday, the Kings Feast, he had to work late that evening after they returned home. The financial report was due in Parliament and could not be put off any longer.

He finished tallying the last column, rechecked his figures, gathered the pile of papers, tapping the bottom edge against his desk to straighten the stack, and tucked them neatly in the open folder marked "Privé-Vertrouwelijk" or private-confidential. He locked it in the cabinet and looked across the large marble foyer and up through the railing to his bedroom door as he flicked the light off and pulled the door shut behind him. His heart sank; a sliver of light beamed across the floor from underneath the door. He took the wide marble stairs three at a time, then hesitated just before opening the door. He took a deep breath, rotated his neck, arched his shoulders a couple of times and put on a smile.

His smile disappeared as she flew at him and buried her face in his neck, sobbing.

"They are all over the roof, clawing at the windows trying to get in, hundreds of them!"

"There now, it is not real." He soothed, holding her tight. "It is only a dream. You are safe."

"I am now. Please, make them go away. They only leave when you are with me."

He scooped her up and put her on the bed, lying down next to her. He stroked her hair and hummed quietly to her until she fell asleep.

Soft whispers of morning light filtered through the curtains, setting a glowing backdrop to Charles' silhouette. She yawned and stretched.

"I am sorry; I did not mean to wake you."

"It's alright, silly. You don't have to dress in the dark." She jumped up and flipped the light on.

"Oh my!" She gasped. "You're a mess." She stifled a giggle at the sight of his wrinkled clothing. "You slept in your clothes." Then she remembered why. "That's my fault. I'm sorry I'm such a baby." Everything seemed better in daylight and it was hard to believe she had let her fears get so far out of hand.

Charles tried to delegate his out-of-town assignments to others as much as he could and when he had an overload of work, he got up early so that he could be with Anna during the evening hours as much as possible.

This schedule was as agreeable to him as it was for her. He could think of nothing he would rather do than to cuddle with her by the fire, especially as the winter snow started to fly. Evenings with Charles and the festive Christmas spirit seemed to be just the thing to put her wolf dreams into hibernation for awhile.

* * *

Anna sat in the parlor struggling to master the art of knitting woolen scarves on a bright Saturday morning. Charles stood quietly watching her from the doorway with a smirk on his face. She squeezed her eyes shut tight in an attempt to control her frustration.

"You are not enjoying your new hobby very much."

"It's all I can do to keep from throwing it into the fire." She held up her foot-long creation that started at six inches wide and narrowed to about four inches.

"I keep dropping stitches and I don't know how to fix it. It looks dreadful. Your mother makes it look so easy, but it's not. She will be disappointed in me."

"My mother dislikes knitting as much as you do; she only learned it because her mother made her do it." He laughed. "Put it away and come with me."

She stuffed her yarn and needles into her bag and left them in the chair, hoping someone would put them where she could never find them again while she was gone!

"Where are we going?"

"Today is December 5, Sinterklaas comes in the night tonight and I think we need our own Christmas tree in our room to put our shoes beneath!"

"But I thought shoes were left by the fireplace for Sinterklaas to fill?" She questioned as she slipped into the fur cloak he held for her.

"Well, we are going to Americanize this Christmas just a bit." He knew how she loved the smells of Christmas. A day spent out in the fresh air and sunshine in a sleigh ride to the woods to cut a tree and some fresh cedar boughs was the perfect way to bring those smells home.

She held her hand as a visor to shield the bright glint of the sun off the sparkling white snow as they sped across the field and into the woods. The glittering diamond crust crunched and sprayed aside as the horses' hooves and the blades of the sleigh plowed through, turning to an opalescent glow as they passed under the darkening umbrella of pines, aspens and wild oaks.

Charles helped her down, lifted the ax from the back seat of the double sleigh and threw it over his shoulder. They trudged through the deep snow, passing up this tree and that in search of the perfect size and shaped tree. The sharp heels of Anna's boots sunk deep, making each step difficult.

She stopped at a thin small tree, its growth stunted by the massive overpowering pines surrounding it.

"Can we take this one home?" She knelt beside it, shaking the snow off its lower branches and scraping it from around the base.

"Are you sure you want this one?" He said raising one brow. "We have passed up several trees better than this. Its branches are so sparse and lopsided." He walked around it shaking his head.

"It can't get enough sunlight or nourishment here. If we dug up the roots with it, we could plant it in the-"

"We are not here to get more trees for the greenhouses." He held up his hands and turned away. "We can not provide a home for every scruffy tree in this forest." He broke a small cluster of needles from the large hovering pine and absently chewed the sticky end as he watched her stroke and fluff the branches of her…"project." She always needed a project. He smiled.

She finally stood and went to Charles and took his arm, looking back at the lonely little shrub.

"I will cut it for you if you really want me to, but we don't have the equipment to dig it and haul it home." He tossed his pine chew and picked up the ax.

"No!" She quickly shook her head. "Let it live."

"Oh, now I am an ax murderer if I cut a Christmas tree?!"

"Are you making fun of me?" She narrowed her eyes as she detected his tell-tale smirk. "Fine, cut down that one. I won't stop you." She pointed back to one they had considered earlier. He walked over to it. It measured up to his chin, nice and full, but not too large in diameter.

"Are you sure? This is the one you want?" He looked back at her as he drew the ax into the air.

"Strike it down in its prime..." she waved dramatically, "if you can live with yourself." She smiled innocently as he dropped the ax to the ground and folded his arms.

"You do not really want to do this do you? I thought you liked Christmas trees."

"I do, I love them." She went to him. "I'm just teasing you...really...sort of. I thought it would be fun to come here and cut it ourselves, but it's like...enjoying a delicious roast chicken placed before you or having to cut its head off and pluck it first."

He threw his head back and laughed.

"May I just pluck a few feathers without killing the chicken?" He chuckled as he pruned a few lower branches and bundled them under his arm.

"They will look and smell nice on our fireplace mantle since we will not have a tree beside it."

The eerie, haunting, howl of wolves in the distance interrupted their playful bantering. Anna tightened her grip on his arm and Charles quickened his pace back to the sleigh. His intention in coming here certainly was not to cause a return of her wolf nightmares. The deep snow and lack of food at higher elevations had driven the wolves closer to civilization. Their search for the perfect Christmas tree, or the avoidance of cutting any tree, had taken them deeper into the woods than was safe.

The howling was moving in the direction where they were headed. Dark shadows flitted through the trees ahead and the whinnying and snorting of the horses confirmed their fears. Charles was practically dragging her as his long strides flew over fallen logs and thick underbrush. Through the trees they watched the pair of matching jet black Arabians rear up and paw the air before bolting back across the field toward home.

The wolves chased the horses and sleigh a short distance and Charles stopped short as they gave up and returned to the woods. It wouldn't be long before they caught their human scent and began circling them. He wrapped his arm around her waist and veered to the left. Maybe if they circled wide around the wolves they could get out into the open field before they were detected. Snarls, crunching snow and snapping twigs grew louder behind them but were nearly drowned out by the pounding of Anna's heart. Shadows passed them on both sides. How many were there? Her lungs were on fire. Her foot caught in a tangle of vines and she went down, pulling Charles to one knee. As he frantically clawed at the vine to free her foot, a large grey mass of claws and teeth lunged from behind a fallen spruce, landing on his back. She opened her mouth to scream, but her lungs and throat were paralyzed. She couldn't breathe. She couldn't think.

He needed a weapon. He had dropped the ax and branches while they were running. He grabbed a small log, raised and spun around, throwing the wolf off his back and cracked it across the jaw as it charged at him again. He kept his eyes on it as he reached down and pulled Anna to her feet. It cowered only for a moment before it began circling, curling its lips into a menacing snarl. Its companions began to take courage and close in as well.

He moved quickly toward a tight clump of aspens; he wanted protection on at least one side so they couldn't be surrounded. As they dashed across the small clearing, a small reddish brown wolf skittered out and gripped Anna's ankle in his jaws, tripping her again. Charles turned and kicked it hard, sending it whimpering into the brush. She nearly flew through the air as he pulled her to the trees and pushed her behind himself. He swung his club from side to side to keep them at bay while he shoved his other hand into each of his pockets. He hoped his revolver hadn't fallen out somewhere. Anna didn't know he routinely carried a gun and he was sorry she would find out like this, but he was relieved when he felt the cold steel.

Three large wolves and four smaller ones were closing in, with the large grey one that had attacked him in the lead. He pulled out his revolver and fired it into the air. Anna clutched the sides of his coat and buried her face in his back.

They fell back, but not far. Hunger had made them bold and unwilling to put safety over a fine meal. They cautiously crept closer, spreading out around them. A small one had circled behind them and wedged its upper body through the aspens. Anna wrapped her arms around Charles' middle and shrieked as it bit at her torn, bloody boot.

As he turned back to see what was happening behind him, the big grey leaped at him. He held up his left arm to block it as he leveled his pistol within inches of the small wolf behind and fired it. He fell back on top of Anna from the weight, with it gnawing at his arm through his thick leather coat. He shoved his gun into its belly and fired again. It writhed, howling and pawing. Charles heaved it off of them and stood. He put his pistol to its head, squeezed the trigger and it went limp and still except for the icy breeze ruffling its soft thick fur.

The others bounded off a short distance into the woods, but kept pacing back and forth trying to get up their courage to attack. Charles' wounds were insanely painful and adrenaline was thick in his veins. He hoisted the dead wolf over his head and roared as he heaved it into the middle of the pack, scattering them in all directions. He shoved his revolver back into his pocket and knelt beside Anna. She was leaning against the trees, her arms wrapped around her knees and her face buried in them, sobbing. He gathered her up into his arms.

"We must leave before they return." She wrapped her arms around his neck and held on as he whisked her through the trees and out into the open field. She held her hand to her eyes as the bright sun reflected into them. There was blood on her hand. It was not her own. Charles coat was torn at the neck and shoulder.

"Charles, put me down, you are hurt badly."

"It's nothing." He put his head down into the icy wind and forged ahead toward the main road, rather than across the field toward home. A farmer was coming down the road toward town, his wagon laden with crates of eggs.

"Your Highness?" He was surprised as he pulled on the reigns.

"May we trouble you for a ride into town? We were in the woods cutting a Christmas tree when a pack of wolves frightened away our ride home." He laughed lightly, trying to ease the horrified look on the farmer's face. He leaped from his wagon to help them in.

"Shall I take you to the hospital?" he asked as he swung up into his seat and shook the reigns.

"No, that will not be necessary. If you can just get us back to town, we would appreciate it." He looked down at their tattered bloody clothes. Dr. Pirard, their family physician, would certainly be called in.

"I'm sorry I don't have more dignified traveling accommodations for you sir." The farmer said as they pulled up in front of the palace.

"I am very grateful for you and your wonderful wagon." Charles smiled and shook his hand. He stepped down and carefully lifted Anna from the seat.

"Wait, here please."

"Yes, sir." He sat patiently, wondering why he would have further need of him now that they were safely home.

Pier met them at the front door as they struggled in and a flurry of excitement rippled through the palace. Charles sent Pier out to pay the farmer for his trouble as swarms of family and servants descended upon them.

"We have been so worried. When the team returned without you, we sent out a search party."

"Come in and sit down, look at you!"

"Call the doctor!"

"Boil some water and fetch some clean towels!"

***

The fire crackled comfortingly as they sat, bandaged and wrapped in warm blankets in their room. Anna was nestled under Charles' right arm, his left was stitched, bandaged and elevated on a soft pillow. His right shoulder was stitched in a few places near the base of his neck. Most of the scratches across his shoulder and down his back were not deep and were cleaned, smeared with ointment and wrapped in several layers of gauze.

Anna had two small cuts that needed stitching where teeth pierced her boot and her ankle was sprained. He watched her as she stared into the fire. What could she be thinking? What would this disastrous day do to her? Would she ever get over it?

"A penny for your thoughts?"

"Don't you mean a centime for my thoughts?" She smiled. "I was just wondering how Sinterklaas will come down our chimney with a fire burning beneath it."

He exhaled in relief; she was thinking about Sinterklaas.

"I'm sorry about today. You simply wanted a small tree for our room and I dragged us off into danger." She apologized.

"It was my fault. I should have just taken you to the orphanage. I purchased some chocolates for them and I meant to take you shopping for more treats…"

She sat up, lit with excitement. "Oh really, could we do that, right now?"

"It is too late now, the shops have all closed." He winced as his shoulder moved with her.

"We could pick oranges out in the greenhouses and with the chocolates…at least it's something."

"Alright, let me put a shirt on." His breath caught in his throat as he pulled himself up.

"What am I thinking? We can't go anywhere. You are injured." It was hard to see his pained expression in the flickering firelight.

"I am fine. How is your foot?" He gently pulled the sleeve over his left arm and groaned as he arched his right arm back to the other sleeve. She jumped up to help him, hopping on her good foot.

"My foot is fine too, as long as I can keep my balance." Her eyes watered. Lowering the elevation when she stood made her ankle throb in intense pounding pain with every pulse of her heart.

"We will have to be very quiet. I am sure this excursion is not part of our approved treatment plan." He winked and opened the door a crack. All was dark and quiet, except for the light beneath Leopold and Astrid's door across the main foyer. They helped each other with shoes and coats, grabbed the bag of chocolates and slipped out to the railing that ran around the entire upper floor. Anna hung onto the railing for balance as she hopped. Charles scooped her up and started down the stairs.

"Put me down! You'll tear your stitches out." She whispered loudly.

"Shhhh. You will wake the entire kingdom thumping around on one foot."

Once down the stairs, she insisted he put her down and just support her as she limped painfully across the foyer to the kitchen. As they hobbled out the back entrance to the greenhouses, they stumbled over Nico's muddy garden shoes. There were some crates stacked by the door as well. They took one to put the oranges in.

When they came back, they looked at each other and each picked up one of Nico's shoes and scraped the mud from it. They placed them just inside the door and put an orange and some chocolates in them. On the counter they found an open bag of pepernoten cookies and fruit shaped marzipan, probably left from Leopold and Astrid filling their children's shoes, and tucked them in the crate with the oranges and chocolates.

Pier was just locking up the garages as they crept around the corner.

"Psst, Pier." Charles hissed, his father and Dr. Pirard were standing down the drive by their vehicles, talking.

"What are…" Pier whirled and dropped his keys.

"Shhh." Charles put his finger to his lips and then pointed toward the King and the good doctor.

"I will need a car for about an hour. I will lock up for you." He whispered.

"You are in no—"

"Shhh, please, Pier."

"You are in no condition to drive anywhere." He whispered more quietly. "I will drive you." He unlocked the door and helped them into the nearest car. When the King and Dr. Pirard got into their vehicles and drove away, he pulled out of the garage and turned back to them.

"Where are we going tonight?"

"Please take us to the orphanage in Sint-Jans-Molenbeek."

Pier jerked fully back, searching Charles expression to make sure he was serious. Anna reddened, embarrassed by her behavior involving this same orphanage a year ago.

"We are on a top secret mission under direct orders from Sinterklaas himself." Charles winked and Pier turned and pulled down the driveway shaking his head.

When they arrived at the orphanage they found seventeen tattered pairs of shoes of various sizes lined up on the porch by the front door. There was one stick of gum and a new pencil in each pair.

"We should have brought new shoes for them and warm stockings." He lifted each pair, making a mental note of sizes. "We must return on Christmas Eve."

They carefully stuffed each pair of shoes with an orange, cookies, marzipan and Sinterklaas shaped chocolates wrapped in brightly painted foil. Charles bent down to pick up a small pile of dry grass left for Sinterklaas' horse. He scattered a little across the porch and tossed the rest behind a bush.

"I wish we could see their faces tomorrow morning." Anna smiled and took Pier's arm, leaning heavily on him. Her entire leg felt like knives were stabbing up and down it. Pier stiffened. He was already nervous having brought the injured pair into this part of town at night, but now she was clinging to him.

"Charles is in extreme pain, he just won't admit it." Pier could see a dark spot on Charles' shirt at the neck and chest when his coat flapped back. He nodded, scooped Anna into his arms and placed her in the back seat of the car. He went back to help Charles gather the crate and empty candy and cookie bags. He took the crate from Charles and wrapped his other arm around his middle.

"Put your weight on me."

"My legs are in good condition, Pier, thank you." He smiled in the darkness; what a good friend Pier was.

"I appreciate your help. I am afraid if I had to lift my arms one more time they would fall off entirely."

"You should have allowed me to make this delivery for you."

"Knowing it was done is not nearly as much fun as making the delivery ourselves." Charles smiled and tried to pat him on the shoulder, but groaned and dropped his arm.

"Your wound is bleeding."

"Yes, well, we can look on the bright side, the pain I am suffering now is nothing compared to the stiffness I will feel tomorrow! I should enjoy myself while I can."

Chapter 28

Christmas morning stole across the face of the earth, creeping through windows and rousing sleepy little eyes. As the world pushed forward, ever reaching for the sun and the renewal of a new day dawning, great waves of children yawned, stretched and jumped from their beds in anticipation of what they might find in the stockings they had hung the night before. Some homes would soon be filled with the tantalizing smells of roast goose and stuffing, others would not. Some were grateful for what they had, others were left bitter from the inequalities of life.

Ivo had worked an evening shift and arrived home late the night before. He groaned and rolled toward his wife, Tatiana, draping his arm across her. He could hear the boys giggling and whispering in the next room.

"St. Nickolaas has surely come by now, let's go see."

"No, not yet. Papa said to wait until the sun is up."

"Look, it is getting light out. I want to see if St. Nickolaas brought me a new wagon."

"I want to see if he brought me a rifle, but it is not light enough. The sun must be above the hills."

"St. Nickolaas didn't bring you a rifle. Giliam says he doesn't bring things like rifles to poor people like us."

The flit of excitement inside Ivo turned to fire as he listened to his sons' conversation through their paper thin walls. He was able to procure the rifle his son wanted, but it was used. He had refurbished it himself. He threw back the covers, shoved his legs into his pants and stomped across the frosty stone floor and out through the kitchen to the wood pile for more logs. He stopped on the back porch to pull on his heavy fur lined boots before stepping down into the thick crunchy layer of snow that had fallen in the night. Some of the neighboring stone chimneys rising from the slate rooftops of this overcrowded common neighborhood already had wisps of smoke curling upward, chasing the chill from their homes below.

Ivo's family was better off than some; he had steady work. Times were hard and so many families had so little. It wasn't what he had or didn't have that bothered him as much as the inequality. Some, the ruling class in particular, had so much more.

He opened the stove door and reached in with the poker, stirring the embers to a gentle glow. He tore some bark from a log and blew softly on it until it caught fire before he put the whole log on top. A tickle in his ear temporarily coaxed him from his sour mood. Tatiana kissed and nuzzled his neck.

"Merry Christmas." She whispered. "Did you bring home a duckling last night?"

"Yes, it's hanging on the back porch. Pitifully small, it is."

"It's alright, things will get better. You will see to that my love." She went out the back and came in with the duckling, all plucked and ready to roast.

"Shall we call the boys? They are so anxious."

"Yes. Let's get on with it. I have an important meeting tonight."

"On Christmas!"

"Alfons is leaving right after the holidays and I have to work a double shift tomorrow." He slammed the door to the stove and kicked the extra logs into the corner beside it.

"I work as hard as anyone. You would think we could afford a decent goose for Christmas dinner." He mumbled to himself.

* * *

Josef, Heinrich and Erwin were huddled around the fire. Alfons and Ernst were talking over some maps and documents on the small desk in the opposite corner in the back room of Heinrich's Village Market. When Ivo entered, they all gathered at the desk.

"We are ready here." Heinrich offered excitedly.

The others looked at Erwin for confirmation. He smiled and nodded.

"No, we need evidence." Alfons demanded.

"We have evidence."

"We need more. When we strike, it must be a lethal blow. Multiple minor accusations will only alert them to our plan."

Ivo stared at the wall as if he could see through it into the future, while the others argued distantly. A triumphant smile curled one side of his face.

"I will get your evidence." He looked back at Alfons. "It will take time to set it up."

"How much time?"

Ivo leaned forward and tapped rapidly on the desk with his index finger, then straightened.

"Two months...at the most."

Alfons looked directly into each face, nodding.

"Very good then. We will be in touch."

Chapter 29

Charles was busy in the office with last minute preparations, as he would be going out of town early next morning. Anna couldn't sleep. She was accustomed to sleeping next to Charles and was dreading his being away for two weeks. She decided to slip down to the kitchen to see if she could find something to snack on. The door to the office was open and the light was on. She was cautious not to be seen, as she was in her nightgown. She peeked in, Charles was alone. He looked up and saw her. He smiled, pushed back his chair and beckoned her to come in. She climbed onto his lap, drawing her knees up, her hair down, loose about her shoulders.

"I miss you already."

"Did the wolves come back?"

"No, I don't think they're coming back."

He raised a hopeful, questioning eyebrow. Sometimes she seemed so strong and courageous and other times so fragile and delicate. Still not quite 20 years old, she wasn't much more than a child. He wished to shelter her from all the unpleasantness of the political unrest he faced.

"Last night I dreamed I heard a noise and went to the window, the wolves were all down in the courtyard below celebrating. I don't know what or why they were celebrating and I don't know why they aren't coming back." She hesitated, trying to understand the strange dream. "The thing that really bothers me is that I don't feel relieved that it's over."

"Maybe you are just distraught because I'm going away." He took her hand and stroked it tenderly. "I have no choice this time." He gently lifted her chin, searching her with troubled eyes. She didn't wish to cause him more concern; he already had so much to worry about.

"I know." She snuggled deeper into his embrace. "I'm not afraid of anything when you are with me."

"Will you be alright? Do you want me to have someone stay with you while I am away?"

"I can have a bed brought in for Adelheid. She will stay with me if I need her to." She sat up and looked in his eyes. "Sometimes I'm more trouble than I am worth."

"I don't know," he smiled, "you are worth a lot of trouble!" He laughed. "What would I do with myself if I didn't have you to rescue?" He wrapped his arms around her and held her close. "The moon is nearing full. I will look at it every night as I imagine you are in my arms." He didn't know how much joy, being in love would bring him, or he wouldn't have fought it with so much determination. He sat, caressing her, until she fell asleep. Then he gently carried her to bed and returned to his work.

It was so late when he finished that he left then, instead of waiting until morning. When Anna woke, he was gone.

She tried to stay busy to pass the time. When Klaas sent word that he needed her assistance, she welcomed the diversion. She hadn't seen Klaas and Hilde for over a year now. They weren't asking her to go to a part of town in which Charles wouldn't approve. She had no intention of defying his authority now.

Klaas blew on his fingers as he stood on the platform in his shabby, worn coat waiting for Anna while his family huddled in a corner under the eaves of the train station. Short puffs of steam rose into the cold February morning air. He hurried toward her when he saw her making her way through the groups and bunches of people.

"Thank you, for assisting us. My brother, in Germany, he has been in a terrible accident." His eyes darted from her to the station behind her, down the tracks and back to her again. "He is not expected to live much longer." He stamped his feet and blew on his hands.

"You are going there now?"

"Yes, well, that was our intention." He looked over at his family and nodded. "But we don't..." He looked away again and rubbed his furry chin. "Will you lend me money to buy the tickets? I will pay you as soon..."

"Of course. Don't worry about it. It will be my gift to your family." She put her hand on his and squeezed. "I hope you get there in time."

"Danke, vielen Dank." He ducked his head and hurried to his family.

It must be humiliating for a man to have to ask for help, Anna thought. She tried to save his dignity as much as possible as she quickly purchased their tickets and helped them settle their little ones on the train. She hugged them and wished them well before exiting to the platform.

A group of young men in uniforms stepped forward and bowed to her.

"Your Highness, what brings you here?" The blonde one with a camera hung around his neck and a sheaf of papers under one arm, removed his hat and stepped forward.

"Are you traveling alone?" He raised an eyebrow in suspicion. She was getting used to people recognizing her that she had never met before, but this young man was different; there was no admiration in his eyes.

"No, I'm not traveling; I'm just helping some friends."

"They are friends of yours?" He further interrogated as he tipped his head toward the train.

"Yes, and I am not alone, my driver is out front."

"Does he know what you are up to?"

"Up to?" she replied incredulously.

He held her gaze before answering with deliberation.

"I apologize, Your Highness. Good day." He smiled and the icy chill that sent shivers down her spine and forced its way out through her skin leaving tiny bumps across her arms and legs, was not from the winter weather. The impression he left was not unlike that of the wolf at her window.

Anna watched them as they hurried off, unable to move or think. Numbing pain spread like poison with each thundering pound of her heart, slowing to a deafening near stop. The whistle of the train and mountains of billowing steam hissing beside her faded along with the chatter of the masses to a distant corner of her awareness. She was barely conscious of Pier at her elbow, his questions and concern, or their return to the palace.

* * *

Charles had only been gone one week, but the days dragged on so slowly, it seemed much longer. Anna decided to go to the Galleries St. Hubert, a large, glass covered shopping center. She took Adelheid with her and Pier drove them.

Anna and Adelheid shopped for awhile, buying only some chocolates, while Pier followed at a short distance. Shopping was a poor substitute for Charles.

Victor Hugo's Notre Dame de Paris was playing at Le Theatre des Galleries. She had purchased his book, of the same name, at Café de la Renaissance. She wanted to read it since she had been to Notre Dame when she and Charles were in Paris. She had cried through the book and would probably cry through the play, but she was in the mood to cry.

As they were exiting the theatre, the girls wiping their eyes and noses, a group of policemen approached them. She bristled as she recognized their leader as the same young man that was spokesman of the group she had encountered at the train station a few days earlier.

She was getting better at understanding Dutch, if it was spoken slowly. These men spoke rapidly, so she only caught parts of what they said. She was being arrested, but she didn't understand why.

"There must be some mistake. Do you know who I am?"

"Ivo, do you know who she is?" One of them laughed sarcastically.

By the fear in Pier's expression, Anna knew she was in trouble.

"Pier, take Adelheid home, and get word to Charles." She cried as she was handcuffed and dragged away.

Chapter 30

The door swung open. It was Charles.

"You're back! Now you can clear this up and we can go home." She had only been incarcerated for four days, but it seemed an eternity. The relief that washed over her quickly disappeared as she ran to him and he caught her arms and asked her to sit.

"Ivo's men are watching."

"Charles, what is wrong? You look so tired and you haven't shaved." She couldn't remember him ever looking so bedraggled and unkempt. "What is going on? Use your influence and get me out!" Apprehension began to creep over her. He had always been able to fix any trouble she had gotten into previously, but his demeanor suggested otherwise this time.

"I got back two days ago and I have been using my influence. I've done everything in my power." His voice cracked with emotion. "I can not set you free." He sat down across from her, his elbows resting on his knees, hands nervously clasped, with desperate apology in his eyes.

"But I haven't done anything!"

"You have done everything they say you have done. You helped Klaas get out of the country."

He stood and began to pace anxiously.

"You were set up. They knew you would help him. You help every stray puppy that comes to you—without checking backgrounds or asking questions." He shook his head in desperation. "Klaas is an extreme enemy to this nation. He acquired vital military information and you posted it to Germany. They have witnesses and absolute proof."

Anna felt faint as the blood drained from her face. There was only one letter it could have been.

"Klaas asked me to post a letter to his brother more than a year ago. He was in trouble. It was just money to help his brother." She squinted trying to force more memory to her mind.

"Did you see the contents of the letter?"

"No, it was sealed. But he told me…" Her heart sank as she realized how misplaced her trust in Klaas had been. "But I didn't know. Tell them I was set up."

"They know you were. The communist party wants control of the government. They planned this very carefully."

"We'll make them understand."

"You don't understand" he bellowed, quaking with more intensity than he would normally allow himself. He looked down and regained his composure.

"You are being charged with treason." He could hardly say the word. "They will get a conviction," He paused, not wanting to finish the sentence. "and you will be executed!"

The silence strangled her. How could she have been such a fool? How could this be happening?

Finally he spoke in a quiet voice, "Our only hope is to leave this country as soon as arrangements can be made. This shouldn't be hard because this is exactly what they are hoping we will do."

Now Anna stood and went to the small barred window, looking across the government park to the town hall in the distance. She loved this country, the people, the culture, the history. She couldn't take Charles away.

"No, this country needs you. I will not be the downfall of you or your country. I will not be your Delilah!" She turned to faced him. "You know you can't turn your back on your people."

"What kind of man do you think I am to bring you here, away from your homeland, your safety, your life, and turn my back on you and allow you to be executed for something you did not understand?" He didn't mean to allow so much emotion into his voice. "If we don't leave, you will die!"

"Everybody dies, Charles!" She shot back before catching herself, forcing her emotions under control. "Nobody lives forever," she said with quiet intensity as the reality of what was happening settled over her and tears began to form. "And when we die, we leave behind a legacy of honor, courage and integrity," she swallowed the lump in her throat, "or of cowardice. We will not run. You were a strong leader before I came here and you will continue to lead your people through these difficult times after I am gone."

He had learned to put his responsibilities ahead of his own needs and desires. He ran his fingers through his hair as he paced. He had always thought he could do whatever he was called upon to do. But she had brought a new dimension to his life that he never expected or even dared to dream of. It would be like returning to a silent, black and white life after living this Technicolor talkie with Anna. He wasn't so sure he could go on without her. These past two days had taken their toll as this beautiful dream world he had been living in began to slip through his fingers.

Anna was gazing out the window again and silent tears fell on the window ledge. Charles stood mutely behind her. What words of comfort could he offer?

"Greater love hath no man than this, that a man lay down his life for his friends?" She whispered.

"No." He grasped her shoulders and turned her to face him, squeezing tighter than he should have. "No. I will not let you die. How can you give up so easily? I will find a way." He dropped his grip and backed away, working his jaw. He turned and called to the guard.

He had explored every option, checked out every angle, every loophole, everything he could possibly think of. With Anna's rejection of his plan to leave the country, he didn't know where to go or what to do. He wandered aimlessly through the streets going over every aspect of her case in his mind.

He ended up at the church where he and Anna were married and went inside. He slid quietly into the back row and buried his face in his hands. He sat pleading from the depths of his heart. As the night dragged on, the chapel slowly emptied. The priest began putting out the lights and making a final inspection of the chapel for the night when he noticed the tortured soul in the back corner. He slid next to him and had his arm around him before he recognized who this anguished young man was.

"I did not seek this trouble, it found me. I have always tried to do what was best for my country, my people. Even my marriage, I was not looking for romance. I agreed to this marriage for the protection of our government. I was willing to go through life not knowing what other men know, feeling what they feel. Now I have dragged Anna into this, she is so naive and innocent. She is not a traitor to this country, but now she will give her life for it. How can I live with myself after this? I would gladly give my life for hers." He buried his face in his hands again. "I am not a bad person, I did not mean for this to happen to her." Charles clutched at the priest's arm begging him to believe his desperate confession. "She is the pinnacle of joy, the very source of my happiness, the embodiment of everything that is good in my life. Why is this happing to us?"

The glow of candlelight reflected from the priest's moist eyes. "That is an age old question: Why do bad things happen to good people?" He patted Charles' knee. "Christ said, 'What manner of men ought ye to be? Even as I am'. If we look at our time on this earth as an educational period, a time to learn to be 'as Christ is', then we must look at each difficulty in our lives as a learning experience. We learn and develop a Christ-like character more from our trials than when everything is going smoothly. We are not here to see how much money we can amass or how much pleasure we can experience. We are here to become 'even as He is.' Do not lose your faith. God will sustain you and comfort you even if He does not let this cup pass from you."

The priest sat with him for awhile before finishing his responsibilities. A gentle warmth slowly settled over him as he pondered the words of this kind follower of Christ.

* * *

In the dark, quiet loneliness of her cell, Anna's thoughts tumbled over each other all through the night. Klaas and Hilde were not her friends. The letter she had posted for them was used to incriminate her. They had made friends with her only so they could use her to destroy Charles. Erwin was probably the supplier of information to Klaas. She had thought Charles was so cruel to him and so judgmental of Klaas and Hilde. If only she had trusted Charles and followed his instructions.

She had done everything in her power to make him love her, against his better judgment. She couldn't allow him to choose between his heart and his country. She had to find a way out of all of this. But the weight of what she had done, the pain she was causing, her exquisite happiness coming to an abrupt end, was crushing her.

* * *

Charles spent a great deal of time trying to solve this insurmountable problem, but he came to visit Anna as often as he could. He was just getting up to leave when the door opened for Filip, his trusted friend and attorney. He looked as if he carried a momentous burden as he shook their hands.

"I have some important news. They have decided that since Anna is a foreign national, she will not be executed."

"What caused them to have such mercy?!" Anna's eyes widened. Did she dare hope that this nightmare would all disappear? She wanted to jump up and down, but Filip's demeanor didn't suggest good news. He continued to speak directly to Charles.

"She will be deported. She will be considered an Enemy of the State and anyone having any contact with her whatsoever will be considered also an Enemy of the State and will be tried for treason and executed."

He turned to Anna with condemnation in his eyes. "It is not mercy." He spat out in disgust. "You did not run as they had hoped. If you are dead, what hope do they have? They will tail you both, knowing that when, not if, but when contact is made, Charles will be executed, the royal family will be implicated and the government will be theirs. They don't want you, they want your husband."

Charles dropped onto a chair and buried his face in his hands. He was overcome with relief and gratitude that Anna's life would be spared.

Their situation was still grave, but the devastating thought of her being executed ebbed.

Anna, however, focused more on what Filip said about Charles being executed when they made contact. She grasped Filip by his wrists, her eyes pleading with his.

"Please, do something. Protect him." She whispered.

The door clanked and swung open.

"Sir," Charles looked up. "I have papers for you to sign. Come with me." He followed the guard down the hall to the desk at the end.

"Send me somewhere that no one will suspect. Don't let Charles know where I am." Anna hurried to make her plea before Charles returned. "I won't make contact."

"It will not matter if actual contact has been made. They do not have to be honest, just believable."

She dropped his hands and staggered to the window, clinging to the sill for support. Her breath jerked out in tight palling gusts. Her mind reeled with the knowledge that his life would be traded for her own. Her heart pounded in rhythm to her sobbing pulsations. There had to be some way out of this. She couldn't allow him to die for her mistake. She slumped to her bed, her strength drained with the flow of tears.

* * *

It had been two weeks, since Anna's arrest. Tomorrow would be the trial. Then it would all be over. There was nothing more they could do. She leaned against the wall as she stood watching Charles. He stepped inside and stood looking at the floor, shoulders slumped, his hands in his pockets. The guard clanked the door shut and locked it before disappearing into the dark hallway. What had she done to him? Her heart was breaking for him. What could she say to help him get through this?

"I am sorry I brought you here." He finally broke the silence. "I had no right to involve you in all of this." He spoke without looking up.

"I'm not sorry." She nearly choked on the idea that he was blaming himself. "I have seen more, done more and loved more in this last year and a half since you came into my life than I would have done in a hundred years if you had not."

"You will soon be living in America again, as you would have been had I not interfered with your life. The difference being you would not have suffered all this pain and humiliation."

"Everything that is happening to me is my own fault. If only I had trusted you from the beginning."

"You did not know what you were doing; it is entirely my fault. I drove you away. If I had…"

"Let's not spend our last night together agonizing over whose fault it is. I would suffer twice what I have, to hold you even once more."

She looked at the ceiling and blinked hard as stinging tears filled her eyes. "For all sad words of tongue and pen, the saddest are these, it might have been." She quoted Whittier. Charles reached for her and she pushed away, looking nervously through her barred door and down the hallway.

"Don't put yourself at risk for me." She ordered.

"It's alright; they are no longer watching us. They want our last moments together to be so poignant, that when you leave, I go with you." He took her in his arms. "I am afraid that their plan is working. I don't think I can let you go."

She squeezed with all her might before relaxing. She reached into his inside breast pocket for his handkerchief. He sat on her bed and pulled her onto his lap, leaning against the cinderblock wall. She wrapped her arms around his chest and nuzzled his neck. His muscles were taut and she stretched up to kiss his jaw.

"Well, you don't need to worry about that now." She assured him with such confidence, that he looked at her with part hope, part suspicion as she buried herself in his embrace again, committing every aspect of him to memory.

"Worry doesn't solve anything. All I know is that I am in your arms, and I'm not afraid of anything now. I can do whatever I have to do," she said, reveling in the strength of his arms around her.

"There will be many full moons." She added softly.

Chapter 31

Anna looked around the courtroom as she was led to the front. The courtroom was packed. Ivo, her main accuser, and his followers, were on one side, at the front, the extended Royal family and friends were on the other. Everyone she knew, and many that she did not know, were there.

She sat fidgeting, trying to keep her thoughts from landing on anything long enough to stir memories or focus on the future. She studied the intricate carving of the heavy wooden railings that separated her from everyone else and the pattern on the tile floor. The flag posted in front, to the side of the judge's podium, stood as limp and lifeless as she felt. The heavy draperies hanging at the row of windows behind the front stand were suffocating as the room closed in on her. On the walls hung paintings of former adjudicators, glaring down at her in disapproval. She felt burning humiliation in this room full of people she cared so much for. She darted from face to face, avoiding eye contact. Don't think; just keep moving, clothing, furniture, anything to keep her thoughts in motion.

Suddenly, she was hoisted to her feet by the two guards, one on each side of her, as everyone in the room stood. The royal family entered and all were seated except the king and Charles. Her heart leapt into action and raced wildly as this elegant being strode in and took his place beside his father. Why did he have to wear his white uniform, was torture part of her sentence? Her arms ached to hold him again. If she could just feel his arms about her one more time, smell his neck, taste his lips one last time. His eyes found her and looked quickly away. The exquisite pain in her chest tightened; he couldn't even look at her. The dishonor she had brought upon him and his family must be unbearable.

Her mind, as though running through water, slowed to a dreamlike pace. She saw only one person, a perfect specimen of discipline and self control. He could have been standing at attention at a coronation or any military event, except for the muscles in his neck pulsing and the agony in his eyes. She couldn't look away. The pain in his eyes seared into her conscience. Closing her eyes did not help. Charles, his name, his family, must be protected. Nothing else mattered.

Charles, stone-faced, standing perfectly erect beside his father, Albert King of the Belgians represented all of Belgium as victims of her traitorous actions. How ironic that the two men that knew her character and appreciated her most, should be forced to be plaintiffs for these ridiculous charges.

Charles wanted to look at Anna, absorb every detail of her face and form, as this was his last chance. This afternoon she would leave his life forever. She was looking back at him with her big, watery eyes. His throat started to swell tight; the force of pent up emotion was incredible. He shut his eyes tight, strangling any tears before they could escape. His brain had been treading water for these last days and he felt it slowly, numbly slipping below the surface. Not daring to think or focus, he stared at the large clock on the back wall, every jerk of the second hand dragging him closer to the inevitable agony of separation from the most beautiful part of his life.

The verdict and sentence were read. Treason—she was pronounced an Enemy to the State. Because she was a foreign national, the death penalty would be waved. She would be permanently exiled from the country. Anyone to contact her in any way would be considered a conspirator and traitor as well and would be executed. She would be deported and returned to her homeland that afternoon. Her name would be stricken from all records, she no longer existed there.

She already knew what the outcome of this trial would be, but hearing it now made it final. The thought of going back to America in humiliation left her empty and cold. She had no one there, no previous life to return to. But the thought of never seeing Charles again was more than she could bear.

Watching him now, knowing that she was the cause of his grief, was torture to her. She was not trained to discipline her emotions, and her tears flowed freely down her cheeks.

When she was asked if she had any final request or statement, she knew what she had to do.

"I would like to apologize," she swallowed hard, "and please," she struggled to contain herself, barely choking out the words, "one final embrace?"

Of course the opposition had no problem with this request. It would only help to cement their plan. How could he possibly let her permanently leave his life now?

Charles looked desperately at the judge, shaking his head. Please don't allow this, I can't bear it, he thought. His heart cried out from the depths of his soul, while his outer shell stood its ground firmly; like a ship in a violent storm tearing at its anchoring. How much more could he take?

As she stumbled forward and threw her arms around him, her streaming tears became violent sobbing.

"I am so sorry for the pain I've caused you. Please, forgive me, but you are stronger than I am. I can't do this."

Ivo jumped to his feet in triumph.

"You can't do what?!" There was no other choice, what did she mean? As Charles stared down at her in confusion, her expression changed from deep sorrow to horror and extreme agony. He could feel her inability to exhale. Her forehead was deeply creased and her eyes were wide before she squeezed them tightly closed. He grasped her shoulders and pushed her back. A dark red stain on the right of her abdomen began swelling and spreading downward as his dagger fell from her hand and clattered onto the tile floor. Her eyes began to roll back and she grew pale, her knees started to buckle.

Still holding her shoulders Charles pulled her to him, wrapping his arms around her tightly, gasping, "What have you done, what have you done!"

He buried his face in her neck as he slowly collapsed to his knees and held her, sobbing. "No Anna please, you can not die now. Please, don't die. Anna hold onto me!" He wailed as she went limp in his arms.

King Albert's heart ached as he cleared the courtroom. He had been unable to protect the man he'd watched grow from infancy into a towering beacon of example. His mind slipped beneath an icy surface, numb as he went through the motions of propriety. He was stunned as he helplessly watched this pillar of strength so many depended on, sway and buckle to the emotional blast, this lofty column as it fell into a heap of emotional rubble.

The entire courtroom looked on in shock. Ivo and his men were stunned as their cunning plan vaporized before their very eyes, while the rest looked on with unrestrained sympathy.

Tomorrow Charles would rebuild, stronger than before with a concrete encasement around his heart. He would belong to his country and fill his duties with integrity and honor. He would feel the pain of his people as they mourned with him. All that knew Anna loved her, and would feel her loss. He would live out his life with nobility and unselfishness. But today, he was prisoner only, to a grief from which none could deliver.

Epilogue

Charles was educated at the Royal Naval College at Osborne on the Isle of Wight and the Royal Naval College in Dartmouth, a cadet training school for future Royal Navy Officers. After completing his naval training in Dartmouth, Prince Charles spent periods on board various British warships. He was awarded knighthood as the 377th Grand Cross of the Order of the Tower and Sword.

His brother, Leopold, married Princess Astrid of Sweden. They had three children Josephine Charlotte, Baudouin, and Albert II.

On February 17, 1934 King Albert I died in a climbing accident in the Ardennes region of Belgium. Six days later Leopold began his reign as King of the Belgians. On August 29, 1935, when he and his wife Astrid were returning from a vacation in Switzerland, Leopold lost control of the car. Astrid was thrown from the car and killed.

In 1941, to the disapproval of the people, Leopold married the lovely, but worldly Lilian Baels. This marriage and his hasty surrender to the German occupation during World War II made him very unpopular with the Belgian people. In 1944, when Belgium was freed from German occupation, Leopold was in exile in Switzerland and Charles was made Prince Regent. He reigned in Leopold's stead from 1944 to 1950.

Some important economic and political decisions were made under the regency of Prince Charles. Belgium participated in the Marshall Plan, which was a system of recovery set up by the United States to aid European countries devastated by the war. Illegal profits gained during the war were targeted by "Operation Gutt." A social welfare system was introduced and women were given the right to vote. Benelux, a union between Belgium, Netherlands and Luxembourg, was formed. Belgium became a member of the UN and the NATO treaty was signed. The headquarters for the North Atlantic Treaty Organization is in Brussels. The first NATO Secretary General, Lord Ismay, stated that their goal was "to keep the Russians out, the Americans in, and the Germans down."

Leopold returned to Belgium and his throne in 1950 which brought about uprisings and protests, particularly in the region of Wallonia. With the country on the brink of civil war, he abdicated his throne to his twenty year old son Boudouin just one year later. Charles disappeared from public life and was notably absent from King Boudouin's wedding.

Everybody Dies (Eventually)
Alternate Ending

The sharp scent of rubbing alcohol burned in Anna's nostrils while she fought through the fog that filled her head. A tall blur of white and a shorter white blur with a white cap of some sort stood off to the right, where the clinking of medical instruments being cleaned and chattering voices hummed softly without clarity of words.

A bright light glared from overhead. Anna squeezed her eyes tight and rolled over to her side in an attempt to sit. Fire ripped through her side with the movement and she cried out.

Albert appeared instantly from somewhere behind her, gently pulling her back down. The two blurry white figures, a doctor and a nurse sharpened fully into focus as they came to her as well.

Not being trained in where to put a dagger to cause a mortal wound, Anna suffered from shock and a substantial loss of blood, but her wound was far from fatal.

Anna moaned as the fog in her head cleared and the bitter memory of her trial seeped into the empty space.

"I can't do anything right, can I?" She squeezed her eyes tight, fighting the painful realities.

The others looked at each other. What could they say? What hope could they offer?

"Killing yourself would not have been right. It was a noble thing to attempt, but I must say I am glad you did not succeed." The king squeezed her arm and then rubbed it briskly to warm her.

"Actually, you have improved our position in this state of affairs. If the opposition thinks you are dead, they will not follow us so closely, expecting contact and pretended contact will not be possible."

"Do you mean I can still be with…" She started to rise again, but clutched her wounded side and laid back.

"No, if you remained here they would certainly find out. Contact with you would still be dangerous for Charles…for any of us for that matter. However, if they never find out that you are alive, it will make life easier for everyone, in that respect."

"Then no one must ever find out." She clutched at his arm and tears stung her eyes again. "I am so sorry." She swallowed a choking sob. "Don't tell Charles I am alive. Since we can never be together, it will be easier for him to move on. Encourage him to remarry. Help him to have a happy life." She held his hand to her face. "I am so sorry. I never meant to hurt anyone."

"You did not mean for any of this to happen. You have been so brave and unselfish." He gently wiped her tears. She held her breath and let it out in short gasps through clenched teeth.

"Doctor, she needs something for pain." The king paced at the foot of her bed while the doctor flipped a syringe and injected yellowish liquid into her arm. He massaged the sight of injection briefly before returning to his surgical cleaning. Anna's eyes and fists squeezed tight and Albert rubbed her hand.

"Try to relax." He soothed. When she opened her eyes again they were sunken and hollow. "Did that ease your pain?" he asked and she nodded.

"What now?" She spoke barely over a whisper.

"I am not sure how to get you back to America without someone finding out that you are really alive. It will be hard to hide."

"What will you do with me if I don't make it?" She rasped again.

"You will be all right. You are much too stubborn to give up now that you have saved Charles." He winked and she flushed crimson.

"What would you have done with me if I had died in the courtroom?"

He paused, finding it hard to speak it. "Your body would have been flown back to America in a coffin."

"Then that is what we will do. Don't try to hide it. Publicly put me on the plane inside my coffin."

"We can do no such thing!" He stepped back aghast at the suggestion. "Close you inside? It would be...How would you breath?"

"Drill inconspicuous holes."

"You would be frightened, locked inside a coffin!"

"The doctor can give me something to sleep. After we are in the air, someone can get me out. We would get rid of the coffin; dump it in the ocean or something. Very few people will have to know the truth."

The king paced around the room pondering her suggestion, shaking his head.

"We will secret you on the plane in the night and publicly place an empty coffin on the plane the next day."

"Suppose someone wants to see inside? If I were sleeping deeply enough I would appear lifeless. Just make sure no one touches me! I won't...feel dead."

He looked at the doctor who then nodded. "Yes, I have something that could do that. It could work."

"It will work." She closed her eyes and her breathing deepened and slowed. Albert left to make arrangements.

Geoffrey, Norbert and Sebastiaan had taken Charles back to the Royal Palace and were sitting with him in the south study. No one spoke. What could be said? What comfort could possibly be offered?

Geoffrey, Norbert and Sebastiaan stood when the king entered the room. Charles merely looked up without seeing. Nothing registered in his mind, nothing made sense, and nothing mattered. His eyes were red, but dry and glossed over.

"Norbert, come with me please. Charles, when I return I will take you to make the final arrangements...choose her coffin and what she will wear."

Charles nodded vacantly. The king turned and left with Norbert following.

"Norbert, I am assigning you to escort Anna back to America. This will be a long-term assignment as you have no dependant family to leave behind. Put your affairs in order, but pack as if you plan to return shortly. No one must know that you will not."

"Yes sir."

"My personal driver will pick you up Thursday morning at 7:00 am."

Norbert hoped for more explanation, but when there was none he saluted and left to begin his preparations.

Norbert was delivered to the back entrance where he was met by the king himself and led to the locked room where Anna was kept.

"She once had feelings for you. If feelings develop between you again, marry her and make her happy." He instructed Norbert before they went inside. He handed Norbert a sturdy case containing enough gold to get them settled.

He ignored the bewildered look on Norbert's face and pulled two keys from his pocket. He gave Norbert one, being the key to the case and unlocked the door with the other. Shock and enlightenment assaulted Norbert as he stepped into the room and saw Anna standing in front of the glass cabinet, straightening her dress in the reflection.

"You can see the bulge of my bandages." She frowned and then giggled when she saw the look on Norbert's face, his mouth gaping.

"I guess it's time." She offered grudgingly as she walked over to the coffin that stood open on the floor. "He picked a pretty one." She fingered the pink satin interior while she rubbed her other hand over the smooth, shiny, white exterior. "Hmm, I don't know." She held the deep forest green skirt of her dress next to the pink satin. "Does it clash?"

Norbert shifted his weight nervously. Can this really be happening?

"I know, I'm stalling." Anna threw her arms around the king's neck and choked back a sob. "Thank you for everything. You are the only father I've ever known. I'm going to miss you, all of you."

"Come now, you must not spoil your make up." He replied, choking on the lump in his throat.

"I suppose it wouldn't do to have our corpse appear as though she had recently been crying." She laughed as she daubed a tear from the corner of her eye very carefully so as not to smear the thick layer of pale flesh colored makeup she had applied to her face to make it appear less alive.

She stepped into the coffin and laid down, straightening her dress and carefully arranging her hair. She folded her hands at her waist, making sure to conceal the thick bulge of bandages with her arms. The doctor administered the injection and soon she was carried away to another world in the deep recesses of her mind.

* * *

Norbert accompanied the king in the black limousine following the hearse. The rest of the guard stood at attention in three straight lines perpendicular to the aircraft that waited to carry Anna's body to her homeland. Charles stood at the head of the front line without emotion, whether because he was numb and past feeling or because his old self control had returned.

Ivo and Alfons were at the front of a crowd gathering to the side, opposite the Guard. They stomped their feet and stuffed their hands into their armpits to warm them. Puffs of white breath streamed from their mouths and nostrils in spite of the bright morning sun.

Six of the guards pulled the coffin from the hearse and carried it somberly and without the pomp of a hero's ceremony, past the row of guards in shiny black dress uniforms toward the waiting aircraft.

Charles joined his father at the front of the coffin as he passed, with Norbert following in the rear.

"She deserves better than this." Charles hissed without relaxing his posture. "She was not a traitor to this country, she was a martyr."

"She offered her own life to protect yours. Do not waste her sacrifice with imprudence now." King Albert glanced at Ivo.

They stopped at the foot of the stairs and the king turned to face the public. He merely stepped aside and waved for the men to proceed with the coffin up the stairs.

"No words, nothing? Father, please." Charles' façade of strength wavered. "At least allow me to see her one last time."

"Yes, we would like to pay our final respects as well." Ivo stepped forward, anxious to confirm that Anna was actually inside. The king hesitated. This could be good or it could end up disaster. Provide witness without contact.

Necks craned to look in as the lid was lifted. Charles fought desperately against the impulse to hold her in his arms, but only the tendons in his neck, labored breathing and clenched fists gave evidence of this battle. Could this be real? Could she actually be gone? Was her tender heart stilled for ever? He reached in to hold her hand as he bent to kiss her cheek. Her hand was soft but cold. Ivo pressed closer.

"Charles!" His father barked. "Stand tall." Charles instantly responded to the order snapping straight and rigid as his father closed the lid and latched it.

"Stand aside. Proper respect and decorum will be exercised here." He ordered the pressing crowd. "This is not a circus side show."

"No farewell kiss for our beloved princess?" Ivo sneered.

"We have shown no improper display of honor, but neither will she be mocked." The king glared at Ivo, a gust of white steam hissed from his lips. He hoped to appear more angry than nervous.

"Proceed." He then waved the pall bearers forward. The coffin was put onboard and all the guard returned to the ground except Norbert. The engines roared to life, billowing white clouds in the frosty air. The aircraft lumbered forward and taxied down to the end of the runway.

The crowd slowly broke into various groups and dispersed. Charles alone remained. He watched the aircraft as it picked up speed and lifted into the air. It soared higher into the western sky. The morning sun glinted off its wings from the east as it rose above the puffy clouds in the distance. It was no more than a dot over the horizon when he felt his father's arm around his shoulders.

"She is gone." Charles said with a quaver in his voice. His father sighed. It sounded like relief, but his eyes glistened as he too watched the dot shrink out of existence.

* * *

Once again, Anna fought through the fog of drug induced unconsciousness. Her nose was cold and she snuggled deeper into the thick wool blanket wrapped around her. She couldn't turn on her side because of the satin walls that tightly confined her. The distant rumble of the engines grew to a roar as she emerged from the fog. She grabbed the side of the coffin and tried to pull herself up, fighting to open her eyes.

Norbert knelt at the side of the coffin that rested on the floor of the aircraft and helped her out. It was good to see his familiar face as she returned to reality.

"How did it go?" Norbert buckled her into her seat and tucked the blanket around her.

"It went well." He buckled himself in. "Very believable." Anna stared at him waiting for more.

"Was anyone there? Were there any witnesses?"

"Yes. There was a large crowd actually." He nodded. "Ivo was there. He was satisfied." He buttoned and unbuttoned his jacket. How could he change the subject before she asked about Charles and started to cry? "Are you warm enough?" She watched him play with his buttons and straighten his tie.

"What happened? How do you know he was satisfied?"

Norbert leaned forward, resting his elbows on his knees, then leaned back and folded his arms. "He saw you." He leaned forward again. "But he never touched you." He shook his head. "He was convinced. He left without incident." He looked at the floor. Change the subject!

"Where in America would you like to live?" He looked up at her. Too late, her eyes were moist.

"Was Charles there?"

"Yes, of course." He pulled his handkerchief from his breast pocket and absently twisted it around his finger.

"Did he see me?"

"Yes."

"Did he touch me?"

"Yes."

"Is that for me?" She reached for the handkerchief and he handed it without words. Silent tears flowed freely and she buried her face in his neck.

* * *

Norbert took good care of Anna. He found her a comfortable place to live and was able to help out financially until she could get a job at a department store. He offered to do more, but she refused. They developed a very close relationship, but it never went beyond friendship.

When Anna found herself with child, he offered to marry her; but again, she refused.

Anna made friends quickly both where she lived and worked. Catharina was her closest friend. She and Norbert got to know each other well as they were both with Anna a good deal of time. Anna could tell they were interested in each other, but they never courted.

* * *

Geoffrey talked Charles into joining their polo game. It wasn't until he got there that he learned it was with Fernand's French team. France won. While his teammates were celebrating, Fernand slipped away to catch Charles.

"Charles" He called as he lit off of his mount. Charles turned, burying his emotions when he saw who it was. He stretched his hand to Fernand to shake. "Congratulations, you played very well today." He offered before he turned to leave. Fernand held tight. "Charles please, I have not come to gloat over your loss today. It is a different loss I have come to discuss." Charles turned back to him with hooded eyes.

"I have heard many rumors, most of which I do not believe. I do not believe Anna was a traitor. I am very sorry for your loss." Fernand's deep sincerity caught Charles off guard. He studied for a moment before deciding that Fernand truly meant it.

"She was not a traitor. She should be highly honored; she gave her life for this country...for me. She knew I would eventually try to contact her and be executed for it. She gave her life to save mine. I must live with that guilt."

"Anna could be impulsive at times. I was the recipient of her impulses. Trust me; I know how frustrating she could be." He half laughed. "But her impulsive behavior reflected the desires of her heart." He looked intently into Charles eyes. "I tried to win her heart; but it was solidly yours. She was loyal to you and your country. That I definitely believe."

They both were lost in their memories for a moment when Fernand shook his head. "Do not feel guilty, there was probably nothing you could have done. She could appear to be helpless and in need of protection, but she could hold her own. You probably never saw the stubborn side of her that I saw." Charles smiled as he recalled the orphanage incident. "Do not waste your time feeling guilt. Remember all the good things. In your heart, she is honored."

"The Wolf of Europe challenged her to a duel and he did not win. Finishing her battle keeps me going." He shook Fernand's hand again.

"Thank you...thank you."

It felt good to talk about her with someone else that understood, to remember happier times, to smile again.

* * *

Norbert took Anna to the hospital that cold October night. He and Catharina sat in the waiting room while little Albert Theodore Meinrad was born. They visited her there and cared for her and the baby after they brought them home.

Norbert offered to marry her again. "The Prince needs a father."

"I love you, Norbert. You are a very dear friend. But I still love Charles. I don't love you like I love him; and you don't love me like you could love Catharina." He looked at her curiously.

"I can tell you have feelings for her; and she for you. It is your promise to the King that holds you back from her. You can still help me and influence little Albert...Uncle Norbert!?" She winked.

"Does Catharina know your situation? Have you told her?"

"No. I haven't told anyone. Most people wouldn't believe it, but if anyone did..." She shook her head. "We can't take a chance of any rumor getting back there. It would mean certain execution for Charles and his father for hiding the truth. Norbert wanted to tell Catharina, but he honored Anna's wish.

Norbert increasingly spent more time with Catharina and by Christmas they were engaged. They were married on Valentines Day. They were still on their honeymoon trip three days later; one year from her trial...and the last time she held Charles in her arms. It was a difficult day for her, but at least she had his son. He was a comfort to her over the years.

Anna listened to the news on the radio regularly; but seldom was there anything about Belgium. Occasionally, Norbert heard from Diederik, and brought her the news. He was the only connection they had with Belgium. It was too risky to communicate directly with the king. Besides the doctor and nurse that cared for her there and the pilot, Diederik and the king were the only two in Belgium that knew Anna was alive.

* * *

Charles' father entered the office with his hiking clothes on. "Charles, surely you aren't working today, it's Saturday! We are going for a hike; come with us."

"Thank you, Father, but I'm not feeling up to it." Charles didn't smile and he didn't look up.

"What is wrong?" The king pried. Charles' somber countenance had become the norm, but he seemed worse today. "If you are not feeling well, we will postpone our outing."

"No, go ahead, I would rather be alone." Charles pencil snapped in his hands. He placed it in the desk drawer and took out another.

"You are thinking about Anna." He squeezed Charles shoulder. "You hide your emotions most of the time and I forget that you still carry this sorrow.

"It was two years ago today." Charles shuffled and restacked the papers on his desk. His father watched him gnaw his lower lip, his eyes dull and pained as he tried to focus on the matters of state lying on the desk before him.

"I think there is something I need to tell you." He dropped his backpack, pulled a chair over to face Charles and eased into it. Perhaps he had been wrong to assume Charles would be better off not knowing the truth, that he would get over his heartache and move on. Charles was strong and committed to his country. He would not do anything foolish.

"We thought it would make your situation easier, but perhaps we were wrong." This wasn't something he could drop in his lap and then run off for a day of family fun, but he should know that Anna was alive and well. Knowing that she was quite possibly married to Norbert and happily moving on with a new life of her own, might help Charles to do the same.

Just then Leopold stepped in the doorway. "Let's go, we are ready." He called, impatiently tapping the door frame.

"Tonight, when we get home, you and I will talk." Leopold would not be included in this conversation. No one else could know.

* * *

Anna was setting out a new shipment of perfumes at work on Monday, February 19, when Norbert found her. He had gotten a telegram from Diederik.

"Anna, can we talk?" She knocked over a row of bottles and straightened them with shaking hands. His grave expression suggested tragedy. He guided her to a remote corner of the store to talk in private.

"Anna, His Majesty King Albert was killed in a hiking accident last Saturday."

She grasped Norbert's arm as she felt the blood drain from her. She felt light headed and weak. He handed her his handkerchief and found her a chair.

Her thoughts tumbled over each other in her mind. She would never see him again. He had been so kind to her. She wanted to be with Charles during this difficult time for him.

"I'm sorry, when I got the telegram I came straight here. I should have waited until you were at home." He put his hand on her shoulder. She stood, throwing her arms around his neck and sobbed. He held her without speaking. What could he say? There was nothing that could be done. She could send no condolences, offer no comfort and no one but he, could understand her grief.

"Catharina!" He gasped, pushing Anna back into the chair and straightening his clothing.

"What? Where? We're not doing anything wrong." Anna was confused by Norbert's behavior.

"Do you want to explain why you are in my arms in this back corner, why I am not at work, why you are crying over the death of some king no one has ever heard of?"

"Norbert, Anna?" Catharina wound around the circles of hanging clothing. She might not have suspected anything were it not for Norbert's nervousness. "What is wrong? Anna, you're crying."

Norbert and Anna looked at each other. What could they tell her? Anna slowly rose to her feet, drying her eyes. How could they explain why this news should be so important that Norbert would leave work and come to her immediately, without revealing the whole story? It wasn't fair that Norbert should have to keep this secret from his wife. She could be trusted.

Catharina began to back away shaking her head and blinking back tears. Their silence and guilty appearance started to sink in.

"You are not really brother and sister are you?"

Anna reached for her hand, but she pulled away.

"My best friend?" She choked out.

"Catharina, this is not what you think." Norbert reached for her.

"You are not what I think! I thought I could trust you. I thought you were so honorable and good and perfect." She slapped his hands away, whirled around and ran from the store. Anna caught his arm and stopped him as he lunged after her.

"This is my mess. Let me clean it up. You wanted to tell her from the start."

The incident turned out to be a blessing. Anna needed a friend she could turn to with all the pain she bore, a woman, someone that could fully understand the holes in her heart. Catharina was just that person, on more occasions than one.

Eighteen months later tragedy struck the royal family again. Leopold, now the king, and his queen, Astrid, were returning home from their vacation in Switzerland. He was distracted momentarily and lost control of their car. They plunged off the road into a meadow where they were both thrown from the car. Leopold suffered a broken arm and minor injuries while Astrid was thrown into a tree, killing her instantly.

While most of the country was unaware of the mourning in the Belgian royal family, Anna suffered with them. September 1, 1939 as World War II began, she devoured any information she could get about Europe. In 1940, Germany occupied Belgium, putting Leopold on house arrest in Brussels. On September 11, 1941 Leopold married a commoner, the very beautiful and worldly, Lillian Baels.

* * *

Little Albert was growing tall and strong. He was so much like his father, but with a love for baseball rather than polo. On his 9th birthday,

October 6, 1941, Anna took him to the World Series game at Ebbets Field.

The Yankees were ahead 3-1 in the series. They had pulled ahead at the end of the ninth inning the day before. The Dodgers had a 4-3 lead and 2 outs in the 9th, when Henrich stole 1st on an error. DiMaggio followed with a single and Charlie Keller with a 2-run double.

Albert had his hot dog and soda and settled in for the Yankees final series-clinching win.

The crisp autumn weather set in as the holidays drew near. They had Thanksgiving dinner with Norbert, Catharina and their two children. Their oldest son was just more than a year younger than Albert and shared a common love for baseball.

Anna had been saving to buy a mitt and bat for Albert for Christmas. Monday morning she stopped on her way to work to check the prices. With just 17 days left until Christmas, she knew she would have to get it soon before they were gone.

Everyone in the store was talking about the events of the day before. Anna and Albert had spent the evening after their church meetings, with Norbert and his family. Anna hadn't listened to the radio since Saturday. She hadn't heard the news about the bombing of a naval station on an island of Hawaii at Pearl Harbor!

* * *

With the U.S. fully entrenched in the war, Anna trained as a nurse's assistant at a hospital for disabled veterans. She loved her work there, she felt very needed and useful. The war stimulated the economy; there were jobs available and a common purpose. The effects of the great depression began to subside.

In June 1944 Norbert came with the news that Leopold had been deported to Germany. He had no news of Charles. No one seemed to know of his whereabouts.

"I'm sure he is safe. He must be in hiding."

Anna was not convinced.

"If he were captured or killed, that would be in the news. We would receive word of that." Anna tried to believe Norbert and prayed continually for Charles' safety. She kept herself busy, but she grew thin and pale. Anna tried not to become a nuisance by constantly begging for information. She knew that if Norbert knew anything he would tell her. News from Belgium was sparse and rare. She could tell without asking, by the apologetic look in his eyes, when he had none.

Norbert found Anna and Albert at Macy's on the first Saturday that September. Albert was in the fitting room trying on a pair of trousers for his first day of school. He would start sixth grade on Tuesday, the day after Labor Day, that next week.

"The allies are in Belgium! They are fighting to gain control of Antwerp. They need the port."

Tuesday morning as Anna walked Albert to school on her way to work, she stopped at the news stand and bought a paper. Belgium is free! But where is Charles? Please, let him be safe. Surely news of him will surface now that the country is free.

"Mother, why are you hugging that newspaper?" Albert questioned. "And why are you crying? Did something bad happen?"

"No, something good, something very good. We are winning the war, son. Our soldiers are moving across Europe freeing them from German control."

"Good, I hate Germans."

"Oh, you mustn't hate Germans. Many of them hate what is happening as much as we do. Only some of them are bad, not all."

Christmas was difficult that year as Germany had attacked Belgium in the Ardennes Forest hoping to divide the allies from the port of Antwerp. The Battle of the Bulge lasted from December 16 until January 25, 1945 with the allied countries emerging victorious.

Norbert received a letter from Diederik two days before Christmas, but he saved it until Christmas Day to show Anna. It was the bright spot of the entire season.

On the liberation of Belgium, Charles had been made Regent of the Kingdom by the Combined Chambers of Parliament. On September 20, 1944, Prince Charles took the constitutional oath and began to exercise the royal prerogatives. Economic activity was quickly re-established. Women were given the right to vote, a social security system was implemented and reconstruction of the property destroyed by the war was begun. Anna was proud of him. This reconfirmed her decision to do whatever was necessary to keep him in a position to serve his people.

* * *

Working at the veterans' hospital gave Anna the opportunity to know the ravages of war even after the dust has settled and the bombs have quieted. She was patient and compassionate to all the men struggling to learn how to care for themselves without all their faculties.

Anna especially liked Harvey. He lost his left arm, leg and eye to a grenade. He had been so dependant and down hearted, but Anna cheered and encouraged him every day. He was happy and positive now, learning new ways to accomplish everyday tasks.

One hot August day she decided he needed a picnic. Albert came along to help with Harvey's wheel chair. He was nearly 13 years old and quite tall and strong for his age. After they ate, Albert played catch with Harvey while Anna sat on a blanket watching them. She brought her radio along on almost every outing. When she turned it on, she could hardly believe her ears; the U.S. had bombed Hiroshima.

The massive destruction was the topic of every gathering. Three days later Nagasaki met the same fate and five days after that, Japan surrendered. On September 2, the war was over!

"What will all of this mean for Belgium…for Charles?" Anna questioned Norbert.

"Leopold's hasty surrender to Germany as well as his marriage to Lillian has made him very unpopular with the people. He and his family are exiled in Switzerland. Charles continues to reign in his place."

* * *

The economy progressed and happier times were on the scene for most Americans. But for Anna, loneliness prevailed. Every November, she went to Times Square and sat where she had sat with Charles the first day they met, so many years and lifetimes ago. She had good friends and neighbors and had kept busy raising her son. But now as he got older and more independent, she missed Charles more than ever.

Albert was seventeen and was graduating from high school, with honors. Anna was so proud of him. In the fall he would be going to the University. But tonight he was excited to be going to his graduation dance.

Anna wished Norbert could be there with Albert at his graduation, since his father could not. Albert looked up to Norbert with great respect. Norbert treated him like one of his own sons. But Norbert had been away on business for the past two weeks.

She straightened his tie, tipped her cheek up for him to kiss and stepped out onto the front porch to watch him leave. The moon was full again. She wondered, as she had every full moon for the last 18 years, if Charles stood watching it with her. Of course he wasn't. He was 6 hours ahead of her and he didn't know she lived. But, somehow, she felt closer to him knowing that he might be looking at it, thinking of her.

* * *

Memories flooded Norbert's heart as he drove through Brussels. He hadn't been there for over eighteen years. He walked slowly up the steps of the palace, letting his memories replay on the stage of his mind. He loved his wife and children. But he had given up the land of his birth and left a piece of his heart there when he went to America to honor the request of his king.

The young guard did not know Norbert and did a security check; then led him to the office where Charles was working. It took Charles a moment to recognize Norbert when the guard announced him. He jumped up and gave Norbert a warm hand shake and clap on the back. "My father said you were permanently stationed abroad. I don't remember where or why. It is good to see you again."

"It is good to see you as well. I have been in America these many years. There are many changes since I was last here. You look the same…I have come to find out if your heart is the same."

Charles raised a questioning eyebrow.

"I have kept up on the news of my homeland as much as possible. I am sorry for your losses; your father and sister-in-law. I have not heard any news of remarriage for you." He searched Charles' expression and found a distant sorrow, a wound that refused to heal.

"You still love her, don't you?"

"My enemies didn't quite destroy me—so my friend comes all the way from America to finish the job?"

"She still loves you as well." Norbert said opening the book he brought with him. Each page was covered with pictures and newspaper clippings from the last eighteen years. The specters rose from the pages daring his mind to believe what his eyes were seeing, as page by page he watched his Anna grow eighteen years older and the baby in the pictures with her grow to manhood.

"That is your son; Albert Theodore Meinrad." Norbert nodded, confirming what Charles dared not ask.

He tenderly caressed each image, as his heart tried to process the pain he had learned to live with. Why hadn't he been in on this secret? Was this what his father wanted to tell him the day he died? Was it easier, living these eighteen years without her, thinking she was dead? Would it have been easier knowing the truth, that she was alive and well and raising their son without him?

"Influence the people to vote in favor of Leopold's return. Anna needs you and Albert should know his father. You have given everything to your country; now it is their turn." Norbert stood, closed the book, and put it firmly in Charles hands. Charles looked up at him, eyes glistening, as Norbert nodded with profound understanding.

After Albert left, Charles sat back, holding the book reverently in his bosom. He closed his eyes, squeezing out one tear that slowly made its way over the creases of his face and dropped silently onto his weathered hand.

It was time for peace and happiness in his own life. He would transition his brother back into his rightful place. If the people would not accept him, surely they would accept his son, Boudin, who was now a fine young man.

He had fought a good fight; he had served his people well.
He had done his part.

* * *

Anna went to the front desk to request a fan for the men in the room
under her care. The end of July was the peak heat of the summer so far
and she wished to ease their suffering all she could. The permanently
disabled had enough misery already. There was only one fan left, on the
top shelf of the closet. She had to stand on a chair to reach it. She had
just returned the chair behind the front desk, when the door opened and
a tall, straight, fully functioning gentleman walked in. Most of the men
that came in were on crutches or in a wheel chair.

When he removed his hat, Anna stared; except for the gray hair at his
temples, he could have been Charles. She slowly drew closer, not daring
to blink for fear he would disappear, a figment of her imagination. She
was trembling. Was she suffering from heat exhaustion? Was he merely
a vision?

Then he smiled. "Anna?" In just two long strides he had her in his
arms.

"Tell me you are real! Tell me I'm not dreaming!" she cried.

As they stood holding each other, the years melted away. A cooling
balm washed over them. No more wolves, no more full moons apart.
They were together; life was good again.